'The wittiest, angriest, most exacting and most desolate work of fiction we've yet had about life in New York and London after the World Trade Centre fell. I devoured it in three thirsty gulps, gulps that satisfied a craving I didn't know I had'
New York Times

'*Netherland* is so expertly woven that it is impossible for a reader not to admire what it essentially is – a beautifully written exploration of memory and self' *Sunday Telegraph*

'A novel full of vividly descriptive passages that possess a heightened, almost hallucinatory, brilliance. A great American novel with an ordinary European everyman at its centre. O'Neill has created an unlikely hero for our uncertain times'
Observer

'The reader, almost imperceptibly, becomes little by little scorched by the novel's brilliance' SEBASTIAN BARRY

'Suspenseful, artful, psychologically pitch-perfect'
JONATHAN SAFRAN FOER

'A rare combination of ambition and humility. The best novel about cricket you'll read in a long time' *Literary Review*

'Sensitive and intelligent, *Netherland* tells the fragmented story of a man in exile – from home, family and, most poignantly, from himself' *Washington Post*

By the same author

This is the Life
The Breezes
Blood-Dark Track: A Family History

JOSEPH O'NEILL

Netherland

HARPER PERENNIAL
London, New York, Toronto, Sydney and New Delhi

Harper Perennial
An imprint of HarperCollins*Publishers*
77–85 Fulham Palace Road, Hammersmith, London W6 8JB

www.harperperennial.co.uk
Visit our authors' blog at www.fifthestate.co.uk

This Harper Perennial edition published 2009
4

First published in Great Britain by Fourth Estate in 2008

A catalogue record for this book is available from the British Library

ISBN 978-0-00-727570-0

Set in Minion by
Palimpsest Book Production Ltd, Grangemouth, Stirlingshire

Printed and bound in Great Britain by Clays Ltd, St Ives plc

Mixed Sources

Product group from well-managed
forests and other controlled sources
www.fsc.org Cert no. SW-COC-1806
© 1996 Forest Stewardship Council

FSC

To Sally

I dream'd in a dream, I saw a city invincible to
  the attacks of the whole of the rest of the earth;
I dream'd that was the new City of Friends

Whitman

The afternoon before I left London for New York – Rachel had flown out six weeks previously – I was in my cubicle at work, boxing up my possessions, when a senior vice president at the bank, an Englishman in his fifties, came to wish me well. I was surprised; he worked in another part of the building and in another department, and we were known to each other only by sight. Nevertheless, he asked me in detail about where I intended to live ('Watts? Which block on Watts?') and reminisced for several minutes about his loft on Wooster Street and his outings to the 'original' Dean & DeLuca. He was doing nothing to hide his envy.

'We won't be gone for very long,' I said, playing down my good fortune. That was, in fact, the plan, conceived by my wife: to drop in on New York City for a year or three and then come back.

'You say that now,' he said. 'But New York's a very hard place to leave. And once you do leave . . .' The SVP, smiling, said, 'I still miss it, and I left twelve years ago.'

It was my turn to smile – in part out of embarrassment, because he'd spoken with an American openness. 'Well, we'll see,' I said.

'Yes,' he said. 'You will.'

His sureness irritated me, though principally he was pitiable – like one of those Petersburgians of yesteryear whose duties have washed him up on the wrong side of the Urals.

But it turns out he was right, in a way. Now that I, too, have left that city, I find it hard to rid myself of the feeling that life carries a taint of aftermath. This last-mentioned word, somebody once told me, refers literally to a second mowing of grass in the same season. You might say, if you're the type prone to general observations, that New York City insists on memory's repetitive mower – on the sort of purposeful post-mortem that has the effect, so one is told and forlornly hopes, of cutting the grassy past to manageable proportions. For it keeps growing back, of course. None of this means that I wish I were back there now; and naturally I'd like to believe that my own retrospection is in some way more important than the old SVP's, which, when I was exposed to it, seemed to amount to not much more than a cheap longing. But there's no such thing as a cheap longing, I'm tempted to conclude these days, not even if you're sobbing over a cracked fingernail. Who knows what happened to that fellow over there? Who knows what lay behind his story about shopping for balsamic vinegar? He made it sound like an elixir, the poor bastard.

At any rate, for the first two years or so of my return to England, I did my best to look away from New York – where, after all, I'd been unhappy for the first time in my life. I didn't go back there in person, and I didn't wonder very often about what had become of a man named Chuck Ramkissoon, who'd been a friend during my final East Coast summer and had since, in the way of these things, become a transitory figure. Then, one evening in the spring of this year, 2006, Rachel and I are at home, in Highbury. She is absorbed by a story in the newspaper. I have already read it. It concerns the emergence of a group of tribespeople from the Amazon forest in Colombia. They are reportedly tired of the hard jungle life, although it's noted they still like nothing better than to eat monkey, grilled and then boiled. A disturbing photograph of a boy gnawing at a blackened little skull illustrates this fact. The tribespeople have no idea of the existence of a host country named Colombia, and no idea, more hazardously, of diseases like the common cold or influenza, against which they have no natural defences.

'Hello,' Rachel says, 'your tribe has come to light.'

I'm still smiling when I answer the ringing phone. A *New York Times* reporter asks for Mr van den Broek.

The reporter says, 'This is about Kham, ah, Khamraj Ramkissoon . . . ?'

'Chuck,' I say, sitting down at the kitchen table. 'It's Chuck Ramkissoon.'

She tells me that Chuck's 'remains' have been found in the Gowanus Canal. There were handcuffs around his wrists and evidently he was the victim of a murder.

I don't say anything. It seems to me this woman has told an obvious lie and that if I think about it long enough a rebuttal will come to me.

Her voice says, 'Did you know him well?' When I don't answer, she says, 'It says somewhere you were his business partner.'

'That's not accurate,' I say.

'But you were in business together, right? That's what my note says.'

'No,' I say. 'You've been misinformed. He was just a friend.'

She says, 'Oh – OK.' There is a tapping of a keyboard and a hiatus.

'So – is there anything you can tell me about his milieu?'

'His milieu?' I say, startled into correcting her mooing pronunciation.

'Well, you know – who he hung out with, what kind of trouble he might have gotten himself into, any shady characters . . .' She adds with a faint laugh, 'It is kind of unusual, what happened.'

I realise that I'm upset, even angry.

'Yes,' I finally say. 'You have quite a story on your hands.'

The next day a small piece runs in the Metro section. It has been established that Chuck Ramkissoon's body lay in the water by the Home Depot building for over two years, among crabs and car tyres and shopping carts, until a so-called urban diver made a 'macabre discovery' while filming a school of striped bass. Over the next week there is a trickle of follow-up items, none of them informative. But apparently it is interesting to readers, and reassuring to certain traditionalists, that the Gowanus Canal can still turn up a murder victim. There's death in the old girl yet, as one commentator wittily puts it.

The night we receive the news, Rachel, in bed next to me, asks, 'So who's this man?' When I don't immediately answer, she puts down her book.

'Oh,' I say, 'I'm sure I've told you about him. A cricket guy I used to know. A guy from Brooklyn.'

She repeats after me, 'Chuck Ramkissoon?'

Her voice contains a detached note I don't like. I roll away onto one shoulder and close my eyes. 'Yes,' I say. 'Chuck Ramkissoon.'

Chuck and I met for the first time in August 2002. I was playing cricket at Randolph Walker Park, in Staten Island, and Chuck was present as one of the two independent umpires who gave their services in return for a fifty-dollar honorarium. The day was thick as a jelly, with a hot, glassy atmosphere and no wind, not even a breeze from the Kill of Kull, which flows less than two hundred yards from Walker Park and separates Staten Island from New Jersey. Far away, in the south, was the mumbling of thunder. It was the kind of barbarously sticky American afternoon that made me yearn for the shadows cast by scooting summer clouds in northern Europe, yearn even for those days when you play cricket wearing two sweaters under a cold sky patched here and there by a blue tatter – enough to make a sailor's pants, as my mother used to say.

By the standards I brought to it, Walker Park was a very poor place for cricket. The playing area was, and I am sure still is, half the size of a regulation cricket field. The outfield is uneven and always overgrown, even when cut (once, chasing a ball, I nearly tripped over a hidden and, to cricketers, ominous duck), and whereas proper cricket, as some might call it, is played on a grass wicket, the pitch at Walker Park is made of clay, not turf, and must be covered with coconut matting; moreover the clay is pale sandy baseball clay, not red cricket clay, and its bounce cannot be counted on to stay true for long; and to the extent that the bounce is true, it lacks variety and complexity. (Wickets consisting of earth and grass are rich with possibility: only they can fully challenge and reward a bowler's repertoire of cutters and spinners and bouncers and seamers, and only these, in turn, can bring out and fully test a batsman's repertoire of defensive and attacking strokes, not to mention his mental powers.) There is another problem. Large trees – pin oaks, red oaks, sweet-gums, American linden trees – clutter the fringes of Walker Park. Any part of these trees, even the smallest hanging leaf, must be treated as part of the boundary, and this brings randomness into the game. Often a ball will roll between the tree trunks, and the fielder running after it will partially disappear, so that when he reappears, ball in hand, a shouting match will start up about exactly what happened.

By local standards, however, Walker Park is an attractive venue. Tennis courts said to be the oldest in the United States neighbour the cricket field, and the park itself is surrounded on all sides by Victorian houses with elabor-ately planted gardens. For as long as anyone can remember, the local residents have tolerated the occasional crash of a cricket ball, arriving like a gigantic meteoritic cranberry, into their flowering shrubbery. Staten Island Cricket Club was founded in 1872, and its teams have played on this little green every summer for over a hundred years. Walker Park was owned by the club until the 1920s. Nowadays the land and its clubhouse – a neo-Tudor brick structure dating back to the 1930s, its precursor having been destroyed by fire – are the property of the New York City

Department of Parks and Recreation. In my time, a parks department employee, a phantom-like individual who was never seen, reportedly lived in the attic. The main room was rented out to a nursery school and only the basement and the beaten-up locker room were routinely made available to cricketers. Nevertheless, no other New York cricket club enjoys such amenities or such a glorious history: Donald Bradman and Garry Sobers, the greatest cricketers of all time, have played at Walker Park. The old ground is also fortunate in its tranquillity. Other cricketing venues, places such as Idlewild Park and Marine Park and Monroe Cohen Ballfield, lie directly beneath the skyways to JFK. Elsewhere, for example Seaview Park (which of course has no view of a sea), in Canarsie, the setting is marred not only by screeching aircraft but also by the inexhaustible roar of the Belt Parkway, the loop of asphalt that separates much of south Brooklyn from salt water.

What all these recreational areas have in common is a rank outfield that largely undermines the art of batting, which is directed at hitting the ball along the ground with that elegant variety of strokes a skilful batsman will have spent years trying to master and preserve: the glance, the hook, the cut, the sweep, the cover drive, the pull, and all those other offspring of technique conceived to send the cricket ball rolling and rolling, as if by magic, to the far-off edge of the playing field. Play such orthodox shots in New York and the ball will more than likely halt in the tangled, weedy groundcover: grass as I understand it, a fragrant plant wondrously suited for athletic pastimes, flourishes with difficulty; and if something green and grass-like does grow, it is never cut down as cricket requires. Consequently, in breach of the first rule of batting, the batsman is forced to smash the ball into the air (to go deep, as we'd say, borrowing the baseball term) and batting is turned into a gamble. As a result, fielding is distorted too, since the fielders are quickly removed from their infield positions – point, extra cover, midwicket and the others – to distant stations on the boundary, where they listlessly linger. It's as if baseball were a game about home runs rather than base hits and its basemen were relocated to spots deep in the outfield. This degenerate version of the sport – bush cricket, as Chuck more than once dismissed it – inflicts an injury that is aesthetic as much as anything: the American adaptation is devoid of the beauty of cricket played on a lawn of appropriate dimensions, where the white-clad ring of infielders, swanning figures on the vast oval, again and again converge in unison towards the batsman and again and again scatter back to their starting points, a repetition of pulmonary rhythm, as if the field breathed through its luminous visitors.

This is not to say that New York cricket is without charm. One summer afternoon years ago, I sat in a taxi with Rachel in the Bronx. We were making the trip to visit friends in Riverdale and were driving up Broadway, which I had no idea extended this far north.

'Oh! Look, darling,' Rachel said.

She was pointing down to our right. Scores of cricketers swarmed on a tract of open parkland. Seven or eight matches, eleven-a-side, were under way in a space that was strictly large enough for only three or four matches, so that the various playing areas, demarcated by red cones and footpaths and garbage barrels and foam cups, confusingly overlapped. Men in white from one game mingled with men in white from another, and a profusion of bowlers simultaneously whirled their arms in that windmill action of cricket bowlers, and multiple batsmen swung flat willow cudgels at once, and cricket balls chased by milky sprinters flew in every direction. Onlookers surrounded the grounds. Some sat beneath the trees that lined the park at Broadway; others, in the distance, where trees grew tall and dense at the edge of the common, gathered by picnic tables. Children milled, as it's said. From our elevated vantage point the scene – Van Cortlandt Park on a Sunday – appeared as a cheerful pell-mell, and as we drove by Rachel said, 'It looks like a Brueghel,' and I smiled at her because she was exactly right, and as I remember I put my hand on her stomach. It was July 1999. She was seven months pregnant with our son.

The day I met Chuck was three years later. We, Staten Island, were playing a bunch of guys from St Kitts – Kittitians, as they're called, as if they might all be followers of some esoterically technical profession. My own teammates variously originated from Trinidad, Guyana, Jamaica, India, Pakistan and Sri Lanka. That summer of 2002, when out of loneliness I played after years of not playing, and in the summer that followed, I was the only white man I saw on the cricket fields of New York.

A while back, the parks department had put a rivalrous baseball diamond in the south-west corner of Walker Park. Cricketers were not licensed to take the field until the completion of any authorised softball game. (Softball, my teammates and I observed with a touch of snobbery, was a pastime that seemingly turned on hitting full tosses – the easiest balls a cricket batsman will ever receive – and taking soft, glove-assisted catches involving little of the skill and none of the nerve needed to catch the cricket ball's red rock with bare hands.) The match against the Kittitians, due to start at one o'clock, did not begin until an hour later, when the softball players – ageing and overweight men much like ourselves, only white-skinned – at last shuffled away. The trouble started with this hold-up. The Kittitians brought a large number of followers, perhaps as many as forty, and the delay made them restless, and they began to entertain themselves with more abandon than was usual. A group formed round a Toyota parked on Delafield Place, at the northern border of the ground, the men flagrantly helping themselves to alcoholic drinks from a cooler, and shouting, and tapping keys against their beer bottles in rhythm to the soca that rattled insistently from the Toyota's speakers. Fearful of complaints, our president, a blazer-wearing Bajan in his seventies named Calvin Pereira, approached the men and said with a smile, 'Gentlemen, you are very welcome, but I must ask you to exercise discretion. We cannot have trouble with the parks department. Can I invite you to turn off the music and come join us inside the ground?' The men gradually complied, but this incident, it was afterwards agreed, influenced the confrontation for which those present will always remember that afternoon.

Before the start of play, one of our team, Ramesh, drew us into a circle for a prayer. We huddled with arms round one another's shoulders – nominally, three Hindus, three Christians, a Sikh and four Muslims. 'Lord,' said the Reverend Ramesh, as we called him, 'we thank You for bringing us here today for this friendly game. We ask that You keep us safe and fit during the match today. We ask for clement weather. We ask for Your blessing upon this game, Lord.' We broke up in a burst of clapping and took to the field.

The men from St Kitts batted for just over two hours.

Throughout their innings their supporters maintained the usual hullabaloo of laughter and heckling and wisecracks from the field's east boundary, where they congregated in the leaves' shadows and drank rum out of paper cups and ate barbecued red snapper and chicken. 'Beat the ball!' they shouted, and 'The man chucking!' and, raising their arms into the scarecrow pose that signals a wide ball, 'Wide, umpire, wide!' Our turn came to bat. As the innings wore on and the game grew tighter and more and more rum was drunk, the musical din started up again from the Toyota, where men had gathered once again, and the shouting of the spectators grew more emotional. In this atmosphere, by no means rare for New York cricket, the proceedings on and off the field became more and more combative. At a certain moment the visitors fell prey to the suspicion, apparently never far from the mind of cricketers in that city, that a conspiracy to rob them of victory was afoot, and the appeals of the fielders ('How's that, umpire? Ump!') assumed a bitter, disputatious character, and a fight nearly broke out between a fielder in the deep and an onlooker who had said something.

It did not surprise me, therefore, when I took my turn to bat, to receive three bouncers in a row, the last of which was too quick for me and whacked my helmet. There were angry shouts from my teammates – 'Wha' scene you on, boy?' – and it was at this point that the umpire recognised his duty to intervene. He wore a panama hat and a white umpire's coat that gave him the air of a man conducting an important laboratory experiment – which, in his own way, he was. 'Play the game,' Chuck Ramkissoon evenly told the bowler. 'I'm warning you for the last time: one more bumper and you're coming off.'

Apart from spitting at the ground, the bowler didn't respond. He returned to his mark, ran in to bowl, and delivered another throat-ball. With roars and counter-roars of outrage coming from the boundary, Chuck approached the captain of the fielding team. 'I warned the bowler,' Chuck said, 'and he disregarded the warning. He's not bowling any more.' The other fielders ran in and noisily surrounded Chuck. 'What right you have? You never warn him.' I made a move to get involved, but Umar, my Pakistani batting partner, held me back. 'You stay here. It's always the same with these people.'

Then, as the argument on and off the field continued – 'You thiefing we, umpire! You thiefing we!' – my eye was drawn to a figure walking slowly in the direction of the parked cars. I kept watching him because there was some-thing mysterious about this person choosing to leave at such a moment of drama. He was in no hurry, it seemed. He slowly opened the door of a car, leaned in, reached around for a few moments, then stood up straight and shut the door. He appeared to be holding something in his hand as he strolled back into the ground. People started shouting and running. A woman screamed. My team-mates, grouped on the boundary, set off in every direction, some into the tennis courts, others to hide behind trees. Now the man was ambling over somewhat uncertainly. It occurred to me he was very drunk. 'No, Tino,' somebody shouted.

'Oh shit,' Umar said, starting towards the baseball diamond. 'Run, run.'

But, in some sense paralysed by this unreal dawdling gunman, I stayed where I was, tightly gripping my Gunn & Moore Maestro bat. The fielders, meanwhile, were backing away, hands half raised in panic and imploration. 'Put it down, put it down, man,' one of them said. 'Tino! Tino!' a voice shouted. 'Come back, Tino!'

As for Chuck, he now stood alone. Except for me, that is. I stood a few yards away. This required no courage on my part, because I felt nothing. I experienced the occasion as a kind of emptiness.

The man stopped ten feet from Chuck. He held the gun limply. He looked at me, then back at Chuck. He was speechless and sweating. He was trying, as Chuck would afterwards relate, to understand the logic of his situation.

The three of us stood there for what seemed a long time. A container ship silently went through the back gardens of the houses on Delafield Place.

Chuck took a step forward. 'Leave the field of play, sir,' he said firmly. He extended his palm towards the clubhouse, an usher's gesture. 'Leave immediately please. You are interfering with play. Captain,' Chuck said loudly, turning to the Kittitian captain, who was a little distance away, 'please escort this gentleman from the field.'

The captain tentatively came forward. 'I coming now, Tino,' he called out. 'Right behind you. No foolishness, now.'

'Don't worry,' Tino muttered. He looked overcome by exhaustion. He dropped the gun and left the field slowly, shaking his head. After a short break, play resumed. Nobody saw any reason to call the cops.

When the match ended, both teams came together by the old clubhouse and shared Coors Lights and whisky Cokes and Chinese takeout and talked gravely about what had taken place. Somebody called for quiet, and Chuck Ramkissoon stepped forward into the centre of the gathering.

'We have an expression in the English language,' he said, as silence began to establish itself amongst the players. 'The expression is "not cricket". When we disapprove of something, we say "it's not cricket." We do not say "it's not baseball." Or "it's not football." We say "it's not cricket." This is a tribute to the game we play, and it's a tribute to us.' By now, all chatter had ceased. We stood round the speaker, solemnly staring at our feet. 'But with this tribute comes a responsibility. Look here,' Chuck said, pointing at the club crest on a Staten Island player's shirt. '"*Lude*

Ludum Insignia Secundaria," it says here. Now I do not know Latin, but I'm told it means, and I'm sure you'll correct me, Mr President, if I'm wrong' – Chuck nodded at our club president – 'it means, "Winning isn't every-thing. It's only a game." Now, games are important. They test us. They teach us comradeship. They're fun. But cricket, more than any other sport, is, I want to say' – Chuck paused for effect – 'a lesson in civility. We all know this; I do not need to say more about it.' A few heads were nodding. 'Something else. We are playing this game in the United States. This is a difficult environment for us. We play where we can, wherever they let us. Here at Walker Park, we're lucky; we have locker-room facilities, which we share with strangers and passers-by. Most other places we must find a tree or bush.' One or two listeners exchanged looks. 'Just today,' Chuck continued, 'we started late because the baseball players have first right to play on this field. And now, when we have finished the game, we must take our drinks in brown paper bags. It doesn't matter that we have played here, at Walker Park, every year for over a hundred years. It doesn't matter that this ground was built as a cricket ground. Is there one good cricket facility in this city? No. Not one. It doesn't matter that we have more than one hundred and fifty clubs playing in the New York area. It doesn't matter that cricket is the biggest, fastest-growing bat-and-ball game in the world. None of it matters. In this country, we're nowhere.

We're a joke. Cricket? How funny. So we play as a matter of indulgence. And if we step out of line, believe me, this indulgence disappears. What this means,' Chuck said, raising his voice as murmurs and cracks and chuckles began to run through his audience, 'what this means is, we have an extra responsibility to play the game right. We have to prove ourselves. We have to let our hosts see that these strange-looking guys are up to something worthwhile. I say "see". I don't know why I use that word. Every summer the parks of this city are taken over by hundreds of cricketers but somehow nobody notices. It's like we're invisible. Now that's nothing new, for those of us who are black or brown. As for those who are not' – Chuck acknowledged my presence with a smile – 'you'll forgive me, I hope, if I say that I sometimes tell people, You want a taste of how it feels to be a black man in this country? Put on the white clothes of the cricketer. Put on white to feel black.' People laughed, mostly out of embarrassment. One of my teammates extended his fist to me, and I gave it a soft punch. 'But we don't mind, right, just so long as we can play? Just leave us alone, and we'll make do. Right? But I say we must take a more positive attitude. I say we must claim our rightful place in this wonderful country. Cricket has a long history in the United States, actually. Benjamin Franklin himself was a cricket man. I won't go into that now,' Chuck said quickly, because a frankly competing hubbub had broken out amongst the players.

18

'Let us just be thankful that it all ended well, and that cricket was the winner today.'

There the umpire stopped, to faltering applause; and soon after, everybody headed home – to Hoboken and Passaic and Queens and Brooklyn and, in my case, to Manhattan. I took the Staten Island Ferry, which on that occasion was the *John F. Kennedy*; and it was on board that enormous orange tub that I ran once again into Chuck Ramkissoon. I spotted him on the foredeck, amongst the tourists and romantics absorbed by the famous sights of New York Bay.

I bought a beer and sat down in the saloon, where a pair of pigeons roosted on a ledge. After some intolerable minutes in the company of my thoughts, I picked up my bag and went forward to join Chuck.

I couldn't see him. I was about to turn back when I realised he was right in front of me and had been hidden by the woman he was kissing. Mortified, I tried to retreat without attracting his attention; but when you're six feet five, certain manoeuvres are not easily accomplished.

'Well, hello,' Chuck said. 'Good to see you. My dear, this is –'

'Hans,' I said. 'Hans van den Broek.'

'Hi,' the woman said, retreating into Chuck's arms. She was in her early forties with blond curls and a plump chin. She wiggled a set of fingers at me.

'Let me introduce myself properly,' Chuck said. 'Chuck

Ramkissoon.' We shook hands. 'Van den Broek,' he said, trying out the name. 'South African?'

'I'm from Holland,' I said, apologising.

'Holland? Sure, why not.' He was disappointed, naturally. He would have preferred that I'd come from the land of Barry Richards and Allan Donald and Graeme Pollock.

I said, 'And you are from . . . ?'

'Here,' Chuck affirmed. 'The United States.'

His girlfriend elbowed him.

'What do you want me to say?' Chuck said.

'Trinidad,' the woman said, looking proudly at Chuck. 'He's from Trinidad.'

I awkwardly motioned with my can of beer. 'Listen, I'll leave you guys to it. I was just coming out for some fresh air.'

Chuck said, 'No, no, no. You stay right here.'

His companion said to me, 'Were you at the game today? He told me about what happened. Wild.'

I said, 'The way he handled it was quite something. And that was some speech you gave.'

'Well, I've had practice,' Chuck said, smiling at his friend.

Pushing at his chest, the woman said, 'Practice making speeches or practice with life-and-death situations?'

'Both,' Chuck said. They laughed together, and of course it struck me that they made an unusual couple: she,

20

American and white and petite and fair-haired; he, a portly immigrant a decade older and very dark – like Coca-Cola, he would say. His colouring came from his mother's family, which originated in the south of India somewhere – Madras, was Chuck's suspicion. He was a descendant of indentured labourers and had little firm information about such things.

An event for antique sailing ships was taking place in the bay. Schooners, their canvas hardly distended in the still air, clustered around and beyond Ellis Island. 'Don't you just love this ferry ride?' Chuck's girlfriend said. We slipped past one of the ships, a clutter of masts and ropes and sails, and she and Chuck joined other passengers in exchanging waves with its crew. Chuck said, 'See that sail there? That triangular sail right at the very top? That's the skyscraper. Unless it's the moonsail. Moonsail or skyscraper, one of the two.'

'You're an expert on boats, now?' his girlfriend said. 'Is there anything you don't know about? OK, smarty-pants, which one is the jolly jumper? Or the mizzen. Show me a mizzen, if you're so smart.'

'You're a mizzen,' Chuck said, fastening his arm around her. 'You're my mizzen.'

The ferry slowed down as we approached Manhattan. In the shade of the huddled towers, the water was the colour of a plum. Passengers emerged from the ferry lounge and began to fill up the deck. Banging against the wooden bumpers of the terminal, the ship came to a stop. Everybody disembarked as a swarm into the cavernous terminal, so that I, toting my cricketer's coffin, became separated from Chuck and his girlfriend. It was only when I'd descended the ramp leading out of the terminal that I saw them again, walking hand in hand in the direction of Battery Park.

I found a taxi and took it straight home. I was tired. As for Chuck, even though he interested me, he was older than me by almost twenty years, and my prejudices confined him, this oddball umpiring orator, to my exotic cricketing circle, which made no intersection with the circumstances of my everyday life.

Those circumstances were, I should say, unbearable. Almost a year had passed since my wife's announcement that she was leaving New York and returning to London with Jake. This took place one October night as we lay next to each other in bed on the ninth floor of the Hotel Chelsea. We'd been holed up in there since mid-September, staying on in a kind of paralysis even after we'd received permission from the authorities to return to our loft in Tribeca. Our hotel apartment had two bedrooms, a kitchenette, and a view of the tip of the Empire State Building. It also had extraordinary acoustics: in the hush of the small hours, a goods truck smashing into a pothole sounded like an explosion, and the fantastic howl of a passing motorbike once caused Rachel to vomit with terror. Around the clock, ambulances sped eastward on West 23rd Street with a sobbing escort of police motor-cycles. Sometimes I confused the cries of the sirens with my son's night-time cries. I would leap out of bed and go to his bedroom and helplessly kiss him, even though my rough face sometimes woke him and I'd have to stay with him and rub his tiny rigid back until he fell asleep once more. Afterwards I slipped out onto the balcony and stood there like a sentry. The pallor of the so-called hours of darkness was remarkable. Directly to the north of the hotel, a succession of cross-streets glowed as if each held a dawn. The tail lights, the coarse blaze of deserted office buildings, the lit storefronts, the orange fuzz of the street lanterns: all this garbage of light had been refined into a radiant atmosphere that rested in a low silver heap over Midtown and introduced to my mind the mad thought that the final twilight was upon New York. Returning to bed, where Rachel lay as if asleep, I would roll onto my side and find my thoughts forcibly embroiled in preparations for a sudden flight from the city. The list of essential belongings was short – pass-ports, a box full of photographs, my son's toy trains, some jewellery, the laptop computer, a selection of Rachel's favourite shoes and dresses, a manila envelope filled with official documents – and if it came down to it, even these items were dispensable. Even I was dispensable, I recognised with an odd feeling of comfort; and before long I would be caught up in a recurring dream in which, finding myself on a subway train, I threw myself over a ticking gadget and in this way sacrificed my life to save my family. When I told Rachel about my nightmare – it qualified as such, for the dreamed bomb exploded every time, waking me up – she was making some adjustment to her hair in the bathroom mirror. Ever since I'd known her, she had kept her hair short, almost like a boy's. 'Don't even think of getting off that lightly,' she said, moving past me into the bedroom.

She had fears of her own, in particular the feeling in her bones that Times Square, where the offices of her law firm were situated, would be the site of the next attack. The Times Square subway station was a special ordeal for her. Every time I set foot in that makeshift cement underworld – it was the stop for my own office, where I usually turned up at seven in the morning, two hours before Rachel began her working day – I tasted her anxiety. Throngs endlessly climbed and descended the passages and walkways like Escher's tramping figures. Bare high-wattage bulbs hung from the low-lying girders, and temporary partitions and wooden platforms and posted handwritten directions signalled that around us a hidden and incalculable process of construction or ruination was being undertaken. The unfathomable and catastrophic atmosphere was only heightened by the ever-present spectacle, in one of the principal caverns of that station, of a little Hispanic man dancing with a life-size dummy. Dressed entirely in black and gripping his inanimate partner with grotesque eagerness, the man sweated and pranced and shuffled his way through a series, for all I know, of foxtrots and tangos and fandangos and paso dobles, intently twitching and nuzzling his puppet to the movements of the music, his eyes always sealed. Passersby stopped and gawked. There was something dire going on – something that went beyond the desperation, economic and artistic, discernible on the man's damp features, beyond even the sexual perverseness of his routine. The puppet had something to do with it. Her hands and feet were bound to her master's. She wore a short, lewd black skirt, and her hair was black and unruly in the manner of a cartoon gypsy girl. Crude features had been inscribed on her face, and this gave her a blank, bottomless look. Although bodily responsive to her consort's expert promptings – when he placed his hand on her rump, she gave a spasm of ecstasy – her countenance remained a fog. Its vacancy was unanswerable, endless; and yet this man was nakedly in thrall to her . . . No doubt I was in an unhealthy state of mind, because the more I witnessed this performance the more troubled I grew. I reached the point where I was no longer capable of passing by the duo without a flutter of dread, and quickening ahead into the next chasm I'd jog up the stairs into Times Square. I straightaway felt better. Unfashionably, I liked Times Square in its newest incarnation. I had no objection to the Disney security corps or the ESPN Zone or the loitering tourists or the kids crowded outside the MTV studio. And whereas others felt mocked and diminished by the square's storming of the senses and detected malevolence or Promethean impudence in the molten progress of the news tickers and in the fifty-foot visages that looked down from vinyl billboards and in the twinkling shouted advertisements for drinks and Broadway musicals, I always regarded these shimmers and vapours as one might the neck feathers of certain of the city's pigeons – as natural, humble sources of iridescence. (It was Chuck, on Broadway once, who pointed out to me how the rock dove's grey mass, exactly mirroring the shades of the sidewalk concrete and streaked with blacktop-coloured dorsal feathers, gratuitously tapers to green and purple glitter.) Perhaps as a result of my work, corporations – even those with electrified screens flaming over Times Square – strike me as vulnerable, needy creatures, entitled to their displays of vigour. Then again, as Rachel has pointed out, I'm liable to misplace my sensitivities.

Lying on her side in the darkness, Rachel said, 'I've made up my mind. I'm taking Jake to London. I'm going to talk to Alan Watson tomorrow about a leave of absence.'

Our backs were turned to each other. I didn't move. I said nothing.

'I can't see any other way,' Rachel said. 'It's simply not fair to our little boy.'

Again, I didn't speak. Rachel said, 'It came to me when I thought about packing up and going back to Tribeca. Then what? Start again as though nothing has happened? For what? So we can have this great New York lifestyle? So I can keep risking my life every day to do a job that keeps me away from my son? When we don't even need the money? When I don't even enjoy it any more? It's crazy, Hans.'

I felt my wife sit up. It would only be for a while, she said in a low voice. Just to get some perspective on things. She would move in with her parents and give Jake some attention. He needed it. Living like this, in a crappy hotel, in a city gone mad, was doing him no good: had I noticed how clinging he'd become? I could fly over every fortnight; and there was always the phone. She lit a cigarette. She'd started smoking again, after an interlude of three years. She said, 'It might even do us some good.'

There was another silence. I felt, above all, tired. Tiredness: if there was a constant symptom of the disease in our lives at this time, it was tiredness. At work we were unflagging; at home the smallest gesture of liveliness was beyond us. Mornings we awoke into a malign weariness that seemed only to have refreshed itself overnight.

27

Evenings, after Jake had been put to bed, we quietly ate watercress and translucent noodles that neither of us could find the strength to remove from their cartons; took turns to doze in the bathtub; and failed to stay awake for the duration of a TV show. Rachel was tired and I was tired. A banal state of affairs, yes – but our problems were banal, the stuff of women's magazines. All lives, I remember thinking, eventually funnel into the advice columns of women's magazines.

'What do you think? Hans, say something, for God's sake.'

My back was still turned to her. I said, 'London isn't safe either.'

'But it's safer, Hans,' Rachel said, almost pityingly. 'It's safer.'

'Then I'll come with you,' I said. 'We'll all go.'

The ashtray rustled as she stubbed out her cigarette. 'Let's not make too many big decisions,' my wife said. 'We might come to regret it. We'll think more clearly in a month or two.'

Much of the subsequent days and nights was spent in an agony of emotions and options and discussions. It is truly a terrible thing when questions of love and family and home are no longer answerable.

We talked about Rachel giving up her job or going part-time, about moving to Brooklyn or Westchester or, what the hell, New Jersey. But that didn't meet the problem of

28

Indian Point. There was, apparently, a nuclear reactor at a place called Indian Point, just thirty miles away in Westchester County. If something bad happened there, we were constantly being informed, the 'radioactive debris', whatever this might be, was liable to rain down on us. (Indian Point: the earliest, most incurable apprehensions stirred in its very name.) Then there was the question of dirty bombs. Apparently any fool could build a dirty bomb and explode it in Manhattan. How likely was this? Nobody knew. Very little about anything seemed intelligible or certain, and New York itself – that ideal source of the metropolitan diversion that serves as a response to the largest futilities – took on a fearsome, monstrous nature whose reality might have befuddled Plato himself. We were trying, as I irrelevantly analysed it, to avoid what might be termed a historic mistake. We were trying to understand, that is, whether we were in a pre-apocalyptic situation, like the European Jews in the thirties or the last citizens of Pompeii, or whether our situation was merely near-apocalyptic, like that of the Cold War inhabitants of New York, London, Washington and, for that matter, Moscow. In my anxiety I phoned Rachel's father, Charles Bolton, and asked him how he'd dealt with the threat of nuclear annihilation. I wanted to believe that this episode of history, like those old cataclysms that deposit a geologically telling layer of dust on the floors of seas, had sooted its survivors with special information.

Charles was, I believe, flummoxed – both by the substance of my enquiry and the fact that I'd chosen to pursue it with him. Many years previously, my father-in-law had been the Rolls-Royce-driving financial director of a British conglomerate that had collapsed in notorious circumstances. He had never entirely resurfaced from his consequent bankruptcy and, in the old-fashioned belief that he'd shot his bolt, he lurked about the house with a penitent, slightly mortified smile on his face. All financial and domestic powers now belonged to his wife, who, as the beneficiary of various trusts and inheritances, was charged with supporting the family, and there came into being, as the girl Rachel grew up, an axis of womanly power in the house from whose pull the sole male was excluded. From our earliest acquaintance Charles would raise a politely enquiring man-to-man eyebrow to suggest slipping off for a quiet pint, as he called it, in the local pub. He was, and remains, an immaculately dressed and most likeable pipe-smoking Englishman.

'I'm not sure I can be much use to you,' he said. 'One simply got on with it and hoped for the best. We weren't building bunkers in the garden or running for the hills, if that's what you mean.' Understanding that I needed him to say more, he added, 'I actually believed in deterrence, so I suppose that helped. This lot are a different kettle of fish. One simply doesn't know what they're thinking.' I could hear him tapping his pipe importantly. 'They're likely to take some encouragement from what happened, don't you think?'

In short, there was no denying the possibility that another New York calamity lay ahead and that London was probably safer. Rachel was right; or, at least, she had reason on her side, which, for the purposes of our moot – this being the structure of most arguments with Rachel – was decisive. Her mythic sense of me was that I was, as she would point out with an air of having discovered the funniest thing in the world, a rationalist. She found the quality attractive in me: my cut-and-dried Dutch manner, my conversational use of the word 'ergo'. 'Ergonomics,' she once answered a third party who'd asked what I did for a living.

In fact, I was an equities analyst for M——, a merchant bank with an enormous brokerage operation. The analyst business, at the time of our displacement to the hotel, had started to lose some of its sheen, certainly as the source of exaggerated status for some of its practitioners; and soon afterwards, in fact, our line of work became mildly infamous. Anyone familiar with the financial news of the last few years, or indeed the front page of the *New York Post*, may remember the scandals that exposed certain practices of stock tipping, and I imagine the names Jack B. Grubman and Henry Blodget still ring bells in the minds of a number of so-called ordinary investors. I wasn't personally involved in these controversies. Blodget and Grubman worked in telecommunications and technology; I analysed large-cap oil and gas stocks, and nobody outside the business knew who I was. Inside the business, I had the beginnings of a reputation as a guru: on the Friday of the week Rachel declared her intent to leave for London, *Institutional Investor* ranked me number four in my sector – a huge six spots up from the year before. To mark this accolade, I was taken to a bar in Midtown by some people from the office: my secretary, who left after one drink; a couple of energy analysts named Appleby and Rivera; and a few sales guys. My colleagues were both pleased and displeased with my achievement. On the one hand it was a feather in the bank's hat, which vicariously sat on their heads; on the other hand the feather was ultimately lodged in my hatband – and the supply of feathers, and the monetary rewards that went with them, were not infinite. 'I hate drinking this shit,' Rivera told me as he emptied into his glass the fifth bottle of champagne I'd bought, 'but seeing as you'll be getting most of my year-end fucking bonus, it gives me satisfaction on a wealth-redistribution basis.'

'You're a socialist, Rivera,' Appleby said, ordering another bottle with a tilt of thumb to mouth. 'That explains a lot.'

'Hey Rivera, how's the e-mail?'

Rivera was involved in an obscure battle to keep his office e-mail address unchanged. Appleby said, 'He's right to stand his ground. Goddamn it, he's a brand. Have you registered yourself down at the trademarks bureau yet, Rivera?'

'Register this,' Rivera said, giving him the finger.

'Hey, Behar says he's going to tell the funniest joke he ever heard.'

'Tell the joke, Behar.'

'I said I'm *not* going to tell it,' Behar said slyly. 'It's offensive.'

There was laughter. 'You can describe the joke to us without telling it,' Appleby counselled Behar.

'It's the nigger-cock joke,' Behar said. 'It's hard to describe.'

'Just describe it, bitch.'

'So the Queen's on *Password*,' Behar said. 'And the password is "nigger-cock".'

'Somebody tell Hans about *Password*.'

'Somebody tell Hans about nigger-cock.'

'So the Queen says' – here Behar went into a twittering Englishwoman's voice – '"Is it edible?"'

Rivera said, 'Jesus, Hans, what's going on?'

Panicking, I had suddenly lurched to my feet. I said, 'I've got to go. You guys keep going.' I gave Rivera my credit card.

He said, stepping away from the others, 'You sure you're OK? You're looking . . .'

'I'm fine. Have fun.'

I was sweating when I arrived back at the hotel. After a tormenting wait for the single working elevator, I hastened to our front door. Inside the apartment, all was quiet. I went directly to Jake's room. He was askew in a mess of sheets. I sat down on the edge of his IKEA child's bed and righted his body and covered him up. I was a little drunk; I couldn't resist brushing my lips against his flushed cheeks. How hot his two-year-old skin was! How lovely his eyelids!

I went to my bedroom in a new state of excitement. A lamp burned by the bed, in which Rachel, prone, motionlessly faced the window. I circled the bed and saw that her eyes were open. Rachel, I said quietly, it's very simple: I'm coming with you. Still in my coat, I knelt beside her. We'll all go, I said. I'll collect my bonus and then we'll head off together, as a family. London would be just fine. Anywhere would be fine. Tuscany, Tehran, it doesn't matter. OK? Let's do it. Let's have an adventure. Let's live.

I was proud of myself as I gave this speech. I felt I had conquered my tendencies.

She didn't move. Then she said quietly, 'Hans, this isn't a question of geography. You can't geographise this.'

'What "this"?' I said masterfully, taking her hand. 'What's this "this"? There is no "this". There's just us. Our family. To hell with everything else.'

Her fingers were cool and limp. 'Oh, Hans,' Rachel said.

Her face wrinkled and she cried briefly. Then she wiped her nose and neatly swung her legs out of bed and went quickly to the bathroom: she is a helplessly brisk woman. I removed my coat and sat down on the floor, my back resting against the wall. I listened intently: she was splashing running water over her face and brushing her teeth. She returned and sat in the corner armchair, clutching her legs to her chest. She had a speech of her own to give. She spoke as one trained in making legal submissions, in short sentences made up of exact words. One by one, for what must have been several minutes, her words came bravely puffing out into the hotel room, conveying the history and the truth of our marriage. There had been much ill feeling between us these last months, but now I felt great sympathy for her. What I was thinking about, as she embraced herself ten feet away and delivered her monologue, was the time she'd taken a running jump into my arms. She had dashed forward and leaped with limbs splayed. I nearly fell over. Almost a foot shorter than me, she clambered up my body with ferociously prehensile knees and ankles and found a seat on my shoulders. 'Hey,' I said, protesting. 'Transport me,' she commanded. I obeyed. I wobbled down the stairs and carried her the length of Portobello Road.

Her speech arrived at its terminus: we had lost the ability to speak to each other. The attack on New York had removed any doubt about this. She'd never sensed herself so alone, so comfortless, so far from home, as during these last weeks. 'And that's bad, Hans. That's bad.'

I could have countered with words of my own.

'You've abandoned me, Hans,' she said, sniffing. 'I don't know why, but you've left me to fend for myself. And I can't fend for myself. I just can't.' She stated that she now questioned everything, including, as she put it, the narrative of our marriage.

I said sharply, 'Narrative?'

'The whole story,' she said. The story of her and me, for better and for worse, till death did us part, the story of our union to the exclusion of all others – the story. It just wasn't right any more. It had somehow been falsified. When she thought ahead, imagined the years and the years . . . 'I'm sorry, darling,' she said. She was tearful. 'I'm so sorry.' She wiped her nose.

I was sitting on the floor, my shoes stupidly pointing at the ceiling. The yelping of emergency vehicles welled up from the street, flooded the room, ebbed one yelp at a time.

I said disastrously, 'Is there anything I can say that'll make you change your mind?'

We sat opposite each other in silence. Then I tossed my coat onto a chair and went to the bathroom. When I picked up my toothbrush it was wet. She had used it with a wife's unthinking intimacy. A hooting sob rose up from my chest. I began to gulp and pant. A deep, useless shame filled me – shame that I had failed my wife and my son, shame that I lacked the means to fight on, to tell her that I refused to accept that our marriage had suddenly collapsed, that all marriages went through crises, that others had survived their crises and we would do the same, to tell her she could be speaking out of shock or some other temporary condition, to tell her to stay, to tell her that I loved her, to tell her I needed her, that I would cut back on work, that I was a family man, a man with no friends and no pastimes, that my life was nothing but her and our boy. I felt shame – I see this clearly, now – at the instinctive recognition in myself of an awful enfeebling fatalism, a sense that the great outcomes were but randomly connected to our endeavours, that life was beyond mending, that love was loss, that nothing worth saying was sayable, that dullness was general, that disintegration was irresistible. I felt shame because it was me, not terror, she was fleeing.

And yet that night we reached for each other in the shuttered bedroom. Over the following weeks, our last as a family in New York, we had sex with a frequency that brought back our first year together, in London. This time round, however, we went about it with strangeness and no kissing, handling and licking and sucking and fucking with dispassion the series of cunts, dicks, assholes and tits that assembled itself out of our successive yet miserably several encounters. Life itself had become disembodied.

My family, the spine of my days, had crumbled. I was lost in invertebrate time.

An awful sensibleness descended upon us. In December, we found the will to visit our loft to fetch some belongings. There were stories going round of abandoned downtown apartments overrun by vermin, and when I opened our door I was braced for horrors. But, dust-clouded windows aside, our old home was as we'd left it. We retrieved some clothes and at Rachel's insistence picked out items of furniture for the hotel apartment, which I was to continue renting. She was concerned for my comfort just as I was concerned for hers. We'd agreed that whatever else happened, we wouldn't be moving back to Tribeca. The loft would be sold and the net proceeds, comfortably over a million dollars, would be invested in government bonds, a cautious spread of stocks and, on a tip from an economist I trusted, gold. We had another two million dollars in a joint savings account – the market was making me nervous – and two hundred thousand in various checking accounts, also in our joint names. It was understood that nobody would take any legal steps for a year. There was a chance, we carefully agreed, that everything would look different after Rachel had spent some time away from New York.

The three of us flew together to England. We stayed with Mr and Mrs Bolton at their house in Barnes, in south-west London, arriving on Christmas Eve. We opened gifts on Christmas morning, ate turkey with stuffing and potatoes and Brussels sprouts, drank sherry and red wine and port, made small talk, went to bed, slept, awoke, and then spent an almost unendurable further three days chewing, swallowing, sipping, walking and exchanging reasonable remarks. Then a black cab pulled up in front of the house. Rachel offered to accompany me to the airport. I shook my head. I went upstairs, where Jake was playing with his new toys. I picked him up and held him in my arms until he began to protest. I flew back to New York. There is no describing the wretchedness I felt, which persisted, in one form or another, throughout my association with Chuck Ramkissoon.

On my own, it was as if I were hospitalised at the Chelsea Hotel. I stayed in bed for almost a week, my existence sustained by a succession of men who arrived at my door with beer and pizzas and sparkling water. When I did begin to leave my room – as I had to, in order to work – I used the service elevator, a metal-clad box in which I was unlikely to meet anyone other than a muttering Panamanian maid or, as happened once, a very famous actress sneaking away from an encounter with a rumoured drug dealer on the tenth floor. After a week or two, my routine changed. Most evenings, once I'd showered and put on some casual clothes, I went down to the lobby and fell listlessly into a chair by the non-operational fireplace. I carried a book but did not read it. Often I was joined by a very kind widow in a baseball cap who conducted an endless and apparently fruitless search of her handbag and murmured to herself, for some reason, about Luxembourg. There was something anaesthetising about the traffic of people in the lobby, and I also took comfort from the men at the front desk, who out of pity invited me behind the counter to watch sports on their television and asked if I wanted to join their football pool. I did join, though I knew nothing about American football. 'You did real good yesterday,' Jesus, the bellman, would announce. 'I did?' 'Sure,' Jesus said, bringing out his chart. 'The Broncos won, right? And the Giants. That's two winners you got right there. OK,' he said, frowning as he concentrated, 'now you lost with the Packers. And the Bills. And I guess the 49ers.' He tapped a pencil against the chart as he considered the problem of my picks. 'So I'm still not ahead?' 'Right now, no,' Jesus admitted. 'But the season's not over yet. You could still turn it around, easy. You hang in there, you get hot next week? Shit, anything could happen.'

Not counting the lobby, the Chelsea Hotel had ten floors. Each was served by a dim hallway that ran from an airshaft on one side to, on my floor, a door with a yellowing pane of frosted glass that suggested the ulterior presence of a private detective rather than, as was actually the case, a fire escape. The floors were linked by a baronial staircase, which by virtue of the deep rectangular void at its centre had the effect of installing a precipice at the heart of the building. On all the walls was displayed the vaguely alarming artwork of tenants past and present. The finest and most valuable examples were reserved for the lobby: I shall never forget the pink, plump girl on a swing who hovered above the reception area gladly awaiting a push towards West 23rd Street. Occasionally one overheard by-the-night visitors – transients, as the management called them – commenting on how spooky they found it all, and there was a story that the hotel dead were secretly removed from their rooms in the middle of the night. But for me, returning from the office or from quick trips to Omaha, Oklahoma City, Cincinnati – Timbuktus, from my New Yorker's vantage point – there was nothing eerie about the building or the community that was established in it. Over half the rooms were occupied by long-term residents who by their furtiveness and ornamental diversity reminded me of the population of the aquarium I'd kept as a child, a murky tank in which cheap fish hesitated in weeds and an artificial starfish made a firmament of the gravel. That said, there was a correspondence between the looming and shadowy hotel folk and the phantasmagoric and newly indistinct world beyond the Chelsea's heavy glass doors, as if the one promised to explain the other. On my floor

41

there lived an octogenarian person of indeterminate gender – it took a month of surreptitious scrutiny before I'd satisfied myself she was a woman – who told me, by way of warning and reassurance, that she carried a gun and would kick the ass of anybody who made trouble on our floor. There was also an old and very sick black gentleman (now dead), apparently a legendary maker of prints and lithographs. There was a family with three young boys who ran wild in the hallways with tricycles and balls and trains. There was an unexplained Finn. There was a pit bull that never went out without a panting, menacing furniture dealer in tow. There was a Croatian woman, said to be a famous nightlife personality, and there was a revered playwright and librettist, whom it almost interested that I knew a little Greek and who introduced me to Arthur Miller in the elevator. There was a girl with gothic make-up who babysat and walked dogs. All of them were friendly to me, the crank in the suit and tie; but during the whole time I lived at the hotel, I had only one neighbourly visitor.

One February night, somebody knocked on my door. When I opened it, I found myself looking at a man dressed as an angel. A pair of tattered white wings, maybe two feet long and attached to some kind of girdle, rose behind his head. He wore an ankle-length wedding dress with a pearl-adorned bodice, and white slippers with dirty bows. Mottled foundation powder, applied over his whole face, failed to obscure the stubble around his mouth. His hair fell in straggles to his shoulders. A tiara was out of kilter on his head and he seemed distraught.

'Excuse me,' he said. 'I am looking for my cat.'

I said, 'What kind of cat?'

'A birman,' the angel said, and the noun flushed out a foreigner's accent. 'A black face, and white, quite long fur. His name is Salvator – Salvy.'

I shook my head. 'Sorry,' I said. 'I'll look out for him.' I started to shut the door, but his despairing expression made me hesitate.

'He's been gone for two days and two nights,' the angel said. 'I'm worried he's been kidnapped. These cats are very beautiful. They are worth a lot of money. All kinds of people come through this hotel.'

I said, 'Have you put up a notice? In the elevator?'

'I did, but somebody tore it down. That's suspicious, don't you think?' He produced a cigarette from a niche in his outfit. 'You have a light?'

He followed me into my apartment and sat down to smoke. I opened a window. The flossy edges of his wings trembled in the air current.

'This is a nice apartment,' he observed. 'How much are you paying?'

'Enough,' I said. My rent was six thousand a month – not a terrible deal for a two-bedroom, I'd thought, until I found out it was far more than anybody else was paying.

The angel occupied a studio on the sixth floor. He'd

moved in two weeks previously. His name was Mehmet Taspinar. He was Turkish, from Istanbul. He had lived in New York for a number of years, drifting from one abode to another. New York City, he informed me, was the one place in the world where he could be himself – at least, until recently. As he spoke, Taspinar sat very still on the edge of his chair, his feet and knees properly pressed together. He stated that he'd been asked to leave his last apartment by the landlord on the grounds that he was scaring the other tenants. 'I think he believed I might be a terrorist,' the angel said mildly. 'In a sense, I can understand him. An angel is a messenger of God. In Christianity, Judaism, Islam, angels are always frightening – always soldiers, killers, punishers.'

I gave no sign of having heard this. I was making a show of reading work documents I'd pulled out of my briefcase.

Taspinar looked in the direction of the kitchenette. 'You're drinking wine?'

I said without enthusiasm, 'Would you like a glass?'

Taspinar accepted and by way of recompense explained that he had dressed as an angel for two years now. He bought his wings at Religious Sex, on St Mark's Place. He owned three pairs. They cost him sixty-nine dollars a pair, he said. He showed me his right hand, on each finger of which he wore a large yellow stone. 'These were two dollars.'

44

'Have you tried looking on the roof?' I said.

The angel raised his misplucked eyebrows. 'You think he might be up there?'

'Well, the door at the top of the stairs is sometimes left open. Your cat could have got out.'

'Will you show me?' The wings wobbled as he stood up.

'Just go right up the stairs until you come to the door. It's very easy.'

'I'm a little afraid,' Taspinar said, hunching his shoulders pathetically. Although at least thirty, he had the slight, defenceless frame of a batboy.

I reached for my coat. 'I've only got a few minutes,' I said. 'Then I've got to do some work.'

We climbed the stairs to the tenth floor and continued up to the small landing at the entrance to the roof. As I'd suspected, the door was open. We went through. I'd been up to the roof once before. It was divided into plots belonging to the people who occupied the mansard apartments, and they had turned it into a garden of sun decks, brick enclosures, potted plants and small trees. In the summer, it was a lovely place; it was winter now, and the cold was shocking. I carefully trod the frozen snow. Taspinar, wearing only his angel's outfit and barefooted apart from his slippers, headed off elsewhere with small skipping steps. He began calling for his cat in Turkish. I advanced in the direction of a tree dotted with fairy lights and found a spot out of the wind. The lighted peak of the Empire State Building loomed ashen and sublime. I regretted not bringing a hat. Turning, I saw the angel disappear behind a turret and then reappear in madly feathery profile against the red glow of the YMCA sign across the street. He cried out the cat's name: Salvy! Salvy!

I went inside.

If I thought I'd shaken him off, I was mistaken. A nocturnal individual, Taspinar took to joining me in the lobby in the late evenings, assuming a prim upright position on a massive wooden armchair next to mine. Needless to say, his appearance provoked surprise and laughter from the transients. Taspinar enjoyed the attention but rarely responded. When a drunk Japanese asked if he could fly, he gave the man his usual dazed smile. 'Of course, I would *like* to fly,' Taspinar confided to me afterwards, 'but I know I can't. I'm not cuckoo.'

Actually, this last assertion was doubtful. I learned that before he'd become possessed by his angelic compulsion, Taspinar had spent some time in a mental asylum in New Hampshire. His father, a rich man who owned factories, had paid the fees, just as he now paid the allowance that permitted his son to live in frugal idleness. The sustaining fiction in this arrangement was that Taspinar was at graduate school at Columbia University, where he'd enrolled years ago. Once I had overcome the thought that midway through my life the only companionship I could count on was that of a person who, as he put it, could no longer bear the masculine details of his life, I grew to mildly enjoy the angel's unexpectedly serene company. He and I and the murmuring widow in the baseball cap sat in a row like three crazy old sisters who have long ago run out of things to say to one another. Taspinar, it turned out, was a rather artless man who, in spite of his morbid confusion, easily accepted the small offerings of pleasure that daily life provided. He savoured his coffee, read newspapers avidly, found amusement in inconsequential events. With regard to my own situation, about which he made occasional enquiries but offered little comment, he was considerate. As my fondness for him grew, so did my anxiety. When his baroque anguish, too awful and strange for me to think about, became acute, he neglected himself. His frock (he owned three or four) went unchanged for days, his silver fingernail polish deteriorated to a fishy shimmer, his waxed back surrendered to emergent cohorts of hard little hairs. Most distressing of all was the state of his wings. His favourite white pair, in which he had first met me, somehow developed a list, and he took to wearing black bedraggled ones that made him look like a crow. One Saturday I took it upon myself to go to the East Village and buy him fresh plumage. I chose a white, rather magnificent set with shining long vanes. 'Here,' I said, stiffly tendering him the package in the lobby that evening. 'I thought you might find these useful.' Taspinar seemed very pleased, but I had made an error. My gift was never seen again. As for the cat, it was never seen again either.

Meanwhile I was making efforts to promote my own well-being. At Rachel's transoceanic urging, I went to see a shrink, a nice fellow who offered me a peppermint every twenty minutes and subscribed to the fine, progressive notion that each day we have lived is a kind of possession and, if we are its alert custodian, brings us ever closer to knowledge of the slipperiest kind. I lasted three sessions. I started to take yoga classes at the YMCA across the street from the hotel. This went better, and when I touched my toes for the first time in years I felt a larger movement of life at my fingertips. I was determined to open myself to new directions, a project I connected with escaping from the small country of fog in which, at a point I could not surely trace, I'd settled. That country, I speculated, might have some meaningful relation to my country of physical residence, and so every second weekend, when I travelled to London to be with my wife and son, I hoped that flying high into the atmosphere, over boundless massifs of vapour or small clouds dispersed like the droppings of Pegasus on an unseen platform of air, might also lift me above my personal haze. That is, I would conduct a retrospective of our affable intercontinental dealings and assemble the hope and theory that the foundation of my family might after all be secure and our old unity still within reach. But each time Rachel materialised at her parents' door she wore a preemptive expression of weariness, and I understood that the haze had travelled all the way to this house in west London.

'How was the flight?'

'Good.' I fidgeted with my suitcase. 'I managed to get a couple of hours of sleep.' A hesitation, and then an English peck for each cheek; whereas once it had been our loving tic to kiss triply – left, right, and left again – in the Dutch style she found so amusing.

She would never, in the old days, have expressed curiosity about something as prosaic as a flight. Her truest self resisted triteness, even of the inventive romantic variety, as a kind of falsehood. When we'd fallen for each other it had not been a project of bouquets and necklaces and strokes of genius on my part: there were no ambushes by string quartets or surprise air tickets to a spit of Pacific coral. We courted in the style preferred by the English: alcoholically. Our love started in drink at a party in South Kensington, where we made out for an hour on a mound of dark woollen overcoats, and continued in drink a week later at a pub in Notting Hill. As soon as we left the pub she kissed me. We went to my flat, drank more, and grappled on a sofa squeakily adrift on four wheels. 'What's that horrible noise?' Rachel exclaimed with a ridiculous jerk of the head. 'The castors,' I said, technically. 'No, it's a mouse,' she said. She was casting us in a screwball comedy, herself as Hepburn, whose bony beauty I recognised in her, me as the professor with his head up his ass. I looked the part: excessively tall, bespectacled, given to nodding and smiling. I have never entirely shed the gormlessness of that early role. She said, 'Isn't there somewhere less mousy we can go?' Later that night, she said, 'Talk to me in Dutch,' and I did. '*Lekker stuk van me*,' I growled. 'On second thoughts,' she said, 'don't talk to me in Dutch.' When, months later, we sobered up and began to see others as a couple, her public fluency mesmerised me. She spoke in complete sentences and intact paragraphs and almost always in the trope of the tiny, well-constructed argument. She was obviously a brilliant lawyer. My own way with English she found moving for its clunking lexical precision; and she especially loved for me to spout a scrap of remembered Latin, the more nonsensical the better. *O fortunatos nimium, sua si bona norint, agricolas.*

One windy Sunday afternoon in March 2002, when I was in London for a long weekend, we van den Broeks went for a walk on Putney Common. It was the kind of uncomplicated family outing that fortified my belief that our physical separation might yet turn out to have been a bad joke. I suggested to Rachel, as we watched Jake ride ahead on his tricycle, that things were not going too badly. Her eyes were fixed forward and she made no reply. I said, 'What I mean is –'

'I know what you mean,' Rachel said, cutting me short.

Jake got off his tricycle and ran to a swing. I lifted him into the seat and set him in motion. 'Higher,' he joyfully urged me.

Rachel stood beside me, hands in pockets. 'Higher,' Jake repeated every time he swung up to my hand, and for a while his was the only voice among us. His happiness on the swing was about the relief of communication as much as anything. He cleanly uttered his wish and cleanly it was granted. Our son, we'd recently been told, was tongue-tied: the arrival of certain consonants caused his tongue to scuttle back to the innermost parts of his mouth, re-emerging only in the safety of a vowel. An operation to cure this had been discussed and, in the end, rejected; for my own speech impediment, however, there was no optional quick fix. From our beginning, it had been Rachel's place to talk freely and airily, mine to carefully listen and utter only solid things. This bargain acted as a kind of guarantee of our sentimental valuables and, in our minds, set us apart from bantering couples whose trinkety talk felt like a form of emotional dissipation. Now, searching for words as I propelled Jake skyward, I felt at a disadvantage.

'We said we'd review things,' I finally said.

'Yes, we did,' she said.

'I just want you to know —'

'I already know, darling,' Rachel said quickly, and she

waggled her lowered chin to relax the solid orb of tension that was invariably buried at the junction of her neck and right shoulder. There was an exhaustion about her throat I hadn't seen before. 'Let's not do any reviewing,' she said. 'Please. There isn't anything to review.'

Another little boy appeared among us, followed moments later by his mother. The little boy impatiently jangled the seat of the swing. 'Hold on, hold on,' his mother said. A baby, peeping out of a sling, already burdened her. Fractions of smiles passed between the adults. Ten o'clock approached. Soon the playground would be alive with children.

'Higher,' my son said proudly.

There remained the problem of what to do with my alternate weekends in New York. Rivera decided I should play golf. 'You look like Ernie Els,' he said. 'Maybe you could swing like him too.' Stepping away from my desk, he made a triangle of his arms and shoulders. He was a small, compact lefty. 'It's all about rhythm,' he explained. 'Ernie' – his backswing flew up with the word – 'Els': down, for the duration of the syllable, came the downswing. 'See? Easy does it.' Rivera, who was shopping for a lob wedge, took me to a golf centre by Union Square. At the practice facility, a graduated row of shiny irons stood on a rack. 'Hit a ball,' Rivera said, pushing me into a grotto of netting. A troglodyte, I twice swung and missed.

But a reminder of sports had been given to me, and one late-April day, while lowering a box of papers into the trunk of a taxicab, I noticed a cricket bat nestled against the casing of the spare tyre. It seemed like a mirage and I stupidly asked the driver, 'Is that a cricket bat?' As he drove, the cabbie – my future teammate Umar – told me he played every week for a Staten Island team. His glance entered the rear-view mirror. 'You interested in playing?' 'Maybe,' I said. 'Sure.' 'Come along on Saturday,' Umar said. 'Maybe we can fix you up with a game.'

I memorised the time and the place without ever forming the intention of going. Then the first morning of the weekend came. It was a bright, warm day, European in its mildness, and walking past the flowering pear trees on 19th Street I was riddled by a longing for similar summer days in my youth, which were given over, at every opportunity, to cricket.

For cricket is played in Holland. There are a few thousand Dutch cricketers and they go about their game with the seriousness and organisation that characterises all of Dutch sport. The conservative, slightly stuck-up stratum of society, in which I grew up, especially loves cricket, and the players are ghosts of sorts from an Anglophile past: I am from The Hague, where Dutch bourgeois snobbishness and Dutch cricket are, not unrelatedly, most concentrated. We – that is, my mother and I – lived in a

53

semi-detached house on Tortellaan, a quiet street near Sportlaan. From Houtrust, where the indoor skating rink was located and where I first held a girl's hand in romantic earnest (not on the ice but in the cafeteria, where kids gathered to spend their pocket money on cones of *frites met mayonnaise*), Sportlaan led south towards the dunes and seaside hotels of Kijkduin. It also led, if you exercised your imagination, to Paris: one year, the hunched, bright-shirted racers of the Tour de France zoomed by like fantastically bicycling macaws. On the far side of Sportlaan were woods called the Bosjes van Pex, and in the woods was the home of a venerable football and cricket club, Houdt Braef Standt – HBS. I joined HBS at the age of seven, anxiously attending the membership interview with my mother. I am not sure what these encounters were designed to accomplish, but in any event I had no cause to worry. When the meeting was over the members of the committee gravely shook my hand and said, Welcome to HBS. I was thrilled. I was too young to realise they'd all known my father, who had been a member of the club for nearly forty years, and that it must have given them great pleasure to take his son under their wing. For that's how these sports clubs functioned: they took on scores of boys almost as hatchlings and bestowed parental care and effort on them for years, even on those who were athletically hope-less. From September through April I played football, proudly wearing the club's black shirt and black shorts bought at the sporting goods store on Fahrenheitstraat; and from May through August I played cricket. I loved both sports equally; but by my mid-teens, cricket had claimed its first place. We played on coconut matting wickets, and our outfields, used also for winter games, were sluggish; but there any resemblance to American cricket ended.

What ached me, as I paused on 19th Street two decades later, was the memory of lovely solitary cycle rides, on sunny and tranquil mornings like this one in Chelsea, through the fragmented brilliance of the woods around the HBS grounds, my red Gray-Nicolls bag resting between the handlebars of my bicycle, a lambswool sweater slung over my shoulders. Lacoste polo shirts, bright V-necked sweaters, brogues, diamond-patterned Burlington socks, corduroy trousers: I and men I knew dressed that way, even as teenagers. Then came a second memory, of my mother watching me play. It was her habit to unfold a portable chair by the western sightscreen and to sit there for hours, grading homework and occasionally looking up to follow the game. Although always friendly, she rarely spoke to the other spectators scattered along the boundary's whitewashed planks, which, laid end to end, distantly encircled the batsman and marked the edge of his innings' impermanent heaven. Your innings might be over in a second, as a life in eternity. Out, you trudged off miserably, irrevocably dismissed into the nothingness of the non-participant: the amateur cricketer does not enjoy, as the baseballer does, the glimmering prospect of numerous at-bats. You get only one chance, in the blazing middle. When neither fielding nor batting, I and a team-mate or two would embark on a *rondje* – a stroll round the field – smoking cigarettes and acknowledging various parents and interested parties. My mother was known independently to many of the boys at the club because they were current or former pupils of hers.

'*Dag, mevrouw van den Broek. Alles goed?*'

'*Ja, dank je, Willem.*'

We were cordial, somewhat arrogant young men, in accordance with our upbringing.

My cricket career at HBS dwindled while I studied classics at Leiden University. When my first adult job, with Shell Oil, returned me to The Hague at the age of twenty-four, I had grown away from my club. I would not play cricket again until years later, when I went to London to become an analyst at D—— Bank and joined South Bank Cricket Club, whose home, at Turney Road, was near Herne Hill, in the south of the city. On marvellously shorn Surrey village greens – the smell of grass when mown in May provokes in me pangs of emotion that I still dare not dwell on – we battled gently for victory and drank warm beer on the steps of ancient wooden pavilions. Once, after a shaky start to the season, I booked a private net at Lord's. An elderly coach with the countenance of a butler fed balls into a bowling machine and declared, 'Good shot, sir,' each time my bat connected with one of the long hops and half-volleys the machine amiably spat out. All of it was agreeable, English and enchanting; but I quit after a couple of seasons. With my mother no longer watching, cricket was never quite the same again.

Rachel came to Turney Road once. She approached on foot across the green blankness of the sports ground. My team was fielding, and for an hour she sat by herself on the grass. I could sense her boredom from a hundred yards. Between innings, when the teams drank tea and ate cakes and sandwiches, she and I got together. I brought her a cup of tea and sat down with her, self-consciously detached from the rows of players seated at the main table. 'Sandwich?' I said, offering her one of mine, a gluey, cheesy thing that only a starving player could bring himself to eat. She shook her head. 'How can you bear it?' she blurted. 'All that standing around.' I smiled regretfully. Not wanting to spoil my afternoon, she said, 'Although you do look nice in that hat.' It was her only attempt at spectatorship.

To my surprise, my mother continued attending matches at HBS even when I no longer played. It had not dawned on her son that following his progress might not have been her main purpose. Though comfortable at the club, my mother never discovered the talent for jolliness that animated many of the older characters for whom the place was a home away from home. The clubhouse, with its billiards tables and *borreltjes*, was not for her. At stumps she would fold up her chair and make her way directly to the car park, smiling at the many familiar faces she saw. Only now do I appreciate how for her, too, there must have been balminess in the sights and sounds and rhythms of a full day's cricket, in which unhurried time is portioned out by the ticking of ball against bat, and only now do I ask myself about the thoughts occupying her mind as she sat there with a red blanket over her knees, sometimes from eleven in the morning till six or seven in the evening. She was unrevealing about such matters. When she spoke about my father, it would only be to mention a small fact or two – how his job at the air ministry had bored him; how he liked to eat raw herring, slathered in onions and dangled vertically into the mouth, in Scheveningen; how he loved Cassius Clay. My father, Marcel van den Broek, was significantly older than my mother. She was thirty-three when they married, in 1966, and he was forty-three. In January, 1970, my father was the front-seat passenger in a car travelling near Breda, in the south of the country. There was an accident and he flew through the windscreen. He was killed. I was not yet two.

So I walked directly from 19th Street to the storage unit by Chelsea Piers where our loft furnishings had been dumped, and searched around for the cricketing gear I'd brought with me from Europe and which it had never occurred to me either to throw out or to use. The Duncan Fearnley trunk was in a corner at the back. The latches flipped up with a snap, releasing that bitter marmalade odour of neglected cricket apparel. It was all there, the old kit: the Slazenger Viv Richards batting pads with stuffing leaking from the seams; thick-fingered, sweat-darkened batting gloves; unwashed white socks; an anti-erotic jockstrap; and my HBS sweater, moth-eaten and shrunken, with the red V between two black Vs at the neck and, over the heart, two black ticks emblemising crows. I pulled out my old bat. It was more cracked than I remembered. The traces of long-gone cricket balls still reddened its blade. I gripped the worn rubber-sleeved handle with bare hands and crouched into a batting stance. Seeing a fast half-volley land by some boxed books, I strode with my left foot to the pitch of the ball and dreamily smashed it.

I checked my watch. It was not too late to catch a taxi to Staten Island.

When I arrived at Walker Park, I thought I'd come to the wrong place. There seemed no room, in the grassy opening visible from Bard Avenue, for cricket; then I saw the orange-pink batting track and realised, to my dismay, that this must be it.

I had made the mistake of being punctual. Except for two figures out in the middle of the field, who laboured with a metal hand-roller on the track – during the week, the locals heedlessly scuffed the clay – there was nobody around. I waited by the clubhouse in a state of discouragement. A full hour after the appointed time, a few more Staten Island players showed up. Umar, my sole contact, was not among them. The metal hatch to the basement was opened, and out of it were fetched plastic chairs, a couple of tables and, dramatically, the twenty-five-yard-long coconut-fibre matting, rolled into a giant bulging cigar-like cylinder. Six men carried the mat out to the middle, bearing it aloft on three stumps. The visiting team suddenly appeared, hanging around in the ominous aura that always surrounds opponents before a match. I decided to walk over to the home players hammering pins into the loops that fringed the mat. 'Umar told me to come along,' I announced. There was a brief discussion among the more senior men. 'Speak to the captain,' one of them said, directing me back to the clubhouse.

The captain, baffled by my presence, told me to wait a while. Now some of the players had changed into whites and were taking practice catches. Most of the home team appeared to be Indians. They spoke a rough English, to my ears barely comprehensible, that I took to be foreign to them. It wasn't until later that I understood they were West Indians, not Asians, and their speech – a spiky dialect of grammatical short cuts and jewel-like expressions I'd never heard before – was conducted in their first and only language.

After a few secretive consultations between the captain and one or two others, it was suggested to me that I come back some other week and play a friendly match; this I did. I continued to play for the rest of the summer. Because my availability coincided with the cycle of away games, every fortnight I found myself going by taxi to Queens or Brooklyn or hitching a ride with teammates to more faraway destinations. We rendezvoused on Canal Street or in Jersey City. The minibus pulled up and a hand hung out of the passenger-seat window, inviting a slap. 'Wh'appening, Hans, baby?' 'Whassup, Joey. Hey, Salim – thanks for picking me up.' 'Any time, man, any time.' I squeezed in next to my teammates. Nobody complained: already I occupied the slot that groups of men reserve for the reticent good egg. Chutney music was playing, and to its relentlessly tinny and cheerful urgings we'd drive off to New Jersey, Philadelphia, Long Island. We sat mostly silently in the van, absorbed into the moodiness that afflicts competitors as they contemplate, or try to put out of their minds, the drama that awaits. What we talked about, when we did talk, was cricket. There was nothing else to discuss. The rest of our lives – jobs, children, wives, worries – peeled away, leaving only this fateful sporting fruit. Women were rarely present. Their moment came on Family Day, held at Walker Park on an August Saturday. Family Day was when the men repaid, at an outrageous bargain, the mothers and children who had suffered their absences during the season. The men cooked – fussily, on enormous transportable barbecue pits – and the wives, with heartbreaking good nature, played a chaotic game of cricket with the kids. There were foot races and hot dogs and paper plates loaded with curry chicken and dal puri. Everybody went home with a trophy.

In the world of men's cricket, I surprised myself. Aged thirty-four, troubled increasingly by backache, I found I could still fling the ball into the wicket-keeper's gloves with a flat throw from forty yards, could still stand under a skyer and hold the catch, could still run up and bowl outswingers at a medium pace. I could also still hit a cricket ball; but the flame of rolling leather, caught up in long weeds, almost always was quickly put out. The bliss of batting was denied to me.

Of course, it was open to me to make adjustments. There was nothing, in principle, to stop me from changing my game, from taking up the cow-shots and lofted bashes in which many of my teammates specialised. But it was, I felt, different for them. They had grown up playing the game in floodlit Lahore car parks or in rough clearings in some West Indian countryside. They could, and did, modify their batting without spiritual upheaval. I could not. More accurately, I would not change – which was uncharacteristic of me. Coming to America (I'd done so willingly, though not primarily on my own account: it was Rachel who'd applied for an opening with the New

York office of her firm, and I who'd had to look for another job), I'd eagerly taken to new customs and mannerisms at the expense of old ones. How little, in the fluidities of my new country, I missed the ancient clotted continent. But self-transformation has its limits; and my limit was reached in the peculiar matter of batting. I would stubbornly continue to bat as I always had, even if it meant the end of making runs.

Some people have no difficulty in identifying with their younger incarnations: Rachel, for example, will refer to episodes from her childhood or college days as if they'd happened to her that very morning. I, however, seem given to self-estrangement. I find it hard to muster oneness with those former selves whose accidents and endeavours have shaped who I am now. The schoolboy at the Gymnasium Haganum; the Leiden student; the clueless trainee executive at Shell; the analyst in London; even the thirty-year-old who flew to New York with his excited young wife: my natural sense is that all are faded, by the by, discontinued. But I still think, and I fear will always think, of myself as the young man who got a hundred runs in Amstelveen with a flurry of cuts, who took that diving catch at second slip in Rotterdam, who lucked into a hat trick at the Haagse Cricket Club. These and other moments of cricket are scorched in my mind like sexual memories, forever available to me and capable, during those long nights alone in the hotel when I sought refuge from the sorriest feelings, of keeping me awake as I relived them in bed and powerlessly mourned the mysterious promise they held. To reinvent myself in order to bat the American way, that baseball-like business of slugging and hoisting, involved more than the trivial abandonment of a hard-won style of hitting a ball. It meant snipping a fine white thread running, through years and years, to my mothered self.

I ran into Chuck again by accident. In the late summer, a friend of mine from a poker game I'd briefly belonged to, a food critic named Vinay, suggested that I might find amusement in joining him on his nightly forays for material. Vinay wrote a magazine column about New York restaurants, specifically, cheap, little-known restaurants: an enervating assignment that placed him on a treadmill of eating and writing and eating and writing that he couldn't face alone. It did not matter to Vinay that I knew nothing about food. 'Fuck that, dude,' he said. Vinay was from Bangalore. 'Just tag along and stop me from going mad. If we eat some fucking Gouda cheese, I'll ask for your opinion. Otherwise just eat and enjoy yourself. It's all paid for.' So from time to time I went with him to places in Chinatown and Harlem and Alphabet City and Hell's Kitchen or, if he was really desperate and able to overcome his loathing of the outer boroughs, Astoria and Fort Greene and Cobble Hill. Vinay was unhappy with his beat. He believed he ought to have been writing about the great chefs in the great restaurants, or educating the public about vintage wines or – his obsession – single malt whiskies. 'I used to hate whisky,' he told me. 'My dad and his friends drank it all the time. But then I found out they weren't drinking real whisky. They were drinking Indian whisky – look-like whisky. McDowell's, Peter Scot, stuff that almost tastes like rum. When I got into Scotch – that's when I began to understand what this drink is really about.' Vinay found it distasteful to deal with the owners and cooks at the cheap places, immigrants who generally spoke little English and saw no particular reason to spend time talking to him. Also, the sheer variety of foodstuffs bothered him. 'One night it's Cantonese, then it's Georgian, then it's Indonesian, then Syrian. I mean, I think this shit is good baklava, but what the fuck do I know, really? How can I be sure?' Yet when he wrote, Vinay exuded bright certainty and expertise. As I repeatedly went forth with him and began to understand the ignorance and contradictions and language difficulties with which he contended, and the doubtful sources of his information and the seemingly bottomless history and darkness out of which the dishes of New York emerge, the deeper grew my suspicion that his work finally consisted of minting or perpetuating and in any event circulating misconceptions about his subject and in this way adding to the endless perplexity of the world.

Similar misgivings, I should say, had begun to infect my own efforts at work. These efforts required me, sitting at my desk on the twenty-second floor of a glassy tower, to express reliable opinions about the current and future valuation of certain oil and gas stocks. If an important new insight came to me, I would transmit it to the sales force at the morning shout, just before the markets opened at eight. I stood at a microphone at the edge of the trading floor and delivered a godless minute-long homily to doubting congregants distributed amongst the computer screens. After the shout, I spent a half-hour on the trading floor going over the particulars.

'Hans, this Gabon joint venture watertight?'

'Maybe.'

Grins all round at this joke. 'Who's the CEO over there? Johnson?'

'Johnson's with Apache now. Frank Tomlinson is the new guy. Used to be with Total. But the FD is still the same guy, Sanchez.'

'Huh. What kind of development costs we talking about?'

'Five dollars a barrel, max.'

'How they going to do that?'

'The tax structure's good. Plus they're only paying a two-buck royalty.'

'Yeah, well, I need a better story.'

'You might want to try Fidelity. I was over there Monday. Tell them something about innovative horizontal drilling technology. That's another story in itself, by the way – Delta Geoservices. Karen's got the details.'

Somebody else: 'I'll take details on horizontal drilling from Karen all day, every day.'

'So what're you saying, Dutch or Double Dutch?'

I smiled. 'I'm saying Double Dutch.' To my disproportionate credit, this informal catchphrase of mine – 'Dutch' described an ordinary recommendation, 'Double Dutch' a strong recommendation – had entered the language of the bank and, from there, of certain parts of the industry.

I liked and respected my colleagues: the mere sight of them – the men close-shaven and prosperously thick about the waist, where ID badges and communication gadgets clustered, the women in subdued suits, all of them shouldering their burdens as best they could – was capable of filling me with joy. But by the fall of 2002, even my work, the largest of the pots and pans I'd placed under my life's leaking ceiling, had become too small to contain my misery. It forcefully struck me as a masquerade, this endless business of churning out research papers, of blast voice-mailing clients overnight with my latest thoughts on ExxonMobil or ConocoPhillips, of listening to oil executives glossing corporate performance in tired jargon, of flying before dawn to meet investors in shitty towns in the middle of America, of the squabbles about the analyst rankings, of the stress of constantly tending to my popularity and perceived competence. I felt like Vinay, cooking up myths from scraps and peels of fact. When, in October, my *II* ranking remained unchanged at number four, my private reaction was almost one of bitterness.

One Friday of that month, I found Vinay in a bad mood. He had, he told me, been asked to write a story about the eating places of taxicab drivers. The theory, apparently, was that here you had a class of men familiar with alien foods who exercised their choices from a vast selection of establishments and had no stake in the bourgeois dining enterprise: men supposedly driven by unfeigned primitive cravings, men hungering for a true taste of homeland and mother's cooking, men who would, in short, lead one to the so-called real thing. Of course, I could not help thinking it simple, this theory of reality. Vinay had objections of a narrower kind. 'Cab drivers?' he said. 'Have you ever heard one of these guys express an opinion that wasn't complete bullshit? I told my editor, Dude, I'm from fucking India. You think in India we take our fucking dining cues from cab drivers? And then I'm like' – Vinay laughed furiously – 'Yo, Mark, the name's not Vinnie, OK? It's Vinay.' Vinay buckled, as one must, and we found a taxi driven by a man from Dhaka who was prepared to take us to a place he liked. This exercise was repeated with several cab drivers. We'd look at a menu, eat a mouthful of food, and head out again in search of another lurching ride. Before long the night had assumed the character of an evil black soup, sampled somewhere along the line, whose bitty, fatty constituents rose sickeningly to the surface before sinking back again into a spoon-deep dark. Just before midnight, a taxi driver took us to Lexington and 20-something and wordlessly pulled up at yet another accumulation of double-parked yellow cars.

'This is the last one, Vinay,' I warned him.

We entered the restaurant. There was a buffet counter, a wilfully haphazard arrangement of chairs and tables and refrigerators, and framed, violently colourful photographs attached to the walls: schoolchildren, sitting under a tree, receiving instruction from a teacher pointing at a blackboard; an idyll in which a long-haired maiden perched on a swing; a city in Pakistan at night. At the rear was a further dining area where men, eating in silence, stared intently at a television screen. Almost all the patrons were South Asian. 'Look at what they're having,' Vinay said despairingly. 'Naan with vegetables. These guys are on a three-dollar budget.' While Vinay examined the menu, I wandered off to look at the television. To my amazement – I'd never seen this before in America – they were showing a cricket match: Pakistan versus New Zealand, broadcast live from Lahore. Shoaib Akhtar, a.k.a. the Rawalpindi Express, was bowling at top speed to the New Zealand captain, Stephen Fleming. I settled ecstatically into a seat.

Moments later, I felt a tap on my shoulder. It took a second or two to recognise Chuck Ramkissoon.

'Hey there, friend,' he said. 'Come join us.' He was showing me a table occupied by a black man wearing a super's shirt embroidered with the address of his building and his name, Roy McGarrell. I accepted Chuck's invitation, and we were joined by Vinay, who arrived carrying a tray of gajrala and chicken karahi.

I urged Chuck and Roy to eat the food. 'Vinay here's paid to eat this stuff. You'd be doing him a favour.'

It turned out that Roy, like Chuck, was from Trinidad. 'Callaloo,' Vinay remarked absently, and Roy and Chuck started chortling with delight. 'You know callaloo?' Roy said. Addressing me, he said, 'Callaloo is the leaves of the dasheen bush. You can't get dasheen easy here.'

'What about that market on Flatbush and Church?' Chuck said. 'You find it there.'

'Well, maybe,' Roy conceded. 'But if you can't get the real thing, you make it with spinach. You put in coconut milk: you grate the flesh of the coconut fine and you squeeze it and the moisture come out. You also put in a whole green pepper – it don't be hot unless you burst it – thyme, chive, garlic, onion. Normally you put in blue crab; others put in pickled pigtails. You cook it and you bring out a swizzle stick and you swizzle it until the bush

70

melt down into a thick sauce like a tomato sauce. That's the old-time way; now we put it in a blender. Pour it on stewfish – kingfish, carite fish: mmm-hmm. You also eat it with yam, sweet potato. Dumpling.'

Chuck said to Vinay, 'He's not talking about Chinese dumplings.'

'Our dumpling different,' Roy said. 'Chinese dumpling soft. We make our dumpling stiff.'

'Callaloo,' Chuck said wistfully.

'We used to eat it at Maracas Bay,' Roy said. 'Or Las Cuevas. Maracas, the water more rough but the beach more popular. In Las Cuevas, the water calm. Easter time? Oh my Lord, it full. Sometime people walk for miles through the mountains to go there. You spend Easter Sunday and Easter Monday on the beach. You pack your bag with ingredients separate. You have your sweet drink – we call sodas sweet drink – and you pack your car and everybody take a bathing suit, and you go to the beach and spend the whole day eating, bathing. Oh my.' He shuddered with pleasure.

'I nearly drowned in Maracas once,' Chuck said.

'Them riptide there dangerous, boy,' Roy said.

Chuck handed a card to Vinay. 'Maybe you could come by my restaurant sometime.'

Vinay examined the card. 'Kosher sushi?'

'That's what we do,' Chuck said proudly. He leaned over to point at the card. 'That's where we are – Avenue Q and Coney Island.'

71

'Business good?' I asked.

'Very good,' he said. 'We cater to the Jews in my neighbourhood. There are thousands and thousands of them, all observant.' Chuck handed me a card, too. 'I have a Jewish partner who has the confidence of the rabbi. Makes things a lot easier. But I tell you, getting kosher certification is a tough business. Tougher than the pharmaceuticals business, I like to say. You wouldn't believe the problems that come up. Earlier this year we had some trouble with seahorses.'

'Seahorses?' I said.

Chuck said, 'You know how you check nori, the seaweed you wrap the sushi in? You examine it over a light box, like an X-ray. And they found seahorse infestation in our supplier's seaweed. And seahorses are not kosher. Neither are shrimps and eels and octopus and squid. Only fish with scales and fins are kosher. But not all fish with fins have scales,' Chuck added. 'And sometimes what you think are scales are in fact bony protrusions. Bony protrusions do not qualify as scales. No, sir.' Roy and he laughed loudly at this. 'What are we left with? Halibut, salmon, red snapper, mackerel, mahi-mahi, tuna – but only certain kinds of tuna. Which ones? Albacore, skipjack, yellowfin.'

Chuck wasn't going to stop there. He believed in facts, in their momentousness and charm. He had no option, of course: who was going to listen to mere opinion coming from him?

'What about fish eggs, roe?' he said, showing off. 'The eggs of kosher fish are generally shaped differently from non-kosher fish. Also, they tend to be red, whereas non-kosher are black. Then there are issues with rice, issues with vinegar. Sushi vinegar will often have non-kosher ingredients, or will be made using a non-kosher process. There are issues with worms in the flesh of the fish, with utensils, with storage, with filleting, with freezing, with sauces, with the broths and oils you pack the fish in. Every aspect of the process is difficult. It's a painstaking business, I'm telling you. But that's my opportunity, you see. I don't mind complication. For me, complication represents an opportunity. The more something is complicated, the more potential competitors will be deterred.'

'So you're a restaurateur,' I said, moving my chair to let pass two dramatically bearded and turbaned men who had risen to their feet to face up to whatever night toil awaited them.

'I'm a businessman,' Chuck quibbled agreeably. 'I have several businesses. And what do you do?'

'I work at a bank. As an equities analyst.'

'Which bank?' Chuck asked, filling his mouth with Vinay's chicken. When I told him, he improbably declared, 'I have had dealings with M——. What stocks do you analyse?'

I told him, eyeing the television: Fleming had just punched Akhtar through the covers for four runs, and a groan of disgust mixed with appreciation sounded in the restaurant.

'Do you think there's much left in the consolidation trend?'

I turned to give him my attention. In recent years, my sector had seen a rush of mergers and acquisitions. It was a well-known phenomenon; nevertheless, the slant of Chuck's enquiry was exactly that of the fund managers who questioned me. 'I think the trend is in place,' I said, rewarding him with a term of professional wiliness.

'And before M—— you worked where?' Chuck said. He was blithely curious.

I found myself telling him about my years in The Hague and London.

'Give me your e-mail address,' Chuck Ramkissoon said. 'I have a business opportunity that might interest you.'

He handed me a second card. This read,

CHUCK CRICKET, INC.
Chuck Ramkissoon, President

He said, as I wrote down my own details, 'I've started up a cricket business. Right here in the city.'

Evidently something showed in my expression, because Chuck said good-naturedly, 'You see? You don't believe me. You don't think it's possible.'

'What kind of business?'

'I can't say any more.' He was eyeing the people around us. 'We're at a very delicate stage. My investors wouldn't like it. But if you're interested, maybe I could use your expertise. We need to raise quite a lot of money. Mezzanine finance? Do you know about mezzanine finance?' He lingered on the exotic phrase.

Vinay had stood up to leave, and I also got up.

'So long,' I said, mirroring Roy's raised hand.

'I'll be in touch,' Chuck said.

We stepped into the night. 'What a crazy son of a bitch,' Vinay said.

After the passage of a week or so, I received a padded envelope at my office. When I opened the envelope, a postcard fell out.

Dear Hans,
    You know that you are a member of the first tribe of New York, excepting of course the Red Indians. Here is something you might like.
    Best wishes,
    Chuck Ramkissoon

Smothered by the attentiveness, I put the envelope back in my briefcase without further examining it.

A few days later, I caught the Maple Leaf Express, bound for Toronto, to Albany, where a group of investors awaited. It was a brown November morning. Rain spotted my window as we pulled away into the tunnels and gorges through which the Penn Station trains secretively dribble up the West Side. At Harlem, the Hudson, flowing parallel to the track, came into view. I had taken this journey before, yet I was startled afresh by the existence of this waterside vista, which on a blurred morning such as this had the effect, once we passed under the George Washington Bridge, of cancelling out centuries. The far side of the river was a wild bank of forest. Clouds steaming on the clifftops foxed all sense of perspective, so that it seemed to me that I saw distant and fabulously high mountains. I fell asleep. When I awoke, the river had turned into an indeterminate grey lake. Three swans on the water were the white of phosphor. Then the Tappan Zee Bridge came clumsily out of the mist, and soon afterwards the far bank reappeared and the Hudson again was itself. Tarrytown, a whoosh of parking lots and ballfields, came and went. The valley slipped back into timelessness. As the morning lightened, the shadows of the purple and bronze trees became more distinct on the water. The brown river, now very still, was glossed in places, as if immense silver tyres had skidded there. Soon we were inland, amid trees. I stared queasily into their depths. Perhaps because I grew up in the Low Countries, where trees grow either out of sidewalks or in tame copses, I only have to look at New York forests to begin to feel lost in them. I drove upstate numerous times with Rachel, and

76

I strongly associate those trips with the fauna whose corpses lay around the road in great numbers: skunks, deer and enormous indecipherable rodents that one never found in Europe. (And at night, when we sat on a porch, gigantic moths and other repulsive night-flyers would thickly congregate on the screen, and my English wife and I would shrink into the house in amazement and fear . . .) My thoughts went back to a train journey I'd often made, in my student days, between Leiden and The Hague. The yellow commuter train ran through canal-crossed fields as dull as graph paper. Always one saw evidence of the tiny brick houses that the incontinent local municipalities, Voorschoten and Leidschendam and Rijswijk and Zoetermeer, pooped over the rural spaces surrounding The Hague. Here, in the first American valley, was the contrary phenomenon: you went for miles without seeing a house. The forest, filled with slender and thick trunks fighting silently for light and land, went emptily on and on. Then, gazing out of the window, my eye snagged on something pink. I sat up and stared.

I'd caught sight of a near-naked white man. He was on his own. He was walking through the trees wearing only underpants. But why? What was he doing? Why was he not wearing clothes? A horror took hold of me, and for a moment I feared I'd hallucinated, and I turned to my fellow passengers for some indication that might confirm what I'd seen. I saw no such indication.

I was relieved, then, at the appearance shortly afterwards of Poughkeepsie. I'd visited the town, with its merry name that sounds like a cry in a children's game – Poughkeepsie! – for the first time that summer. In its bucolic outskirts a colony of Jamaicans maintained a cricket field on a lush hillside. It was the only privately owned ground we played on, and the farthest north we travelled. The trip was worth it. There was a bouncy but true batting track made of cement; rickety four-deep bleachers filled with shouting spectators; and the simplest wooden shack for a locker room. If you smashed the ball down the hill it landed among cows, goats, horses, chickens. After the match – marked by an umpiring crisis, inevitably – every player went to the clubhouse in downtown Poughkeepsie. The clubhouse was a cabin with a small bar. Prominent signs warned against the use of marijuana. Presently women appeared with platters of chicken and rice. We ate and drank quietly, half following a dominoes game being played with the solemnity that often marked the social dealings of West Indian cricket teams in our league. Our hosts were proud to take care of us, to offer us a territory of their own in this remote place, and we were grateful. The tilted pretty cricket ground, the shipshape clubhouse – such pioneering effort had gone into them!

Somewhere beyond Poughkeepsie I opened my briefcase to glance at work documents. Protruding from a pocket was Chuck's gift. I opened the envelope and with-drew a booklet. Titled *Dutch Nursery Rhymes in Colonial Times*, the booklet was a reprint, made by the Holland Society of New York, of the 1889 original edited by a Mrs E. P. Ferris. I turned the pages with some curiosity, because I knew next to nothing about the ancient Dutch presence in America. There was a song in Dutch about Molly Grietje, Santa Claus's wife, who made New Year *koekjes*, and a song about Fort Orange, as Albany was first known. There was a poem (in English) titled 'The Christmas Race, A True Incident of Rensselaerwyck'. Rensselaerwyck was, I surmised, precisely the district through which my train was now travelling. Stimulated by the coincidence, I gave the poem my closer attention. It commemorated a horse race under 'the Christmas moon' at Wolvenhoeck, the corner of the wolves. The owners of the horses were a certain Phil Schuyler and a gentleman referred to only as Mijnheer: 'Down to the riverbank, Mijnheer, his guests, and all the slaves / went trooping, while a war whoop came from all the Indian braves . . . / The slaves with their whale lanterns were passing to and fro, / Casting fantastic shadows on hills of ice and snow.' In addition to this poem there were hymns, spinning songs, cradle songs, churning songs and trotting songs – songs you sang while trotting your child on your knee – apparently in use all over New Netherland, from Albany to Long Island to the Delaware River. One such song caught my attention:

79

Trip a trop a troontjes
  De varkens in de boontjes,
De koetjes in de claver,
  De paarden in de haver,
De eendjes in de water-plas,
  De kalf in de lange gras;
So groot mijn kleine —— was!

You sang your child's name where the blank was. Adapting the melody of the St Nicholas song that every Dutch child hungrily learns (*Sinterklaas kapoentje / Gooi wat in mijn schoentje . . .*), I hummed this nonsense about pigs and beans and cows and clover to my faraway son, tapping my knee against the underside of the lowered tray as I imagined his delighted weight on my thigh.

The week before, Jake and I had played in his grandparents' garden. I raked leaves into piles and he helped me bag the leaves. The leaves were dry and marvellously light. I added armloads to the red and brown and gold crushed in the plastic sack; Jake picked up a single leaf and made a cautious, thrilled deposit. At one point he put on his superhero frown and charged a hillock of leaves. Wading into its harmless fire, he courageously sprawled. ''Ook, 'ook!' he screamed as he rolled in the leaves. I looked, and looked, and looked. Fronds of his yellow hair curled out from the hood's fringe onto his cheeks. He wore his purple quilted jacket, and his thermal khakis with an inch of tartan turn-up, and his blue ankle boots with the zip, and the blue sweater with the white boat, and – I knew this because I had dressed him – his train-infested underpants, and the red T-shirt he liked to imagine was a Spiderman shirt, and Old Navy green socks with rubbery lettering on the soles. We gardened together. I demonstrated how to use a shovel. When I dug up the topsoil, I was taken aback: countless squirming creatures ate and moved and multiplied underfoot. The very ground we stood on was revealed as a kind of ocean, crowded and immeasurable and without light.

Blocks of colour stormed my window for a full minute. By the time the freight train had passed, the sky over the Hudson Valley had brightened still further and the formerly brown and silver Hudson was a bluish white.

Unseen on this earth, I alighted at Albany–Rensselaer with tears in my eyes and went to my meeting.

Sometimes to walk in shaded parts of Manhattan is to be inserted into a Magritte: the street is night while the sky is day. It was into one such dreamlike, double-dealing evening in January 2003, at Herald Square, that I stumbled out of the building occupied by New York's Department of Motor Vehicles. After years of driving rental cars with a disintegrating and legally dubious international licence issued in the United

Kingdom, I had finally decided to buy and insure a car of my own – which required me to get an American driver's licence. But I couldn't trade my British licence (itself derived from a Dutch one) for an American one: such an exchange was for some unexplainable reason only feasible during the first thirty days of an alien's permanent residence in the United States. I would have to get a learner permit and submit to a driving test all over again: which entailed, as a first step, a written examination on the rules of the road of the Empire State.

At the time, I didn't question this odd ambition or my doggedness in relation to it. I can say quite ingenuously that I was attempting to counter the great subtractions that had lessened my life and that the prospect of an addendum, even one as slight as a new licence and a new car, seemed important at the time; and no doubt I was drawn to a false syllogism involving the nothingness of my life and the somethingness of doing. All that said, I didn't let Rachel know what I was up to. She would have taken my actions as a statement of intent, and maybe she wouldn't have been entirely wrong. It would not have helped much to point out that, if I was indeed embracing an American lot, then I was doing so unprogrammatically, even unknowingly. Perhaps the relevant truth – and it's one whose existence was apparent to my wife, and I'm sure to much of the world, long before it became apparent to me – is that we all find ourselves in temporal currents and that unless you're paying attention you'll discover, often too late, that an undertow of weeks or of years has pulled you deep into trouble.

Carried along, then, by the dark flow of those times, I approached the Department of Motor Vehicles. The DMV was in a building coated in black glass and chiefly identifiable by a large sign for Daffy's, an entity I took to be somehow connected to Daffy Duck but which turned out to be a department store. I avoided Daffy's – and Modell's Sporting Goods, and Mrs Fields Cookies, and Hat & Cap, and Payless ShoeSource, other occupants of the eerily unfrequented mall known as the Herald Centre – by taking the express elevator to the eighth floor. A bell for the benefit of the blind burped at intervals as I rose. Then the elevator door halved and slid away and I stood before the DMV premises. There was a static turnstile like a monster's unearthed skeleton, and there was a set of glass doors in constant use. Approaching these, I was barged into by a middle-aged woman making her exit.

'Get out of my way,' she sobbed.

I joined the line to the reception desk, where two sweating men furiously gave directions. 'I'm here for the written test,' I said. 'You got your social security card? ID?' 'Yes,' I said, reaching for my pocket. 'I don't want to see it,' the man snapped, thrusting forms at me.

I entered the main administrative area. The low ceiling

was supported by an extraordinary clutter of columns; so many, in fact, that I could not avoid the perverse impression that the room was in danger of collapsing. An enormous counter ran round three-quarters of the office like a fortification, and behind it, visible between crenellations made by partitions and computer terminals, were the DMV employees. Two of them, women in their thirties, screamed with laughter by a photocopying machine; but as soon as they reached their positions at the counter they wore faces of sullen hostility. One could understand why, for assembled before them was a perpetually reinforced enemy, its troops massing relentlessly on the hard pew-like benches. Many of those seated were hunched forward with hands clasped and heads bowed, raising their eyes only to follow the stupendous figures – E923, A062, C568 – that randomly appeared on screens with the purpose, never achieved, of moderating the agony of suspense in which visitors were placed.

I filled out my application form and stood in the queue of those waiting to be photographed. After my photograph was taken, I was told to sit on a bench and wait: my Green Card, which I'd handed over as proof of identity, would have to be checked by the Department of Homeland Security. An hour or so later, approval was forthcoming. I waited another twenty minutes and then shuffled with a handful of others to the test area, which was furnished with that heart-sinking grid of desks and chairs familiar to examinees everywhere. There were requests for test sheets in Chinese, French, Spanish. I rapidly answered the multiple-choice questions and handed my sheet to the invigilator. It gave me a childish satisfaction to have finished before anyone else. I returned to my desk and waited for the examination period to expire. The invigilator, an obese Hispanic woman, marked erroneous answers with superb strokes of her pencil. When she came to my paper, the pencil hovered and hovered; then she scribbled twenty (out of twenty) and handed it to me with a frown. I experienced a rush of happiness. Now, at last, I could collect my learner permit.

I received a ticket – say, D499 – and further instructions to wait. So I waited. Perplexed and rebuffed Chinese men wandered everywhere. I listened to 106.7 Lite FM and watched a television screen on which 'Entertainment News', rather than actual entertainment, was broadcast. I studied driving-safety posters: YOU SNOOZE, YOU LOSE, it was said. At last my number came up. A balding man in his fifties inspected my paperwork all over again. It fell to applicants to produce proof of identity worth six points: a Green Card scored three points, an original social security card two points, and a credit card or a bank statement or a utilities bill a single point. The man shook his head. 'Sorry,' he said, unapologetically pushing my documents back to me.

'What's wrong?' I asked.

'I can't take the credit card. It's got somebody else's name on it.'

I looked. My name, which by a miracle of typography was fully spelled out on my social security card, is Johannus Franciscus Hendrikus van den Broek. My credit card, for obvious reasons, identified me merely as Johannus F. H. van den Broek – exactly as my Green Card did.

I said, 'That's my name. If you –'

'I don't want to talk about it. Go see the supervisor. Counter ten. Next.'

I went to counter ten. There were three people already in line. Each had an argument with the supervisor, each went away in a rage. Then it was my turn. The supervisor was in his late thirties, with a severely shaved head and a little goatee and an earring. He wordlessly extended his hand and I passed him my documents of identification. In exchange he passed me a notice: ALL FORMS OF IDENTIFICATION MUST SHOW THE SAME NAME.

He quickly compared my papers. 'You got to show me documents with the same name,' he said. 'This Con Ed bill is no good.'

'Wait a minute,' I said. I pulled out a bank statement I'd brought along in case of difficulty. It too was in the name of Johannus F. H. van den Broek, but it contained copies of cheques I'd written. 'You see?' I said. 'The signature on those cheques is exactly the same as the signature on my social security card and Green Card. So it's obviously me in both cases.'

He shook his head. 'I'm not a handwriting expert,' he said. 'I need the same name.'

'OK,' I said calmly. 'But let me ask you this. The Green Card's good, right? And the name on the Con Ed bill and the bank statement is the same as the name on the Green Card.'

The supervisor re-examined my Green Card. 'Actually, you got yourself another problem,' he said with a smile. 'See this? The name on the Green Card is not the same as the name on the social security card.'

I looked: on the Green Card was typed 'Johanus'. I'd never noticed it before.

I said, 'Yes, well, that's just an obvious clerical error made by the INS. The photograph on the Green Card is obviously me.' The supervisor looked unmoved, so I added, 'Either that, or there's somebody out there who looks exactly like me and has exactly the same name, and I happen to have stolen his Green Card.'

'Not exactly the same name,' the supervisor said. 'And that's where we have a problem. You want me to give you a learner permit? OK, but who are you? Are you Johanus' – he pronounced the last two syllables as an obscenity – 'or are you Johannus?'

'Come on, let's not play games,' I said.

'You think I'm playing a game?' He was actually baring

his teeth. 'Let me remind you, sir, you seem to be in possession of somebody else's Green Card – either that, or somebody else's social security card. I might just get suspicious about that. I might just have to start looking into that.'

This man was dangerous, I realised. I said, 'You really want me to go down to the INS and get a new Green Card? That's what you want to get out of this?'

'I don't want you to go there,' the supervisor said. Now he was pointing at my chest. 'I'm forcing you to go there.'

'What about my written test?' I said, pathetically showing him my twenty out of twenty.

He smiled. 'You're going to have to take it again.'

And so I was in a state of fuming helplessness when I stepped out into the inverted obscurity of the afternoon. As I stood there, thrown by Herald Square's flows of pedestrians and the crazed traffic diagonals and the grey, seemingly bottomless gutter pools, I was seized for the first time by a nauseating sense of America, my gleaming adopted country, under the secret actuation of unjust, indifferent powers. The rinsed taxis, hissing over fresh slush, shone like grapefruits; but if you looked down into the space between the road and the undercarriage, where icy matter stuck to pipes and water streamed down the mudflaps, you saw a foul mechanical dark.

Corralled by the black snow ranged along the kerbs, I found myself hastening, for lack of a clear alternative, to the triangular traffic island at Broadway and 32nd Street known as Greeley Square Park. Glowing orange Christmas lights peppered the trees. I came to a statue of one Horace Greeley, a newspaperman and politician of the nineteenth century and, the plaque at the statue's base further asserted, the coiner of the phrase 'Go West, young man, go West.' Greeley, apparently a fellow with an enormous egg-like head, was seated in an armchair. Staring blindly into the void beyond his feet, he wore an expression of devastation, as if the newspaper he clutched in his right hand contained terrible news. I decided to walk homeward down Broadway. The route, unfamiliar to me, passed through the old Tin Pan Alley quarter, blocks now given over to wholesalers and street vendors and freight forwarders and import–exporters – Undefeated Wear Corp, Sportique, Da Jump Off, signs proclaimed – dealing in stuffed toys, caps, novelties, human hair, two-dollar belts, one-dollar neckties, silver, perfumes, leather goods, rhinestones, streetwear, watches. Arabs, West Africans, African Americans hung out on the sidewalks amongst goods trucks, dollies, pushcarts, food carts, heaped trash, boxes and boxes of merchandise. I might have been in a cold Senegal. Black-skinned buyers carrying garbage bags wandered in and out of the stores while overseers and barkers and hawkers, dressed in leather jackets, fur coats, African robes and tracksuits, jingled keys and talked on cellphones and idly heckled passing women and shouted for custom. On 27th Street I turned towards Fifth Avenue: the cold had got to me, and I'd decided to catch a taxi. As I approached Fifth my eye was drawn to a banner hanging from a second-floor window: CHUCK CRICKET INC.

The names of various enterprises were taped to a signboard at the front of the building's entrance: Peruvian Amity Society, Apparitions International, Elvis Tookey Boxing and, at suite 203, Chuck Cricket, Inc., Chuck Import–Export, Inc. and Chuck Industries, Inc. Why not? I thought, and went in. On the second floor I entered a tiny lobby with a receptionist who sat behind a security glass next to a video monitor that colourlessly transmitted, in jerking four-second fragments, dismal images of stairs, elevator interiors and passageways. The receptionist buzzed me in without a word. I walked down a narrow corridor covered in teal carpeting and knocked on the door of suite 203.

Chuck himself opened the door, a telephone at his ear. He tapped on the back of a chair and gestured for me to sit. He seemed wholly unsurprised to see me.

The office consisted of a room with space for a couple of desks and a few filing cabinets. Sheetrock walls were decorated with posters of Sachin Tendulkar and Brian Lara, the greatest batsmen in the world. A strumming sound drifted through from a guitar instructor next door. Chuck winked at me as he dealt with his call. 'It's my wife,' he mouthed. He wore an open-collared shirt and neatly creased trousers that spilled generously over sneakers. I noticed for the first time a couple of large gold rings on his fingers and, running in the dark hair beneath his throat, a necklace's gold drool.

I was startled, in the midst of these impressions, by a strange whistling sound. The whistling was followed, after a few seconds' pause, by a fresh sequence of chirps, and then by a popping like the pop of a bouncing ping-pong ball.

Chuck passed over a CD case. We were listening to Disc Two of *Bird Songs of California*: *Olive-Sided Flycatcher through Varied Thrush*.

As I waited for Chuck to finish his phone call, the muffled guitar music and the birdsong were joined by the ringing of a phone from the other adjoining office. A male voice sounded loudly: 'Hello?' The voice came through again: 'I'm not a mind reader. I can't read your mind.' A pause. 'Stop it. Just stop it. Would you please just stop it.' Another pause. 'Fuck you, all right? Fuck you.' I lowered my eyes. Paper glue-traps for mice, baited with peanut butter and bearing the words ASSURED ENVIRON- MENTS, littered the space under the radiators.

Chuck hung up and I said, 'I was just walking home from the DMV. I happened to see your sign.'

'You live nearby?'

I mentioned the block.

'Well, it's delightful to see you,' Chuck said. He was leaning back in his chair and, my explanation notwithstanding, considering why I, an important man with better things to do, had chosen to drop by. Chuck was too astute not to have detected that somewhere behind this impromptu visit lay some need on my part – and neediness, in business as in romance, represents an opportunity. But how, as I sat before him to the background tweeting of a Townsend's solitaire or black-tailed gnatcatcher, was he going to proceed? He knew that a cold pitch involving sales charts, cash-flow projections and marketing studies wouldn't work. Also, it would have been alien to him to be so uncomplicated in his methods. Chuck valued craftiness and indirection. He found the ordinary run of dealings between people boring and insufficiently advantageous to him at the deep level of strategy at which he liked to operate. He believed in owning the impetus of a situation, in keeping the other guy off balance, in proceeding by way of sidesteps. If he saw an opportunity to act with suddenness or take you by surprise or push you into the dark, he'd take it, almost as a matter of principle. He was a wilful, clandestine man who followed his own instincts and analyses and would rarely be influenced by advice – not my advice, that's for sure. The truth is that there was nothing, or very little, I could have done to produce a different ending for Chuck Ramkissoon.

But it was a while before any of this came to me. Because his deviousness was so transparent and because it alternated with an immigrant's credulousness – his machinating and trusting selves seemed, like Box and Cox, never to meet – I found all of the feinting and dodging and thrusting oddly soothing. Then again, this was a time when I found solace in the patter of Jehovah's Witnesses who stopped me in the street, a time when I was tempted to consult the fat beckoning lady psychic who sat like an Amsterdam hooker in a basement window on West 23rd Street. I was glad of the considerateness, however misconceived. My life had shrunk to very small proportions – too small, certainly, for New York's pickier and more plausible agents of sympathy. To put it another way: I was, to anyone who could be bothered to pay attention, noticeably lost. Chuck paid attention and thus noticed. So, instead of immediately pouncing on me with business details, he came up with a different plan. He was going to fascinate me.

He took another call. When he was done, he said, 'That was my partner, Mike Abelsky. He's just had that stomach reduction operation. You know, they take it and they shrink it to the size of a walnut. He's doing great. Two weeks, and he's already lost thirty pounds.'

A loud commotion sounded on 27th Street. We looked outside. Three men – two Arabs and an African, it looked like – were ineffectually assaulting a black man, aiming kicks and punches that bounced off the suitcase the man held up. They retreated and spontaneously attacked again with loud shouts. Then a fourth party sprinted up to the man with the suitcase and struck him repeatedly with a collapsible chair, knocking him to the ground. A police siren sounded somewhere. The attackers disappeared into a building and the man with the suitcase picked himself up and hurried away.

Chuck Ramkissoon chuckled. 'I love it here. Dog eat dog. No holds barred.'

The neighbour was raising his voice again. 'No, listen to me for once. Just let me say what I have to say. Would you do that for me? Would you just shut the fuck up for one time in your life and just fucking listen?'

Chuck, touching his pockets for his keys, said, 'Usually I have my director of operations here, a nice kid, you'd like him.' As if I might doubt him, Chuck went over to the vacant desk and fetched a business card belonging to MO CADRE, Director of Operations. A fresh burst of twanging came from the guitar instructor. Chuck put on a Yankees cap.

From next door: 'Fuck you! Fuck you, you fucking bitch!'

Chuck picked up his coat. 'Why don't I drop you home? It's on my way.'

We fled towards the elevator. The door of another office was open, and standing at the entry was the woman I'd

seen with Chuck on the ferry – his mistress, I now understood.

She looked up and said, 'Honey, do you –' and then
she recognised me. We traded polite smiles. Chuck said,
'Hans, I believe you've met Eliza. My dear, we were just
on our way out.'

'Okey-dokey,' Eliza said, still with the same smile. 'Have
fun.'

As we walked out of the building into the cold, Chuck
said very gravely, 'Eliza is extremely talented. She composes
photo albums. There's quite a market for this service. People
take all these pictures and they don't know what to do with
them.'

We made our way through animated hordes of men. At
a certain point, Chuck grabbed my arm and said, 'Let's cross
now,' and he trotted quickly across the avenue as a surge of
traffic came roaring up. He had, I realised, waited for a
moment when the pedestrian light showed the fierce red
hand, and then taken his chance. Evidently he felt this gave
him an edge – and it did, because it meant that, walking
on down Sixth Avenue, he and I were signalled forward at
every cross-street by the purposeful white-glowing pedestrian whose missionary stride was plainly conceived as an
example to us all (and whom I cannot help contrasting with
his London counterpart, a green gentleman undoubtedly
rambling with an unseen green golden retriever).

I followed Chuck into an open-air lot. He drove a 1996

Cadillac, a patriotic automobile aflutter and aglitter with banners and stickers of the Stars and Stripes and yellow ribbons in support of the troops. Papers, candy wrappers and coffee cups were strewn over the front-passenger seat. Chuck scrabbled all of it into his arms and dropped it into the junk-filled rear-passenger area, where a pair of field glasses, a laptop, brochures and brown banana peels rested on sheets of old newsprint.

We pulled up across the street from the Chelsea Hotel. I was opening my door when Chuck said, 'Do you have some time? There's something I want to show you. But it's in Brooklyn.'

I hesitated. The truth was, I was done for the day, the Cadillac was warm, and I had a dread of returning to my apartment. Also, as Rachel would be the first to say, I'm easily dragged around.

'We still have an hour of daylight,' Chuck said. 'Come on. You'll find it interesting, I promise.'

'What the hell,' I said, slamming the door shut.

Chuck cackled as he drove off. 'I knew it. You're a fun guy underneath it all.'

'Where are we going?'

'You'll find out. I don't want to spoil the surprise.'

This was acceptable. When was the last time I'd been promised a surprise?

On the West Side Highway, a few blocks north of Houston, the car paused in traffic. Chuck, looking out of the window, leaned forward and exclaimed, 'My God! Look at that. Do you see that, Hans? The ice?'

I did see. Ice was spread out over the breadth of the Hudson like a plot of cloud. The whitest and largest fragments were flat polygons, and surrounding these was a mass of slushy, messy ice, as if the remains of a zillion cocktails had been dumped there. By the bank, where the rotting stumps of an old pier projected like a species of mangrove, the ice was shoddy, papery rubble and immobile; farther out, floes moved quickly towards the bay.

Indeed much of what I was looking at, Chuck informed me as we inched along, was brash ice, the fragments of disintegrating floes that had travelled down from upper parts of the Hudson. Such drifting fields of screeching and groaning ice, as Chuck dramatically put it, were great places to bird bald eagles, which came downriver in search of open water and collected fewer than fifty miles north in order to eat fish. Chuck's fascination with this phenomenon – his interest in naturalism, birds especially, went back to his youth in Trinidad – was, I later came to understand, heightened by the knowledge gained from his enthusiastic and successful studies for the US citizenship exams. He told me that in 1782, after years of argument and indecision, Congress concluded that the bald eagle would make an appropriate symbol of national power and authority, and so it was decided that the bird, depicted with its wings outspread, its talons grasping an olive branch, et cetera, should be adopted as the emblem for the Great Seal of the United States. Chuck dug into his pocket and tossed me a quarter to remind me what the eagle looked like. Not everybody agreed with the decision, Chuck reported. He took back the coin. Benjamin Franklin thought the turkey a better choice and considered the bald eagle – a plunderer and a scavenger of dead fish rather than a hunter, and timid if mobbed by much smaller birds – an animal of bad moral character and in fact a coward. 'I love the national bird,' Chuck clarified. 'The noble bald eagle represents the spirit of freedom, living as it does in the boundless void of the sky.'

I turned to see whether he was joking. He wasn't. From time to time, Chuck actually spoke like this.

As he talked, my thoughts went from the ice on the Hudson, which struck me as a kind of filth, to the pure canal ice of The Hague. Unless I am dreaming, during most winters in the seventies the standing waters of The Hague froze over and for a few days or weeks were the scene of the playful communal activities so familiar from paintings of Dutch life through the centuries. As I sat half listening to Chuck, what struck me most strongly about these remembered glacial shenanigans – the ice-hockey, the pirouetting of a crazed dancing soloist, the hand-in-hand manoeuvres of lovers, the tender pairings of tots and parents, the rich residual silence off which the shouts and laughs and clacks of sticks seemed to bounce – was their peculiar Dutchness. I was gripped by a rare home-sickness. There, by the Hudson, I had what I can only describe as a flashback. What came to me was a water-filled ditch near my childhood home covered in new ice, which is black. The ditch – a *sloot*, as we called it – was a few blocks from home and ran between the white grass of football pitches and, on the opposite bank, the wooded dunes that held back the always-thundering North Sea. I was skating. I should have been at school, learning Greek, but like countless thirteen-year-old schoolboys before me I'd been lured by the freeze into truancy. Nobody else was around. Save for the scraping of my blades, all was noiseless. Forward I skated, past sinking alder trees, past the netless goals in the fields, past what-ever else was contained in the world. I spent an hour or two like this. As my ankles grew sore and my mind turned to the inventing of excuses for my absence from school, a figure approached on the ice. For a moment I was terri-fied. Then I saw that this approaching skater was a woman, a woman who as she drew nearer became my mother. How she'd guessed she would find me in this lonely place is something I still cannot explain. But she had guessed, and here she came now, methodically thrusting sideways and moving with the sweet excess of physical efficiency that is the first and last bliss of ice skating. I was busted; I thought for a moment about sprinting off. When my mother caught up with me, however, she simply said, 'Would you find it terrible if I skated with you?' She and I glided side by side along the edge of the fields of white grass, our hands clasped behind our backs. We pushed in harmony, the one occasionally dropping behind the other where branches leaned into our way or when a cracking sound betrayed a stretch of thin ice. My mother, a large woman and somewhat plodding in shoes, was graceful on runners. It was she who presided over my first wobbling, upright motions on frozen water, who first placed bladed little boots on my feet and, with gentle tugs, pulled tight their criss-crossing white laces.

'OK,' Chuck said. 'See that? That's where I got my cricket idea.'

We had reached Pier 40, a brick, hulking, box-like old shipping terminal that jutted out into the river.

'After the attacks,' Chuck said, 'this was where the Humane Society of New York started up an emergency triage, practically from day one.' We quickened away. 'My God, what a scene. Cats, dogs, guinea pigs, rabbits, pigs, lizards, you name it, they were all here. Cockatoos. Monkeys. I saw a lemur with a corneal inflammation.' Chuck volunteered his services and was put to work 'rehoming' the pets. 'It was a wonderful experience,' Chuck said. 'I made friends with people from Idaho, Wisconsin, New Jersey, New Hampshire, North Carolina, Ireland, Portugal, South Africa. People from out of state came for a couple of days and ended up spending weeks here. Tourists that were vets, even regular tourists, gave up their holidays to help out. And we weren't just looking after the animals. Right over there, you had a feeding area for the rescue personnel, and food and clothing: men would work for days without stopping and their boots and coats would be destroyed.' Chuck said simply, 'I think for many of us it was one of the happiest times of our life.'

I believed him. The catastrophe had instilled in many – though not in me – a state of elation. From the beginning, for example, I'd suspected that, beneath all the tears and the misery, Rachel's leaving had basically been a function of euphoria.

Now we were passing the great downtown vacancy, lit up like a stadium by the faint glow of construction floodlights, and the doomed Deutsche Bank building on Liberty Street, which, with its mournful, poetical drape of black netting, was the object on which the eye helplessly rested.

'Anyhow,' Chuck continued, 'inside the pier is a giant courtyard with two artificial soccer fields. When I found out the whole place was slated for total redevelopment, I had an idea. Why not, I thought, why not –'

He paused and adjusted his Yankees cap. 'I have a question for you.'

'Fire away,' I said.

'How many West Indians would you say lived in the New York metropolitan area? English-speaking West

Indians, now: I'm not talking about Haitians and Dominicans and what have you.'

I told him that I had no idea.

'Well, let me enlighten you,' Chuck said, waving to the frozen cop who guarded the Battery Tunnel turn-off. 'According to the 2000 census, five hundred thousand. You can safely add fifty per cent: so we're talking about seven hundred and fifty thousand, maybe even a million, and growing. We had sixty per cent growth in the 1990s alone. And by the way, West Indians have a better socio-economic profile than Hispanics, and a way better one than African Americans. But that's not the exciting part. The Indian' – he banged a hand against the wheel – 'population in NYC has grown by eighty-one per cent in the last ten years. The Pakistani' – another bang – 'numbers have gone up by one hundred and fifty per cent, and the Bangladeshis, wait for it, five hundred per cent. In New Jersey they're overrun with South Asians. Fort Lee, Jersey City, Hoboken, Secaucus, Hackensack, Englewood: Navratri celebrations in these towns can bring out twenty thousand people. It's the same in New Brunswick, Edison, Metuchen. I'm telling you, I've done the research. I've got all the numbers. And if you think they're coming to mop floors and drive taxis, you're wrong. They're coming to make real money – hi-tech, pharmaceuticals, electronics, healthcare. There's almost half a million South Asians in New York alone. Have you ever visited the Newcomers School in Astoria?

All the kids are from Pakistan. You know what they do in their spare time, these kids? They play cricket. They play at Dutch Kills Playground, over by PS 112, they play in vacant lots, they play in schoolyards up and down Queens and Brooklyn. Just down the block from me, at PS 139, you'll see boys and girls with cricket bats, even in the snow. If I took you there now, I could show you the wicket they've drawn on the wall.' He grinned. 'You see where I'm going with this.'

'You want to build a cricket stadium,' I said. I made no attempt to hide my amusement.

'That's right,' Chuck said. 'But not at Pier 40. That was my first decision. There's no way they're going to let a bunch of black guys take over prime Manhattan real estate. Hate the word stadium, by the way,' Chuck said importantly. We were exiting the yellow gloom of the Battery Tunnel, whose old tiled walls invariably put me in mind of a urinal. 'Stadium spells trouble. Just ask Mike Bloomberg. I'm talking about an arena. A sports arena for the greatest cricket teams in the world. Twelve exhibition matches every summer, watched by eight thousand spectators at fifty dollars a pop. I'm talking about advertising, I'm talking about year-round consumption of food and drink in the bar-restaurant. You're going to have a clubhouse. Two thousand members at one thousand dollars a year plus initiation fee. Tennis, squash, tenpin bowling, indoor facilities, a gymnasium, a swimming pool, a sports bar: something for everyone. But at the centre of it, cricket. The only true cricket club in the country. The New York Cricket Club.'

'That's great,' I said.

Chuck burst out laughing. 'I know what you're thinking: I'm out of my mind. But you haven't heard the kicker.' He looked at me. 'Ready? Global TV rights. A game between India and Pakistan in New York City? In a state-of-the-art arena with Liberty Tower in the background? Can you imagine the panning shots?' Chuck said almost furiously, 'We're thinking a TV and internet viewership of seventy million in India alone. Seventy million. Do you have any idea how much money this would bring in? Coca-Cola, Nike, they're all desperate to get at the South Asian market. We figure we'd break even in three, at most four years. And after that . . .' High on the Gowanus Expressway, now, he waved an arm at the cold bright bay and the mainland beyond. Lights had started shining in Elizabeth and in the Bayonne heights. 'It's an impossible idea, right? But I'm convinced it will work. Totally convinced. You know what my motto is?'

'I didn't think people had mottoes any more,' I said.

'Think fantastic,' Chuck said. 'My motto is, Think fantastic.'

We swung onto the Belt Parkway and for ten minutes followed its semi-circle past Bensonhurst and Coney Island

and Sheepshead Bay, the night now descending over the Rockaways and a blinking jet plane going low over the dismal wetlands of Jamaica Bay.

'Where are you taking me?' I said. 'Queens?'

'We're nearly there,' he said.

We turned south onto the southernmost, quasi-rural section of Flatbush Avenue, where the road was lined only by barren trees. Half a mile or so down, Chuck swung left through a wide gateway onto a concrete private road. This led to a no-man's-land of frozen bushes and scrubland. Another turn, leftward, led to an immense white emptiness. The snow had not been ploughed from this portion of the road, and like a waggoner Chuck steered and bumped us along in the hardened ruts of old tracks. A desolate complex of buildings – warehouses, a tower – was now in view on the left. The sky, aswirl with fleet, darkening clouds, was magnified by the flat null steppe that lay to the east. If a troupe of Mongolian horsemen had appeared in the distance I would not have been shocked.

'Jesus,' I said, 'where are we?'

Chuck, both hands on the wheel, spurted the Cadillac forward. 'Floyd Bennett Field, Brooklyn,' he said.

As he spoke, the tower assumed a familiar outline. This had once been an airfield, I realised. We were on an old taxiway.

Chuck drove past the brick control tower and a pair

of hangars. There were no tyre tracks here. We came to a stop. An indeterminate snowfield, broken only by stands of dwarfish trees, filled three-quarters of the vista. We stepped out into wind and an extraordinary cold.

Chuck said, 'This is it. This is where it's going to be.' He made a gesture at the void in front of us. It was bounded on one side by a vague growth of shrubbery and, glistening behind a row of trees, the streaky lights of Flatbush Avenue. The remaining three sides were bounded by nothing. I thought of a Dutch polder, and then of the Westland, the flat, greenhouse-filled region between The Hague and the Hook of Holland where I played soccer games on bleakly open fields, in gales, against tough teenagers from Naaldwijk and Poeldijk who specialised, for some reason, in offside traps. Westland included the village of Monster. For six weeks, during my incarnation as a seventeen-year-old in need of money, I cycled to Monster at five in the morning in order to work eight hours at a pallet factory. For some reason it bewildered me to think back to him, that boy on the Monsterseweg making his way along the edge of the dunes.

'I have the land, I have the lease, I have the backing,' Chuck said.

I got to hear the story of the property acquisition at a later date, a story involving a grant of a lease by the National Park Service in the 1980s for sporting purposes; a failure to develop the land as envisaged; and, in 2002, a sub-grant of the lease to Chuck, at a price he described as 'minimal', for the purpose of putting the field to use as a cricket field. Chuck had no permission to place any permanent construction upon the land. But he figured that if he built New York's first real cricket ground and installed some removable bleachers, the great India and West Indies teams would be lining up to play here; and once that happened, he reasoned, his application to the Park Service for permission to (1) transform the hangars into a clubhouse and an indoor sports centre, and (2) build grandstands for eight thousand spectators, would have every reason to succeed; and once that happened, the television companies would pile in; and once that happened . . .

But all that was for another occasion. On this occasion, he told me another story.

His first thought had been to call the field Corrigan Field. 'After "Wrong Way" Corrigan,' Chuck said happily. Corrigan, Chuck related, was a 'legendary aviator' who in 1938 flew out of this very airfield to Ireland in an airplane of his own construction. He'd been flatly denied permission to make the crossing but went ahead anyway, afterwards explaining that, confused by fog and a misreading of his compass, he'd erroneously believed himself to be en route to California. 'When he came back, they held a ticker-tape parade for him on Broadway,' Chuck said. But Chuck decided, in the end, to name it

– 'Take a guess. We were just talking about it' – Bald Eagle Field. 'Bald Eagle Field is perfect,' Chuck said. 'It's got scale. It makes it American.' Also, he said, he wanted to pay homage to the eagles and other birds – hummingbirds, herons – that habitually used the nature preserve located in this strange parkland, and homage also to the hundreds of migrant species travelling through here on the Atlantic flyway.

Puffing clouds of breath, he was moved to a moment of silence. 'See how flat it is,' Chuck said, extracting a hand from his pocket and sweeping it across his snowfield. 'The first thing we did, in the summer, was kill everything with Roundup. We brought in a sod cutter to take out all the grass down to the roots, and then we fluffed up the earth and put down a deep layer of topsoil. After that we graded it – you see how it slopes down, like an upside-down saucer? – and after that we aerated it, and after that we seeded it. All by September first. Then we started mowing.'

Needless to say, I was having trouble sharing his vision of this ice and waste. I wanted to get back inside the Cadillac. But there was more. 'Now, look there,' Chuck said, pointing. 'See the stakes?' Short wooden stakes in the middle of the field made a quadrangle.

Under the snow, I was being asked to believe, lay the finest, most fragile area of grass known to sports: a cricket square.

'You're really putting down a turf wicket?' I said.

'The first and best in the country,' Chuck said.

Not for a second did I take him seriously. 'Wow,' I said.

The day, a pink smear above America, had all but disappeared. My feet were frozen. I patted my friend on the back. 'Well, good luck with it,' I said, thinking about the long subway trip back to the hotel.

As a teenager I often bicycled into the centre of The Hague, a half-hour's effort of pedalling made both more difficult and more pleasant by a girlfriend who, in accordance with local romantic tradition, sat leggily side-saddle on the rear seat and accepted this modest transportation with a stalwartness that has, I'm sure, stood her in good stead in later life. She never complained, not even when the bike was shocked by the sunken rails on which the yellow trams drifted. We'd end up at a bar near the Denneweg and drink a few of the gold-and-white gadgets that are Dutch glasses of beer. Later, cycling home past horse chestnut trees and dark-windowed villas, we had the city practically to ourselves: every night a scarcely believable desertedness came over The Hague, as if the night buses, roaring and blazing through the empty streets like ogres, had chased the populace indoors. Those bicycle journeys were always tough going, especially after dark, when the dynamo's friction on the front tyre – source of a white light that spurted, faded, spurted, faded – slowed you down. Into town or back, the most bothersome stretch of the journey was President Kennedylaan, a broad, monotonous thoroughfare where the buildings of the Dutch secret service were said to be located and where one went forward into a near-perpetual sea wind as if into an unseen mob. President Kennedylaan, according to a telephoning policeman, was where my mother, while walking alone, suffered the stroke that killed her almost instantly.

This was in May 2000. Jake, eight months old, was recovering from pneumonia, and Rachel stayed with him in New York while I flew to the Netherlands. Whereas the dealings with the crematorium were my responsibility, my mother's small circle of friends took care of the reception held, as it's said, in her memory; and indeed it was a relief that the burden of remembering her was not yet mine to bear alone. A lawyer came out of the woodwork and, in collaboration with a tearful total stranger who introduced herself as a former colleague of my mother, arranged for the sale of her house and the remittance of all proceeds to my bank account. Provision was made for the charitable disposition of the remainder of her assets. My tax liabilities were calculated. I was back in New York within ten days.

In the months that followed, my grief became disturbed

111

by a guilty sense that very little had changed: with the passage of time Mama was barely less present than she'd been during the many years in which, separated by an airplane journey, we'd spoken once or twice a month on the telephone and seen each other for a week or two in a year. At first, I understood my uneasiness as the product of self-accusation: I had incriminated myself, perhaps inevitably, on a charge of filial absenteeism. But soon a still more disquieting idea took possession of my thoughts – namely that my mother had long ago become an imaginary being of sorts.

Rachel and I spoke about the matter as best we could. Perhaps misunderstanding me, she said, 'It should be a great comfort that you remember her so well.' I wasn't comforted. I kept going back, in my mind, to the visit I'd paid my mother a month before she died, when she'd struck me as a type of stranger. At the least, there was something unsatisfactory about her embodied presence as she went backwards and forwards from the kitchen to the time-shrunken dining room, or passed the cheese slicer over a hunk of cheese, or settled down, as she did on my first night, to watch television until ten o'clock, when she went to bed. And it may well be that my own actuality destroyed expectations of her own. What these were I cannot say, but it is hard not to suspect that she opened the front door hoping to meet someone other than this businessman who stood at the threshold. Towards midnight I climbed like Gargantua up the narrow staircase to my room. I brushed my teeth in the bedroom basin, stripped to my undershorts, turned off the lights. I went to the window – that is, two dormer windows consolidated into a single glass rectangle. It framed a scene which was, I'd decided as a boy, uniquely my property.

The old visual domain was unchanged: a long series of unlit back gardens leading to the almost indiscernible silhouette of dunes. To the north, which was to my right, the Scheveningen lighthouse twinkled for a second, then fell dark, then suddenly produced its beam, a skittish mile of light that became lost somewhere in the blue and the black above the dunes. These sand-hills had been my idea of wilderness. Pheasants, rabbits and small birds of prey lived and died there. On escapades with a friend or two, we would urge our twelve-year-old bodies under the barbed wire lining the footpaths and run through the sand-grass into the wooded depths of the dunes. We made hiding places and climbed trees and fooled around near the old German bunkers. We conceived of ourselves as outlaws, on the run from the *boswachters* – the stewards who wore green woollen jackets and, if I am not mistaken, green Tyrolean hats with small feathers sticking out from the hatband. The stewards never bothered us; but a furious old woman once grabbed a friend by the neck and briefly throttled him. Months later, I recognised her on the street: a stalking witchlike grey-haired woman with sinister sunglasses.

That's her, I excitedly told my mother. That's the woman who strangled Bart.

I was expecting calls to the police, a trial, justice.

My mother looked at the woman. 'Never mind,' she said, leading me away. 'She's just an old lady.'

I stood at the window, waiting for the next arrival of light. The lighthouse had been mesmeric to my boy self. He was an only child and it must be that at night he habitually stood at his bedroom window alone; but my recollection of watching the light travel out of Scheveningen contained the figure of my mother at my side, helping me to look out into the dark. She answered my questions. The sea was the North Sea. It was filled with ships queuing for entry to Rotterdam. Rotterdam was the biggest port in the world. The breakwaters were perpendicular to the beach and stopped the beach from being washed away. The jellyfish in the water might sting you. The blue of the jellyfish was the colour indigo. Seven particular stars made the outline of a plough. When you died, you went to sleep.

Again the beam of the lighthouse swung and went astray. The night's calmness contradicted a long-standing impression of mine, which was that my childhood's nights were invariably given over to tempests. When the loud moaning of air filled the house, I listened for my mother's solid steady footsteps on the stairs coming up to the third floor, which I alone occupied; and in my memory every tempest brought her up to me. (Can you see me, Mama?

I whispered from my bed. Yes, my love, she replied. I told her I was not frightened – *Ik ben niet bang, hoor* – and she stroked my head and said, as if she did not quite believe me, There's nothing to be afraid of.) Now, of course, the stairs were silent. My mother was asleep in bed. I abandoned my lookout. The dunes, the ashen flow of night clouds, the returning ray of light, the exclusive barony granted by this viewpoint, even the little baron himself, and his wonderment: none were any longer in my possession. But if not these things – the question expressed itself as a movement of emotion – then what things?

The following day, my restlessness led me to step out for a stroll in the fading light. It was April and cool, and I wore corduroy trousers and a diamond-patterned sweater, both culled from the teenager's wardrobe that lived on in the pine cupboard of my bedroom. Dressed, then, like Rip Van Winkle, I walked along the curving block. The red-brick houses, semi-detached and built in the 1940s, were arranged as quartets, with two corner houses sandwiching two other houses. Each house was fronted by a small inexpressive garden and a thigh-high red-brick wall, and a pedestrian could peer without diffi-culty through curtainless ground-floor windows, where typically a dense jungle of potted plants met the eye. People lived in these houses for decades: you moved in with young children and you stayed put into your old age.

I turned left onto Kruisbeklaan. Every weekday afternoon a tremor of ball games had run through our quarter; this street was the old epicentre. I passed by the house formerly inhabited by my friend Marc, who, according to my mother, had realised his youthful ambition to become a pharmacist: she had entered a drugstore and had recognised, in the features of the greying man behind the counter, the well-mannered piano-playing youngster who had occasionally rung the doorbell twenty and more years before. They enjoyed a short, friendly conversation, my mother reported, and then each went about his and her business. A little farther down the street was the house in which four brothers, fine sportsmen who for years formed the backbone of our club, had lived in a turmoil of bats and fights and balls and football boots; and other houses I anachronistically identified as the homes of Michael, and of Leon, and of Bas, and of Jeffrey, and of Wim and Ronald who were brothers, and of all the others in our gang. I found it idiotically distressing that a sharp finger-whistle could no longer summon them outdoors into a playful twilight. An ancient discovery was now mine to make: to leave is to take nothing less than a mortal action. The suspicion came to me for the first time that they were figures of my dreaming, like the loved dead: my mother and all these vanished boys. And after Mama's cremation I could not rid myself of the notion that she had been placed in the furnace of memory even when alive and, by extension, that one's dealings with others, ostensibly vital, at a certain point become dealings with the dead.

And it must have been around this time, too, that I became subject to the distractedness that further damaged me and, of course, my family. It is tempting, here, to make a link – to say that one thing led to another. I've never found such connections easy. (It's not a problem I have at work, where I merrily connect dots of all kinds; but the task there is much simpler and subject to rules.) In fairness to my sacked, peppermint-proffering shrink, it may be that this last infirmity goes back to my upbringing. The pleasantness of my Holland was related to the slightness of its mysteries. There obtained a national transparency promoted by a citizenry that was to all appearances united in a deep, even pleased, commitment to foreseeable and moderate outcomes in life. Nowadays, I gather from the newspapers, there are problems with and for alien elements, and things are not as they were; but in my day – age qualifies me to use the phrase! – Holland was a providential country. There seemed little point in an individual straining excessively for or against the upshots arranged on his behalf, which had been thoughtfully conceived to benefit him from the day he was born to the day he died and hardly required explanation. There was accordingly not much call for a dreamy junior yours truly to ponder connections. One result, in a temperament such as my own, was a sense that mystery is treasurable, even necessary: for mystery, in such a crowded, see-through little country, is, among other things, space. It was in this way, it may be supposed, that I came to step around in a murk of my own making, and to be drifted away from my native place, and in due course to rely on Rachel as a human flashlight. She illuminated things I'd thought perfectly well illuminated. To give an example, she was the one, all those years ago, who brought cinema and food to my attention. Undoubtedly I had already watched movies and eaten lunch; but I hadn't located them in the so-called scheme of things.

In my New York confusion I sometimes asked myself if matters might have been different if someone older, or at least someone more attentive than I to the way things are put together, someone with relevant knowledge, had taken my youthful self aside and put him on notice of certain facts; but no such person came forward. My mother, though watchful, and though a teacher, was not one for offering express guidance, and indeed it may be thanks to her that I naturally associate love with a house fallen into silence. It was possible, too, I further speculated, that a father might have done the trick – that is, an active, observable predecessor in experience, one moreover alert to the duty of handing down, whether by example or word of mouth, certain encouragements and caveats; and even now, when I'm beginning to understand the limits of the personal advice business, I am led to consider, especially when I stroll in Highbury Fields with Jake, a skateboarding boy of six these days, what I might one day transmit to my son to ensure that he does not grow up like his father, which is to say, without warning. I still have no firm idea, not least because I have no firm idea whether my own descent into disorder was referable to an Achilles heel or whether it's a generally punishable folly to approach life trustingly – carelessly, some might say. All I know is that unhappiness took me unawares.

There was no question of malaise when I agreed to migrate from London, in 1998: in the American calendar, the year of Monica Lewinsky. I arrived in New York in November, just over a month after Rachel had started at the Times Square office. We were installed in temporary lodgings on the Upper West Side and I had a couple of empty weeks to fill before I took up my position at M———. I had never been to New York before and I was capable of marvelling even at the traffic lights on Amsterdam Avenue, a red muddle that as you crossed the street organised itself into eternally tapering emerald duos. If I was not trying out the part of flâneur I was watching the C-SPAN coverage of the impeachment proceedings. The spectacle, which eventually had at its centre the strange character named Kenneth Starr, grew ever more transfixing and inexplicable. I never puzzled out the hatred apparently inspired by the president, whose administration, so far as I could tell, had done little more than oversee the advent of an extraordinary national fortunateness. It was quickly my impression, in this last regard, that making a million bucks in New York was essentially a question of walking down the street – of strolling, hands in pockets, in the cheerful expectation that sooner or later a bolt of pecuniary fire would jump out of the atmosphere and knock you flat. Every third person seemed to have been happily struck down: by a stock-market killing, or by a dot-com bonanza, or by a six-figure motion-picture deal for a five-hundred-word magazine article about, say, a mystifying feral chicken which, clucking and pecking, had been found roosting in a Queens backyard. I too became a beneficiary of the phenomenon, because the suddenly sunken price of a barrel of oil – it went down to ten bucks that year – helped create an unparalleled demand for seers in my line. Money, then, had joined the more familiar forms of precipitation; only it dropped, in my newcomer's imagination, from the alternative and lucky heavens constituted in the island's exhilaratory skyward figures, about which I need say nothing except that they were the most beautiful sight, never more so than on those nights when my taxi from JFK crested on the expressway above Long Island City and Manhattan was squarely revealed and, guarded by colossal laughing billboards, I pitched homeward into its pluvial lights.

Rachel and I once spotted Monica Lewinsky. She was walking down a street in the Meatpacking District. She wore a tracksuit of some kind and large sunglasses, and made her way across the cobblestones of Gansevoort Street in ordinary little steps. She was smaller than I'd imagined.

'She's put on weight,' Rachel said interestedly. We watched as Monica disappeared round the corner of Washington Street. Rachel said, 'Poor thing,' and we walked on and soon were diverted by something else. But the sighting had served as a luxurious instance of the city's ceaseless affirmation of its salvific worth: even that bizarre class of deliverance fit for poor Monica, it seemed, could be looked for here. And if that were so, one instinctively deduced, then one's own needs, such as they were, might equally be met. Not that we were in much doubt on this score. Our jobs were working out well – much better than expected, in my case – and we'd settled happily into our loft on Watts Street. This had a suitably gritty view of a parking lot and was huge enough to contain, in a corner of our white-bricked bedroom, a mechanical clothes rack with a swooping rail, like a roller-coaster's, appropriated from a dry-cleaning store: you pressed a button and Rachel's jackets and skirts and shirts clattered down from the ceiling like entering revellers. We had plenty to feel smug about, if so inclined. Smugness, however, requires a certain reflectiveness, which requires perspective, which requires distance; and we, or certainly I, didn't look upon our circumstances from the observatory offered by a disposition to the more spatial emotions

– those feelings, of regret or gratitude or relief, say, that make reference to situations removed from one's own. It didn't seem to me, for example, that I had dodged a bullet, perhaps because I had no real idea what a bullet was. I was young. I was not much extracted from the innocence in which the benevolent but fraudulent world conspires to place us as children.

After my mother's death I began taking long walks to Chinatown and Seward Park and the old Seaport area, pushing baby Jake in his stroller. On summery Pearl or Ludlow or Mott I'd find respite from our apartment and its transformation into a kind of parental coalmine, and walk and walk until I reached a state of fancifulness, of indeterminately hopeful receptiveness, which seemed to me an end in itself and as good as it got. These walks were, I guess, a mild form of somnambulism – the product of a coalminer's exhaustion and automatism. Whether that's diagnostically right or wrong, there was a definite element of flight, and an element of capitulation, too, as if I were the one scooting along in the buggy and my mother the one steering it through the streets. For my outings with my baby were taken also in her company. I did not summon her up by way of remembrance but, rather, by fantasy. The fantasy did not consist of imagining her physically at my side but of imagining her at a long distance, as before, and me still remotely swaddled in her consideration; and in this I was abetted by the streets of New York City, which abet desire even in its strangest patterns.

All of which brings me to the second, and last, New York winter I endured on my own, when I wondered what exactly had happened to the unanswerable, conspiratorial place I'd found years earlier, and the desirer who'd walked its streets.

That was a very white winter. A blizzard on Presidents' Day 2003 brought one of the heaviest snows in the city's history. For a day or two, outdoor motions seemed a kind of mummery and the newspapers broke up the Iraq stories with photos of children tobogganing on Sheep's Meadow. I passed the morning of the holiday in an armchair in my hotel apartment, mesmerised by a snowdrift on the wrought-iron balcony that grew and deepened and monstrously settled against the glass door, not completely melting until mid-March. It says something about my empty-headedness that I followed this month-long thaw with something like tension. At least twice a day I peered through the French windows and inspected the dirty, faintly glowing accumulation of ice. I was torn between a ridiculous loathing of this obdurate wintry ectoplasm and an equally ridiculous tenderness stimulated by a solid's battle against the forces of lique-faction. Random mental commotions of this kind constantly agitated me during this period, when I was in the habit, among other strange habits, of lying on the floor of my living room and staring into the space under my brown armchair, a letter-box-shaped crevice out of which, I may have hoped, an important communication would come. I wasn't especially troubled by the hours spent flat on my face. My assumption was that all around me, in the lustrous boxes thickly chequering the night, countless New Yorkers lay stretched out on the floor, felled by similar feelings; or, if not actually poleaxed, stood at their windows, as I often did, to observe the winter clouds rubbing out – so, from my vantage point, it appeared – the skyscrapers in the middle distance. The magnitude of the vanishing was wonderful, even to a spirit such as my own, perhaps because it preluded the seemingly miraculous re-emergence from the clouds of towers dashed from within with light. On Presidents' Day, however, the vaporous, enormously disappearing city provoked a different response. Tiring of my snowdrift vigil, I hauled myself out of the armchair and travelled to my bedroom and, in search of a fresh point of view, wandered to the window there. Snowflakes like coffee grinds blackened the insect screen. Powdered ice, blown up from the window trough, had gained on the sill and now crept up the glass. I was, it will be understood, afflicted by the solitary's vulnerability to insights, so that when I peered out into the flurry and saw no sign of the Empire State Building,

I was assaulted by the notion, arriving in the form of a terrifying stroke of consciousness, that substance – everything of so-called concreteness – was indistinct from its unnameable opposite.

Kicking a rock or patting a dog is, I suppose, enough to rid most people of this variety of bewilderment, which must be as ancient as our species. But I didn't have a rock or a dog to hand. I had nothing to hand – nothing but the glass of a window under assault from a storm. It came as a reprieve to hear the infuriating cheep of my telephone.

It was Rachel. She told me first about the huge anti-war rally that had taken place in London two days before and how Jake had carried a NOT IN MY NAME placard. Next she told me, in the tone of a person discussing a grocery list, that she had definitely decided not to return to the United States, at least not before the end of the Bush administration or any successor administration similarly intent on a military and economic domination of the world. It was no longer a question of physical security, she said, although that of course remained a factor. It was a question, rather, of not exposing Jake to an upbringing in an 'ideologically diseased' country, as she put it, a 'mentally ill, sick, unreal' country whose masses and leaders suffered from extraordinary and self-righteous delusions about the United States, the world, and indeed, thanks to the influence of the fanatical evangelical Christian movement, the universe, delusions that had the effect of exempting the United States from the very rules of civilised and lawful and rational behaviour it so mercilessly sought to enforce on others. She stated, growing more and more upset, that we were at a crossroads, that a great power had 'drifted into wrongdoing', that her conscience permitted no other conclusion.

Ordinarily, I would have said nothing; but it seemed to me that my dealings with my son were at stake. So I said, 'Rach, please let's try to keep things in perspective.'

'Perspective? And what perspective would that be? The perspective of the free press of America? Is that where you get your perspective, Hans?' She made a harsh sound of mirth. 'From TV networks funded by conservative advertisers? From the *Wall Street Journal*? From the *Times*, that establishment stooge? Why not Ari Fleischer, while you're at it?'

Not for the first time, I was finding it hard to believe this was the woman I'd married – a corporate litigator, let's not forget, radicalised only in the service of her client and with not the smallest bone to pick about money and its doings.

'You want Jake to grow up with an American perspective? Is that it? You want him to not be able to point to Britain on a map? You want him to believe that Saddam Hussein sent those planes into the towers?'

Specks of snow, small and dark as flies, swarmed before

me. I said, 'Of course he wouldn't grow up in ignorance. We wouldn't allow it.'

She said, 'Bush wants to attack Iraq as part of a right-wing plan to destroy international law and order as we know it and replace it with the global rule of American force. Tell me which part of that sentence is wrong, and why.'

As usual, she was too quick for me. I said, 'I don't want to get into an argument about this. You're pinning views on me that I don't have.'

Rachel seemed to laugh. 'See? It's pointless having this discussion. It's like playing tennis with someone who insists on playing gin rummy.'

'What are you talking about?'

'You're constantly flailing around and changing the subject and making emotive statements. It's the classic conservative tactic. Instead of answering the point, you sabotage the discussion.'

'Fine,' I said. 'Repeat the point. And stop calling me a conservative.'

'You are a conservative,' Rachel said. 'What's so sad is you don't even know it.'

'If your point is that the US should not attack Iraq,' I managed, 'I'm not going to disagree with that. But if your point is . . .' I trailed off, at a substantive loss. I was distracted, too – by a memory of Rachel and me flying to Hong Kong for our honeymoon, and how in the dimmed cabin I looked out of my window and saw lights, in small glimmering webs, on the placeless darkness miles below. I pointed them out to Rachel. I wanted to say something about these creaturely cosmical glows, which made me feel, I wanted to say, as if we had been removed by translation into another world. Rachel leaned across me and looked down to the earth. 'It's Iraq,' she said.

She said, 'I'm saying the US has no moral or legal authority to wage this war. The fact that Saddam is horrible and should be shot dead today is not the issue. The bad character of the enemy does not make the war good. Think politically, for once. Stalin was a monster. He killed millions of people. Millions. Does that mean we should have supported Hitler in his invasion of Russia? We should have stood shoulder to shoulder with Hitler because he was proposing to rid the world of a mass murderer?'

I should have concurred. I knew better than to argue with Rachel about such things. But I was ashamed and wanted to redeem myself. 'You're saying Bush is like Hitler,' I said. 'That's ridiculous.'

'I'm not comparing Bush to Hitler!' Rachel almost pleaded. 'Hitler is just an extreme example. You use extreme examples to test a proposition. It's called reasoning. That's how you reason. You make a proposition and you follow it to its logical conclusion. Hans, you're supposed to be the great rationalist.'

As I've said, I never laid claim to this trait. I merely

saw myself as cautious about my pronouncements. The idea that I was a rationalist was one Rachel had nurtured – albeit, I must admit, with my complicity. Who has the courage to set right those misperceptions that bring us love?

'This isn't reasoning,' I said. 'This is just aggression.'

'Aggression? Hans, can't you understand? Can't you see this isn't about personal relations? Politeness, niceness, you, me – it's all irrelevant. This is about a life-and-death struggle for the future of the world. Our personal feelings don't come into the picture. There are forces out there. The United States is now the strongest military power in the world. It can and will do anything it wants. It has to be stopped. Your feelings and my feelings' – she was sobbing now – 'are not on the agenda.'

Once again I stared out of my window. The snowfall had come to an end. A cold toga draped the city.

'It's been snowing here,' I said. 'Jake could build a snowman on 23rd Street.'

Rachel sniffled. 'Well, I'm not moving him over there so he can build a snowman. By that logic we should all head for the North Pole. What's left of it.'

I laughed, but I knew Rachel well enough to take seriously everything she had said. However, I had no idea how to respond effectively. The difficulty was not merely that I couldn't think of an alternative to the programme of travelling to London once or twice a month. No, my difficulty was that I could not disarrange the boundless, freezing dismay that undermined every personal motion I attempted. It was as if, in my inability to produce a movement in my life, I had fallen victim to the paralysis that confounds actors in dreams as they vainly try to run or talk or make love.

Naturally, I reproached myself. I should have not allowed this transatlantic stand-off, which had now lasted for more than a year, to persist. I should have moved to London in defiance of my wife's firm but indistinctly explained preference for separateness. More particularly, I should have seen Rachel's telephonic outburst coming, not least because the imminent invasion of Iraq had stimulated an impressive and impassioned opinion in practically everybody I knew. For those under the age of forty-five it seemed that world events had finally contrived a meaningful test of their capacity for conscientious political thought. Many of my acquaintances, I realised, had passed the last decade or two in a state of intellectual and psychical yearning for such a moment – or, if they hadn't, were able to quickly assemble an expert arguer's arsenal of thrusts and statistics and ripostes and gambits and examples and salient facts and rhetorical manoeuvres. I, however, was almost completely caught out. I could take a guess at the oil production capacity of an American-occupied Iraq and in fact was pressed at work about this issue daily, and stupidly. ('What are you saying, two and a half million barrels or three million? Which one is it?') But I found myself unable to contribute to conversations about the value of international law or the feasibility of producing a dirty bomb or the constitutional rights of imprisoned enemies or the efficacy of duct tape as a window sealant or the merits of vaccinating the American masses against smallpox or the complexity of weaponising deadly bacteria or the menace of the neoconservative cabal in the Bush administration, or indeed any of the debates, each apparently vital, that raged everywhere – raged, because the debaters speedily grew heated and angry and contemptuous. In this ever-shifting, all-enveloping discussion, my orientation was poor. I could not tell where I stood. If pressed to state my position, I would confess the truth: that I had not succeeded in arriving at a position. I lacked necessary powers of perception and certainty and, above all, foresight. The future retained the impenetrable character I had always attributed to it. Would American security be improved or worsened by taking over Iraq? I did not know, because I had no information about the future purposes and capacities of terrorists or, for that matter, American administrations; and even if I were to have such information, I could still not hope to know how things would turn out. Did I know if the death and pain caused by a war in Iraq would or would not exceed the miseries that might likely flow from leaving Saddam Hussein in power? No. Could I say whether the right to autonomy of the Iraqi people – a problematic national entity, by all accounts – would be enhanced or diminished by an American regime change? I could not. Did Iraq have weapons of mass destruction that posed a real threat? I had no idea; and to be truthful, and to touch on my real difficulty, I had little interest. I didn't really care.

In short, I was a political-ethical idiot. Normally, this deficiency might have been inconsequential, but these were abnormal times. If New Yorkers were not already jumpy enough from the constant reminders of the code orange level of terrorist threat, there was another peril to concern us: the fires underfoot. The extraordinary quantities of snow and street salt were combining, apparently, to eat away at the municipal electrical system, with the result that, all winter and into the spring, underground wires caught light and flames spreading under the streets blew up thousands of manholes on sidewalks from Long Island City to Jamaica to the East Village, the detonations shooting cast-iron manhole covers fifty feet into the air. It was Chuck Ramkissoon who alerted me to this danger. After our January outing he'd placed me on his electronic mailing list, and two or three times a week I was one of around a dozen – 'Dear friends', he called us – to receive messages about whatever was on his mind: cricket, American history, birding, sales of Brooklyn real estate, meteorological phenomena, interesting economic data, resonant business stories (there was an item, perhaps for my special benefit, about Arctic gas), and eye-catching miscellanea such as the business of the electrical inferno. He signed them all,

CHUCK RAMKISSOON
President, New York Cricket Club

Chuck Cricket Corp. had been replaced by a grander entity.

Often Chuck's e-mails simply provided links to websites he found interesting, but when the message was concerned with his cricket undertaking he might give us the benefit of his own musings. One such memorandum was headed 'NOT AN IMMIGRANT SPORT'. Its text – still preserved in my electronic filing cabinet – was as follows:

Cricket was the first modern team sport in America. It came before baseball and football. Cricket has been played in New York since the 1770s. The first international team sports fixtures anywhere were cricket matches between the USA and Canada in the 1840s and 1850s. In those days cricket matches in New York were watched by thousands of fans. It was a professional sport reported in all the newspapers. There were clubs all over the country, in Newark, Schenectady, Troy, Albany, San Francisco, Boston, Ohio, Illinois, Iowa, Kentucky, Baltimore and Philadelphia. In Philadelphia alone there were dozens of clubs and the magnificent facilities of

Philadelphia Cricket Club, Merion Cricket Club and Germantown Cricket Club are still standing today. (The fields are mostly used for lawn tennis.) It was not until the First World War that the sport went into sharp decline for complicated reasons.

So it is wrong to see cricket in America as most people see it i.e. an immigrant sport. It is a bona fide American pastime and should be regarded as such. All those who have attempted to 'introduce' cricket to the American public have failed to understand this. Cricket is already in the American DNA. With proper promotion, marketing, government support etc awareness of the game could easily be reawakened. American kids could once again play their country's oldest team sport!

One recipient of this missive copied his reply to all of Chuck's addressees:

Whoever
Could you please stop sending me crazy junk mail?!

Although I glanced at them, I didn't respond to Chuck's communications. My instinct was to keep him at a distance, at that distance, certainly, that we introduce between ourselves and those we suspect of neediness. I was wondering, for example, when he was going to ask me for money for his cricket scheme. But I was also drawn to Chuck. I had him down as a lover of contingencies and hypotheses, a man cheerfully operating in the subjunctive mood. The business world is densely margined by dreamers, men, almost invariably, whose longing selves willingly submit to the enchantment of projections and pie charts and crisply totted numbers, who toy and toy for years, like novelists, with the same sheaf of documents, who slip out of bed in the middle of the night to pitch to a pyjama'd reflection in a window-pane. I've never been open to the fantastical aspect of business. I'm an analyst – a bystander. I lack entrepre-neurial wistfulness. In other respects, of course, I'm as faraway as they come. That winter, for example, when the Cricket World Cup was being played in southern Africa and several old teammates of mine played for the Netherlands against the great Indians and Australians, I imagined that events long ago had taken a different turn and that in my youth I'd discovered the great secret of batting – something to do with the position of the head, maybe, or the preliminary movement of the feet, or a special dedication of memory – with the result (I imag-ined further on those black mornings when I woke early to follow the Dutch matches on cricinfo.com's live score-board) that I was now one of those orange-clad Hollanders stationed on the pale lawns of Paarl and

Potchefstroom, and that when Brett Lee, say, took twenty sprinted strides towards me, and leaped, and hurled the white one-day ball at my toes, the ninety-two-mile-per-hour blur came into focus and hung before me like a Christmas bauble and with a simple push of my long-handled bat I sent the ball gliding to the boundary's white rope. How many of us are completely free of such scenarios? Who hasn't known, a little shamefully, the joys they bring? I suspect that what keeps us harmless from them is not, as many seem to believe, the maintenance of a strict frontier between the kingdoms of the fanciful and the actual, but the contrary: the permitting of a benign annexation of the latter by the former, so that our daily motions always cast a secondary other-worldly shadow and, at those moments when we feel inclined to turn from the more plausible and hurtful meanings of things, we soothingly find ourselves attached to a companion far-fetched sense of the world and our place in it. It's the incompleteness of reverie that brings trouble – that, one might argue, brought Chuck Ramkissoon the worst trouble of all. His head wasn't sufficiently in the clouds. He had a clear enough view of the gap between where he stood and where he wished to be, and he was determined to find a way across.

However, and to repeat, this wasn't on my mind at the time – Chuck himself wasn't on my mind. Other people were, among them Rivera. One morning he came into my office and shut the door and told me he was going to be fired.

I gave the statement my consideration. Rivera, I knew, had recently received a disappointing ranking from the sales force, and this had been followed by a poorly received research paper on Nigeria; but he analysed mid-cap stocks, a sector different from mine, and I wasn't on anything like close enough terms with his boss, Heavey, to judge with any certainty what this might mean. That said, Rivera obviously had reason to worry. We all did. The value of analysts is a matter of opinion, and opinions on Wall Street are at least as fickle as they are anywhere else.

'They're giving my job to Pallot,' Rivera said.

He stood by the window looking out at the dropping sleet, a little guy in a clean white shirt. His skinny hairy hands were in the pockets of his pants, gripping and gripping something. Not knowing what to say, I got up and stood next to him, and for a while we surveyed, twenty-two floors down, the roving black blooms of four-dollar umbrellas.

'Sit tight,' I said. 'These things blow up and blow away.'

But in early March I came back from two days in Houston and saw that Rivera was gone; Pallot had indeed taken over his desk. When I telephoned Rivera and offered to take him out for a drink, he found a reason to duck out. He was ashamed, was my impression. 'Listen, I'm OK,' he said. 'I've got a bunch of irons in the fire.'

All of this bothered me a lot. One night I went out with Appleby to a bar on the Lower East Side, anxious to talk about Rivera's fate and scheme in his favour. Appleby, however, had arranged to meet up with friends. He passed the evening telling them jokes I couldn't quite hear or get, and from time to time they stepped out onto the sidewalk to smoke cigarettes and make calls to carousers elsewhere in the city, returning with reports of parties in Williamsburg and SoHo and, as the night whirled away, leaving me on the rim of things. I drank up and left them to it.

No, Rivera was my only true work buddy, perhaps my only true buddy anywhere – even Vinay, my whisky-loving dining friend, had decamped to Los Angeles. In all my time in America I had not received a single social call from those I'd designated as my London friends; and neither, it's true to say, had I called them. With Rivera, I made an effort. I phoned and e-mailed him repeatedly but, as far as getting to meet him was concerned, without success. It wasn't long before he stopped responding. Then I heard he'd moved back to California, where he'd grown up, and then Appleby, who was something of a rumourer, was fairly sure he'd gone down to San Antonio to work for an oil company. But nobody knew one thing or another for a fact, and the moment came when I realised that Rivera had joined those who had disappeared from my life.

I suppose it was this kind of upset, together with that winter's more rhythmical miseries, which drew me into the comforting routine, on those days when I had extra time on my hands, of lingering over breakfast at the Malibu Diner, a restaurant one block east of the hotel. The Malibu was run by Corfiotes – to be exact, by people from an isle off Corfu – and sometimes I would be engaged in conversation by one of the owners, a fellow with heart trouble who read Greek newspapers because, he told me, after nearly thirty years of living in America he was still foxed by the Roman alphabet. The owner's son-in-law had an ex-brother-in-law, and it was this man, a fellow in his late fifties named George, who was my regular waiter. He had a little moustache, a black waistcoat and a red, clean-looking face. My dealings with George were limited by the very depth of our mutual understanding: he automatically brought me scrambled eggs and wholewheat toast and liberally refilled my coffee; I tipped him heavily and without comment. The one fact he disclosed about his life was that he had not long ago become divorced and as a consequence was as happy as he'd ever been. 'I can smoke now,' he explained. 'I smoke five packs a day.' The most remarkable thing about the Malibu was the mirror that covered the entire wall of the back room and duplicated in its glass the whole interior of the diner, with the strange result that newcomers were subject to a powerful temporary illusion that the back room did not actually exist and was no more than a trick of reflection. This unsettling misapprehension perhaps contributed to the relative scarcity of customers at the rear of the diner, where I came to regard a particular table as my own. There were a few other repetitive presences. Every Saturday, people prone to extreme credit card debt and other forms of improvidence convened at the very rear of the restaurant to discuss their squandering ways and give one another encouragement and support. My most constant dining companions, though, were the blind people who lived in a special residence up the street ('A Visionary Community' was inscribed on the frontage) and bravely ventured outdoors with white sticks scratching ahead of them, which is why I came to think of my neighbourhood as the quarter of the blind. Most days two or three unsighted persons – women, almost without exception – would find their way to one of the tables near to me and order huge, complex breakfasts. They ate indelicately, fingering sunny eggs and lowering their faces to the food. My favourites among them were two fast friends, a black woman and a white woman, who both wore bobble hats and swayed from side to side like sailors as they walked. The white woman, in her sixties and the elder by at least ten years, still had a fragment of vision: she examined the menu as if it were a diamond, raising it an inch from her left eye. The black woman, who moved with one hand held fast to the elbow of her consort, went about in utter blindness. When she stretched open her eyelids with her thumbs, yellowish eyeballs turned in the sockets. The two of them always conducted a cheerful, intelligent conversation that I would listen to quite contentedly for an hour or more on those weekends when I had nothing to do. It was during one such session of eavesdropping that a woman I didn't recognise stopped at my table and asked me, in an English accent, if I had once lived in London.

She was a woman of around my age, with pale brown skin and large eyes made a little mournful by the shape of her brow.

'Yes, I have lived in London,' I said.

'In Maida Vale?' she said.

I was about to say no, and then I remembered. About eight years previously, just before I came to know Rachel, I'd stayed at a friend's flat in Little Venice while workmen painted my new place in Notting Hill.

'For about two weeks,' I said, smiling involuntarily.

She smiled back, and in smiling became distinctly pretty. 'I thought so,' she said, wrapping her coat tighter about her. In a polite tone, she went on, 'We once shared a cab. From . . .' She named a nightspot in Soho. 'You gave me a ride home.'

I remembered the club well – it had been something of a haunt of mine – but I didn't remember this woman, or having shared a taxi with anybody like her. 'Are you sure?' I said.

She laughed. Not without embarrassment, she said,

'You're called Hans, right? It was an unusual name. That's why I remember.'

It was my turn to feel embarrassed, but most of all I was amazed.

Although she never took a seat, the woman and I talked for a few minutes longer, and it was very easily agreed that she would drop by one evening. She had, she said, always been curious about the Chelsea Hotel.

If I feel able to state that I didn't give the matter any further thought – that I wasn't planning anything – it's because, a few evenings later, when the house phone in my apartment rang and Jesus at the front desk told me I had a visitor called Danielle, I had no idea what he was talking about. Only at the last second, as I went to answer the cough of my doorbell, did it occur to me who the visitor might be – and that I'd never gotten around to asking her for her name.

I opened the door. 'I was passing by,' she said, and mumbled some further statement. 'If I'm intruding . . .'

'Of course not,' I said. 'Come in.'

She wore a coat that may have been different from the coat I'd first seen her in but had the same effect, namely to make it seem as if she'd just been rescued from a river and blanketed. My own get-up was shabby – bare feet, T-shirt, decaying tracksuit bottoms – and while I changed, Danielle wandered round my apartment, as was her privilege: people in New York are authorised by convention to snoop around and mentally measure and pass comment on any real estate they're invited to step into. In addition to the generous ceiling heights and the wood floors and the built-in closets, she undoubtedly took in the family photographs and the bachelor disarray and the second bedroom with its ironing board and its child's bed covered by a mound of wrinkled office shirts. I imagine this answered some questions she had about my situation, and not in an especially disheartening way. Like an old door, every man past a certain age comes with historical warps and creaks of one kind or another, and a woman who wishes to put him to serious further use must expect to do a certain amount of sanding and planing. But of course not every woman is interested in this sort of refurbishment project, just as not every man has only one thing on his mind. About Danielle, I remember, my feelings were no more specific than a pleasant anxiousness. She hadn't caught me, obviously enough, at a very erotic moment in my life. I had never been much of a pickup artist – a few ghastly encounters in my twenties had seen to that – and the alternative prospect of a euphoric romance not only exhausted me but, in fact, struck me as impossible. This wasn't because of any fidelity to my absent wife or some aversion to sex, which, I like to think, grabs me as much as the next man. No, it was simply that I was uninterested in making, as I saw it, a Xerox of some old emotional state. I was in my mid-thirties, with a marriage more or less behind me. I was no longer vulnerable to curiosity's enormous momentum. I had nothing new to murmur to another on the subject of myself and not the smallest eagerness about being briefed on Danielle's supposedly unique trajectory – a curve described under the action, one could safely guess, of the usual material and maternal and soulful longings, a few thwarting tics of character, and luck good and bad. A life seemed like an old story.

I emerged, fully dressed, from my bedroom. 'Let me show you the building,' I said.

Together we descended, as the wide-eyed transients did, the streaky grey marble steps. While Danielle surveyed the sulphurous, wildly expressive canvases, I found myself freshly eyeing the pipes and wires and alarm boxes and electrical devices and escape maps and sprinklers that cluttered the wall of each landing. These tokens of calamity and fire, taken in conjunction with the fiery and calamitous art, gave a hellishly subterranean aspect to our downward journey, which I had undertaken only once or twice before on foot, and I was almost startled when we reached the bottom of the stairs not to run into chuckling old Lucifer himself and instead to find myself on the surface of the earth and able to walk out directly into the cold, clear night. We stood for a moment under the awning of the hotel, stamping our feet. I could think of nothing better than to suggest dinner.

With no clear sense of a destination we made our way

to Ninth Avenue. At 22nd Street, we entered an Italian restaurant. Danielle removed her coat and I saw that she wore a short skirt, black wool tights, and knee-length leather boots. A tiny metal star was lodged in the crease above a nostril.

A waiter brought pasta and a bottle of red wine. The room's acoustics, which turned surrounding chatter into a roar, forced us to shout to make ourselves heard, so that our conversation formally shared many of the characteristics of a bitter argument. Towards the end of the meal, Danielle, who seemed to be enjoying herself in spite of everything, caught me staring at the first-aid notice that was fixed to the wall behind her. 'Don't you think that's a little bizarre?' I offered. Danielle turned and looked and laughed, because the photographs in the notice made it appear as if the choking victim was actually strangling herself while being attacked from behind by a larger woman. Danielle said something I didn't catch.

I said, 'I'm sorry – what?'

She yelled back, 'Somebody should bring out a book called *The Heimlich Diet*. You know, you eat as much as you want, and then somebody –' She demonstrated the manoeuvre with a jerk of her arms.

'That's a good one,' I said, nodding and smiling. '*The Heimlich Diet*.'

Afterwards, I drifted back towards the chute of white neon letters that spelled HOT L; Danielle walked beside me, smoking a cigarette. It would be difficult for me to overstate the weirdness of that stroll, a weirdness hardly alleviated by the scene that awaited us on our re-entry into the hotel. A party was taking place in the lobby. The occasion was the third birthday of a terrier named Missie who lived on the second floor, and Missie's owner, a friendly man in his sixties whom I knew only as an elevator cohort, placed champagne glasses in our hands and said, 'Missie absolutely insists.' The lobby was crowded with hotel residents human and canine. The angel was there, as was the eminent librettist, and I also recognised an artist who wore dark sunglasses night and day, and two teenaged sisters who had once babysat for Jake, and a concert pianist from Delaware, and a fellow with a seat on the Stock Exchange, and the Iranian husband and wife whose spliffs gave a certain floor its aroma, and the film star who'd recently separated from his film-star wife, and a couple who made baroque wallpaper, and the murmuring widow. Whoever owned a dog had brought that dog down to the lobby. An enormously gentle borzoi was barging around, and I seem to remember a cinnamon-patched mutt, a pair of tiny hairless bright-eyed pugs, an affenpinscher, spaniels, an ancient battered paw-licking chow and, standing by the fireplace, a specimen of one of those miniaturised breeds that are apparently pro-grammed to tremble helplessly. From time to time a chorus of barking broke out and the dog owners would look down and themselves bark reprimands in unison. My immediate inclination was to gulp down one drink and get out. Danielle, however, became involved in a discussion with a maker of papier-mâché dolls and then with a photographer of African scenes, and I found myself in long conferences of my own with, first, a dentist who practised out of a hotel apartment, and second, a ginger-bearded fellow I'd seen around the place who declared himself to be on a 'dog date' with a half-beagle, half-Rottweiler.

'How's it going?' I asked him.

'Pretty good, so far,' the ginger-bearded man said. 'It's only our second date.' He shrugged. 'We've got a week of cohabitation coming up. That's going to be the real test.'

We both looked at the dog. It seemed very friendly. Its shaking tail was permanently at a vertical, exposing a pale pink asshole.

'I wonder if I don't need a more masculine dog,' the man said thoughtfully.

We were standing next to a painting of a horse's face, the very memory of which makes me want to go back and study it once again, for this horse's face, with its pale, dolorous nose set against darkness, seemed to promise to the person who studied it long enough some transcendental revelation. 'You ever groomed a horse?' the ginger-bearded fellow asked, whereupon he was moved to recall his boyhood in Colorado, when he had spent more than one summer working on a dude ranch. He told me you brushed a horse with a variety of brushes, and that the coat of a horse will release small clouds of dirt, and that he used a special mane comb to comb the manes, but very gently, because hairs in a mane break so easily. My eyes were all the while directed at the painted horse, and only when my friend stopped speaking did I turn and see him stroking a tear from his eye.

By the time Danielle and I were reunited – in order, so I assumed, to say goodbye – I'd drunk four or five plastic cups of champagne. Whether it was the alcohol or the unusual texture of the evening (she said with mock bitterness, 'I finally feel like I've arrived in New York. It's only taken me four years'), Danielle was in a state of happy excitement, and it seemed only right that she should follow me into the elevator and into my apartment and that we should begin kissing and, very soon afterwards, fucking.

Viewed narrowly, our first actions were unusual only in that my partner seemed intent, on the one hand, on being held tight, and on the other hand specialised in a squirming manoeuvre that forced me to lunge for her and, in fact, to pursue her onto the floor as she twisted away from me and slid headfirst over the bed's edge. All the while she seemed terribly dazed by some private series of thoughts, and this double slipperiness of body and spirit made it entirely unexpected that she came to lie alongside me in tranquillity, smoking a cigarette.

She said, 'You really don't remember that cab ride?'

I shook my head.

'Why should you?' she said, sending a cloudy zephyr to the ceiling. 'I'm not sure why I remember it myself.'

There followed a pause during which, I decided, this woman was considering the retrospective significance of a taxi journey up the Edgware Road many years ago. Her hand made its way to my thigh and tenderly applied pressure there. 'Anyhow, I think that's why I trust you,' she said, her nearest eye darting at me and then back at the ceiling. 'Because you were a complete gentleman.' The phrase made her laugh loudly, and she began to make a leisurely, more sensual motion with her hand. I reached out to touch her breasts, and it astonished me how much pleasure this gave me. Suddenly, in spite of all the notions with which I'd dismissed the possibility, this woman had my attention. I was fully alert now and fully aware of her particularity. The silver stream of hair bravely flowing from a spring in her crown, the labia like secret crinkled sticks of liquorice, the ins and outs of her Anglo-Jamaican parentage, the few details I'd been told of her New York existence (her apartment on Eldridge Street; her job as a visual creative for an advertising company; her habit of buying lingerie from a tiny, venerable Jewish store on Orchard Street) now struck me as treasurable. Our touching progressed to more purposeful, thrilling contact, and it was in the middle of this subjectively remarkable development – I was being kissed! Kissed by a beautiful woman who wanted to kiss me! – that I became conscious of a kind of vertigo. It arose from the very completeness of my gladness, which was erasing, along with my wretchedness, everything attached to the wretchedness, which was everything of importance to the person I understood myself to be. Once, long ago, an old university friend of mine, a gay man, confided to me that he had only barely survived a cata-strophic depression brought about by a love affair with a woman, the effect of which had been to smash utterly the identity he had constructed at such cost to himself and his parents. I was now in danger of clambering onto the same boat. I dizzily sensed my life to date being set at naught – either that or set on its head, since I was confronted with a turning upside down of my last decade, which very possibly I had completely misread, and whose true sweep, it was now possible to conceive, went from a forgotten London night in 1995 to a serendipitous winter's morning in New York, 2003. This was, perhaps, an extreme reaction to my situation; but nonetheless it was my reac-tion, which I suppose puts me in the romantic camp.

We were once again making love when Danielle whis-pered something I didn't follow. 'I want you to be a gentleman again,' she whispered. 'Will you do that for me?'

I must have signalled some agreement to this incom-prehensible request, because she slipped off the bed and crouched to rummage in the clothes heaped on the floor

– I wasn't watching – and after a few seconds came back to me with refreshed spiritedness. Then she breathed into my ear the assertion, 'Remember, I trust you,' and produced with a little jingle the belt she'd removed from my trousers. I took the belt, a length of black leather that was at once familiar and strange, and saw Danielle lying face down on the bed, and began to perform the act I understood her to need. Every lash was answered by a small moan. If this gave me some unusual satisfaction, I can't remember it now. I do recall a tunneller's anxiety as to where and when it would all end, and that my arm began to tire, and that eventually, as I worked at beating this woman across the back, and the buttocks, and the trembling hams, I looked to the window for some kind of relief and saw the lights of distant apartments mingled in a reflection of the room. I was not shocked by what I saw – a pale white hitting a pale black – but I did of course ask myself what had happened, how it could be that I should find myself living in a hotel in a country where there was no one to remember me, attacking a woman who'd boomeranged in from a time I could not claim as my own. I recall, also, trying to shrug off a sharp new sadness that I'm only now able to identify without tentativeness, which is to say, the sadness produced when the mirroring world no longer offers a surface in which one may recognise one's true likeness.

But, as I've said, I wasn't shocked. The shock came later,

when Danielle failed to respond to the two telephone messages I left for her.

It occurred to me one day that spring had arrived. I was steering my driving instructor's old Buick through the West Village when I noticed flowers splashing colour around the foot of a tree. An idea came to me. I asked Carl, my instructor – this was at the beginning of a two-hour lesson, the first of three I'd booked in preparation for my driving test – if we might drive to Staten Island.

'Fine by me,' Carl said doubtfully.

Carl was a fastidious Guyanese with polished leather shoes and a grey tweed jacket he never wore but instead hung on a hook over the back seat. 'Driving here tricky,' he warned me at the outset. This aside, I discovered, he was reluctant to divulge any specific information relating to the motoring practices of New York. He was, however, keen to discuss his ongoing attempt to secure an appointment at the Bureau of Citizenship and Immigration Services for a fingerprinting session: this was required, he reminded me, of all applicants for Permanent Resident Alien status. Carl told me, as we headed at a lawful speed down the BQE, that he had been waiting two years to have his fingerprints taken. 'They lost the file,' Carl said. 'One day they say it in Texas, the next day they say it in Misery.'

'Misery?' I said.

'Misery,' Carl repeated. He hissed. 'I do not like that place. I do not like it one bit.'

I understood him to be referring, here, not to Missouri but to the Bureau's headquarters at Federal Plaza. I'd been there myself earlier that month in order to cure the typographical error on my Green Card. In the dim, windy early morning I joined the queue of aliens in a cement basin at the foot of the tower. It was a cold wait. Clouds like rats ran across the sky. At last a man in a uniform appeared and goonishly scribbled a light-sensitive mark on the hand each of us offered him, as if we were entering a cheap nightclub – and indeed, within the jurisdiction of the federal building a negative dance was the rage, one which prohibited all blamelessly instinctive movement: in the course of that morning I saw one man removed from the building for looking out of the windows, another for leaning against the heating units, another for taking a telephone call. I duly received a corrected Green Card, which enabled me to return to the DMV to collect my learner permit, which left, as officialdom's final hurdle between me and a driving test, a compulsory presentation on road safety. This turned out to be a four-hour lock-in at a 14th Street basement with ridiculously small classroom desks, behind which the students – we were nearly all foreigners deep into adulthood – sat like imbecilic giants. Our lecturer, a destroyed-looking man in his sixties, appeared apologetically before us, and I am certain that a compassionate understanding tacitly arose among the students that we should do everything to assist this individual, an agreeable and no doubt clever man whose life had plainly come to some kind of ruin. Accordingly we were a well-behaved and reasonably responsive class and, an hour or so later, did our best to abide by his request not to sleep during the screening of two films, the first concerning the impossibility of driving safely when under the influence of drugs or drink, the second concerning the tremendous dangers of night driving. The lights were switched off, a screen was lowered, and the basement was transformed into a crappy bioscope. Unlike many of the others, I managed to stay awake; and could not help thinking, as I endured an ominous dramatisation of the loss of vision produced by alcohol and by nightfall and the disastrous consequences thereof, of my father's life ending in a smash-up presumably just like those presented on the screen, and of the fact, unconsidered by me before, that on top of everything else his early death had given an unfairly morganatic quality to his marriage: he had been posthumously robbed, in his son's sentiments, of a ranking equal to that of his wife. It's our lucky day, my ancestor apparently used to say with that Dutch love of slipping into English phrases. I saw there would come a point when Jake would ask me about his paternal grandparents and it would fall to me to repeat just such scraps relating to my father, and to speak to him about his grandmother and perhaps even her late and only brother, Jake's great-uncle Willem, whom I never knew, and with such small gusts of facts assist in the dispersion of his world's delicious indistinctness – delicious, at least, in retrospect. For my comings and goings were frightening mysteries to my three-year-old son. My arrival, however closely anticipated, startled him; and from our first moment together he would be filled with a dread of my departure, which he could not comprehend or situate in time. He feared that any minute I might be gone; and always the thing he most feared would come to pass.

Carl and I took the top deck of the Verrazano Bridge to Staten Island. A crosswind blew strongly as we soared over the brown water of the Narrows. I wanted to glance left, beyond the towers of Coney Island, because the ocean when glimpsed from New York City is quite something, a scarcely believable slab of otherness; but Carl, sitting to my right, continued to demand my attention.

'Two years they keep me waiting,' he said once more. 'And my lawyer say maybe two years after that.'

'I guess you have to persist,' I said, hoping to bring an end to the topic.

He grinned inexplicably. 'Yes, that's what I have to do. Persist.' The grin grew even more hilarious. 'I have to persist.'

At Staten Island I negotiated the unruly toll plaza and

drove up the slip road to Clove Road, where I turned right and continued up past the Silver Lake golf course to Bard Avenue. Staten Island is hilly, and Bard climbs and descends a hill, and at the bottom of the hill is Walker Park. There I stopped the Buick and got out alone.

My immediate purpose was to find out what had happened to the daffodil bulbs that I and a few other volunteers from the cricket club had buried the previous November along a section of the park's edge. The exercise made no practical difference to the club, since the flowers would bloom and go to ground before our own season got fully under way; but it was felt that an act of elective stewardship would strengthen our claim on the park, a claim which in spite of its longevity we regarded, I believe correctly, as always under threat from unfriendly forces.

Green leaf blades were indeed rising out of the loose earth, and in one or two sunlit places a stem carried a packaged flower bud. For a while I inspected them: botanical dummy that I am, I could hardly believe my eyes. Then, surrendering to another impulse, I walked over mucky grass to the strip of clay at the heart of the field. The clay, altogether battered, was pocked with pools and footprints. Wood fragments were buried in it. Very soon, in early April, our club secretary would pick up two Mexican day-labourers from a street corner and pay them each a hundred bucks plus tip to heave picks and shovels and spread fresh clay, and then the heavy roller that had wintered in chains by the clubhouse would be released and dragged out and pushed slowly over the clay, pressing out moisture and flattening the surface, though not completely: you preserved the very slight convexity needed for the drainage of rainwater. Tufts of grass growing in the clay would be pulled up by hand and countless tiny surfacing stones and pieces of grit would be lightly raked away: then, given a few days of baking sun, you had a track fit for batting on and bowling on. With luck, the parks department would seed the barer parts of the field, and on a dry spring day a man on a lawnmower would wander the acreage lengthwise and trail a faint, fresh swathe of grass and clover. By this time of year, the club's annual general meeting, convened in the clubhouse, will have already taken place. The club officers – president, treasurer, club secretary, first and second vice presidents, fixtures secretary, captain, vice captain, friendly captains – have been elected by those present and those voting by proxy, and the election results have been noted in the minutes of the meeting, which may or may not record the more truculent points of order raised by members fuelled by midday shots of rum. In the second week of April, after all the winter's talking and forward planning and conjecture; after perhaps a Saturday–Sunday tour to Florida, whose lucky cricketers play year round; after all the phone calls and the club committee meetings and the preparatory buying and cleaning of whites and bats; after all of our solitary prefigurative frenzies; after the clocks have jumped forward by an hour; after all these things, the season will actually be upon us. Each of us is a year older. Throwing a ball is harder than we remember, as is the act of turning one's shoulder to bowl a ball. The ball itself feels very hard: skyers struck in catching practice are a little frightening. Bats that were light and wand-like when picked up fantastically during the off-season are now heavy and spade-like. Running between the wickets leaves us breathless. Trotting and bending down after a moving ball hurts body parts we'd thought renewed by months of rest. We have not succeeded, we discover, in imagining out of existence cricket's difficulty. Never mind. We are determined to make a clean try at things. We show in the field like flares.

I've heard that social scientists like to explain such a scene – a patch of America sprinkled with the foreign-born strangely at play – in terms of the immigrant's quest for sub-communities. How true this is: we're all far away from Tipperary, and clubbing together mitigates this unfair fact. But surely everyone can also testify to another, less reckonable kind of homesickness, one having to do with unsettlements that cannot be located in spaces of geography or history; and accordingly it's my belief that the communal, contractual phenomenon of New York cricket is underwritten, there where the print is finest, by the same agglomeration of unspeakable individual longings that underwrites cricket played anywhere – longings concerned with horizons and potentials sighted or hallucinated and in any event lost long ago, tantalisms that touch on the undoing of losses too private and reprehensible to be acknowledged to oneself, let alone to others. I cannot be the first to wonder if what we see, when we see men in white take to a cricket field, is men imagining an environment of justice.

'We better get going,' Carl said. He had materialised at my shoulder. 'The traffic going to be getting heavy.'

He was right; we got caught up in a jam on the BQE beneath Brooklyn Heights. It didn't matter. The clouds in motion over the harbour had left a pink door ajar and surface portions of Manhattan had prettily caught the light, and it appeared to my gaping eyes as if a girlish island moved towards bright sisterly elements.

I was still receptive, apparently, to certain gifts. And I began, in my second Chelsea spring, to take a vague sauntering interest in my neighbourhood, where the morning sun hung over the Masonic headquarters on Sixth Avenue with such brilliance that one's eyes were forced downward into a scrutiny of the sidewalk, itself grained brightly as beach sand and spotted with glossy discs of flattened chewing gum. The blind people were now ubiquitous. Muscular gay strollers were abroad in numbers, and the women of New York, saluting taxis in the middle of the street, reacquired their air of intelligent libidinousness. Vagrants were free to leave their shelters and, tugging shopping trolleys loaded with junk – including, in the case of one symbolically minded old boy, a battered door – to camp out on warmed concrete. I was particularly taken, now that I dwell on these things, by the apparition, once or twice a week, of a fellow in his seventies who fished in the street. He was an employee of the fishing tackle store located beneath the hotel, and from time to time he waded into a bilious torrent of taxis to test fly rods. Always he wore suspenders and khaki trousers and smoked a cigarillo. When he flicked the rod – 'This here is a four-piece Redington with a very fast action. It's a hell of a weapon,' he once explained to me – it became possible, in the mild hypnosis induced by the line's recurrent flight, to envision West 23rd Street as a trout river. The residents of the Hotel Chelsea also stirred. The angel, hitherto trapped indoors by the cold, went out and about in new wings and created a mildly christophanous sensation. March Madness lurched to its climax: the betting activities of the hotel staff assumed fresh vigour and complexity. Soon afterwards, in April and May, there was the peculiar seasonal matter of bodies surfacing in the waters of New York – a question of springtime currents and water temperature, according to the *Times*. The bodies of four drowned boys came out of Long Island Sound. It was reported, too, that the corpse of a Russian woman had been found in the East River under the pier of the Water's

Edge Restaurant on Long Island City. She'd vanished in March while walking her father's cocker spaniel. The cocker spaniel itself had also gone missing, so when a headless dog washed up near Throgs Neck Bridge, people reasoned that this corpse might belong to the Russian woman's dog; but the headless dog turned out to be not a spaniel but a Maltese, or perhaps a poodle. On television, dark Baghdad glittered with American bombs. The war started. The baseball season came into view.

Personally, things remained as they were. I failed my driving test. On the morning in question, Carl showed up in a car I'd never seen before, a 1990 Oldsmobile with a gearshift sprouting from the steering column – 'The Buick being fixed,' he said – and things went downhill from there. We drove in rain to Red Hook, a rotten waterfront district of trucks, potholes, faded road markings, reckless pedestrians. 'Good morning, ma'am,' I said to the examiner as she rolled into the passenger seat. She made no reply and, humming to herself in a way that struck me as psychotic, began tapping my details into a hand-held computer. On her lap, I saw, a portfolio was opened to a page of the Bible and a page of the traffic regulations booklet. 'Drive into traffic,' the woman said. Following her instructions, I went halfway round the block. I executed an uneventful U-turn. The examiner sighed and tittered and tapped on the computer screen with a plastic stylus. 'Turn left,' she said – and I understood she'd just directed me back to the starting point. I said, 'You don't want me to park?' We came to a final stop. The tapping ended and a scrolled ticket emerged from the machine. According to this document, in the course of driving around one block I had shown poor judgement approaching or at intersections; turned wide left; when changing lanes, failed to adequately observe or use caution; failed to yield to a pedestrian; failed to anticipate potential hazards; failed to exercise adequate vehicle control, viz., poor engine acceleration, abrupt braking and poor use of gears. I had, in short, failed over and over and over again.

Carl waited until we'd reached downtown Manhattan before speaking up. He rubbed the windshield. 'Well,' he said, 'I guess you have got to persist.' He cried out with laughter.

There was no movement in my marriage, either; but, flying on Google's satellite function, night after night I surreptitiously travelled to England. Starting with a hybrid map of the United States, I moved the navigation box across the North Atlantic and began my fall from the stratosphere: successively, into a brown and beige and greenish Europe bounded by Wuppertal, Groningen, Leeds, Caen (the Netherlands is gallant from this altitude, its streamer of northern isles giving the impression of a land steaming seaward); that part of England between Grantham and Yeovil; that part between Bedford and Brighton; and then Greater London, its north and south pieces, jigsawed by the Thames, never quite interlocking. From the central maze of mustard roads I followed the river south-west into Putney, zoomed in between the Lower and Upper Richmond Roads, and, with the image purely photographic, descended finally on Landford Road. It was always a clear and beautiful day – and wintry, if I correctly recall, with the trees pale brown and the shadows long. From my balloonist's vantage point, aloft at a few hundred metres, the scene was depthless. My son's dormer was visible, and the blue inflated pool and the red BMW; but there was no way to see more, or deeper. I was stuck.

Coincidentally, whenever I actually arrived in London I'd be treated as though I'd survived a rocket trip from Mars. 'I'm beat,' I'd admit over dinner, and Rachel's parents would bob their heads in assent and mention the arduousness of my journey and – my cue to head upstairs to Jake's room – jet lag. Everyone was grateful for jet lag. I slept with Jake, our mismatched backs pressed together, until I felt small hands heaving at my shoulder and a boy's serious voice informing me, 'Daddy, wake up, it's morning time.' At breakfast I'd express regret about my early bedtime. 'Jet lag,' somebody would wisely say.

Often I did not go to sleep. I lay with an arm in the space beneath Jake's neck, feeling him warm up and drop into fast, whispered breathing. I'd get out of bed and go to the window. The rear of the Boltons' house was separated by gardens from the nearest road, but there was a gap in the vegetation through which passing cars, themselves out of sight, animated fleeting trapezoids of light on the high brick wall of an adjoining property. I'd count off four or five such cartoons and then go back to bed and lie still, listening in like a spy on the conversation that carried up from downstairs along with the clatter of dishes and bursts of television music. I was hunting for clues about Rachel's life. Within six months of returning to England she'd taken a job as a lawyer for an NGO concerned with the welfare of asylum seekers. Consequently she worked civilised hours that permitted her to take lunchtime strolls around Clerkenwell, which she declared to be much changed. This material aside, I had very little information about her. All we talked of, really, was our son: of his white-blond hair, streaked now with browns and golds and growing long, of his friends at nursery school, of his riveting toddler's doings. And, now that the invasion of Iraq had actually taken place, the subject of politics was dropped and with it a connective friction. We rubbed along without touching. Of what one might suppose to be a crucial question of fact – the question of other men – I had no knowledge and did not dare make enquiries. The biggest, most salient questions – What was she thinking? What was she feeling? – were likewise beyond me. The very idea that one's feelings could give shape to one's life had become an odd one.

There came a moment, not long after the Danielle episode and in the first stimuli of spring, when I was taken by light-headed yearning for an interlude of togetherness, a time-out, as it were, during which my still-wife and I might lie together in a Four Seasons suite, say, and work idly through a complimentary fruit basket and fuck at leisure and, most importantly, have hours-long, disinterested, beans-spilling, let-the-chips-fall-where-they-may conversations in which we'd examine each other's unknown nooks and crannies in the best of humour and faith. It's possible that this fantasy originated in a revelation Rachel made one Saturday when she and Jake and I were shopping in Sainsbury's. She'd piled multiple cartons of soya milk into the cart, and this puzzled me.

'I'm lactose intolerant,' Rachel explained.

'Since when?' I said.

'Since forever,' she said. 'You remember how I always had stomach cramps? That was the lactose.'

I was bowled over. I had never considered the possibility of undiscovered factors. Then one night, lying in Jake's bed with ears pricked, I overheard a conversation about Rachel's weekly meetings with her psychotherapist, meetings which, although not secret, were not usually subject to discussion. Nevertheless Rachel's mother, who as a Tory councillor had taken a special interest in the drains and culverts of south-west London and therefore was to be credited with determination, had decided to broach the matter. 'What does he say about Hans?' I heard her ask. 'We're not talking about him,' Rachel replied.

'We're talking about stuff that happened before we ever met.' There was a silence. Rachel said, 'Mum, there's no need to look like that.' My wife's voice dimmed as she travelled from the kitchen to the sitting room. 'This isn't about you and Dad,' I faintly heard. 'There are other –'

Other? Other what? I was too flabbergasted to sleep. So far as I was aware, the course of Rachel's life, prior to its confluence with mine, was almost fully comprehended by the facts set forth in her aptly named curriculum vitae: a private girls' school, a wander-year in India, successful stints at university and law school, and, at Clifford Chance, an articled clerkship that led to the litigator's job she'd very much wanted. Her parents' marriage had throughout stayed intact; she'd benefited from the love of an older brother, Alex, who although living in China for more than a decade had always cheered her on from afar; she'd sailed in and out of a couple of relationships with decent if ultimately merely instructive young men; and of course she'd lived in undisastrous old England. Where, then, was the problem? Where was the intolerable lactose? In the fortnight that followed I became transfixed by this news of my wife's clandestine pre-existent injuries. I'd assumed that some unilateral failing of mine had been at the bottom of our downfall; now it seemed that some malfunction of Rachel's might also have been operative. I concluded, feverishly, that here was a development – an unknown hinterland to our marriage which, if jointly and equally explored, might lead to discoveries that would change everything; and the prospect filled me with a theorist's lunatic excitement and those daydreams of room service and afternoons gobbling blackberries and pineapple slices while we navigated the uncharted reaches of our psyches.

On my next visit to London, therefore, I lay awake until Rachel's parents had gone to bed and she had shut the door of her bedroom – two doors away from Jake's, on the top floor. It was early April; I could hear her sash window rattling as it was raised.

I crept out into the hallway and tapped on her door.

'Yes?'

She was in bed, a novel in her hands. For a second or two I looked around. It was still a young schoolgirl's room. The bookcase was loaded with skinny oversized hardbacks about showjumping. There was a turntable and a dusty stack of LPs. The walls were thronged by identical blue tulips. They had once made a great impression on the two of us, these tulips.

She was regarding me with a dogged expression. Her eyes and cheekbones and T-shirt were drained of colour.

Bedsprings sounded as I sat down on the bed. I said, 'How are things?'

'Me?' she said. 'I'm fine. Tired, but fine.'

'Tired?'

'Yes, tired,' Rachel said.

And it had happened again, one of those planned

conversations that go quickly awry, that leave you alone with rage, a clarifying rage in this instance, in which it all came back in a harsh light: our fading marriage, the two New York years in which she withheld from me all kisses on the mouth, withheld these quietly and steadily and without complaint, averting even her eyes whenever mine sought them out in emotion, all the while cultivating a dutiful domesticity and maternal ethic that armoured her in blamelessness, leaving me with no way to approach her, no way to find fault or feelings, waiting for me to lose heart, to put away my most human wants and expectations, to carry my burdens secretly, she not once in my mourning mentioning my mother, even that time when I wept in the kitchen and dropped a bottle of beer on the floor out of pure sorrow. She merely wiped the floor with paper towels and said nothing, brushing her free hand against my shoulder blade – my shoulder blade! – as she carried the soaked paper to the trash can, never holding me fast, refraining not out of lack of humanity but out of fear of being drawn into a request for further tenderness, a request that could only bring her face to face with some central revulsion, a revulsion of her husband or herself or both, a revulsion that had come from nowhere, or from her, or perhaps from something I'd done or failed to do, who knew, she didn't want to know, it was too great a disappointment, far better to get on with the chores, with the baby, with the work, far better to leave me to my own devices, as they say, to leave me to resign myself to certain motifs, to leave me to disappear guiltily into a hole of my own digging. When the time came to stop her from leaving, I did not know what to think or wish for, her husband who was now an abandoner, a hole-dweller, a leaver who had left her to fend for herself, as she said, who'd failed to provide her with the support and intimacy she needed, she complained, who was lacking some fundamental wherewithal, who no longer wanted her, who beneath his scrupulous marital motions was angry, whose sentiments had decayed into a mere sense of responsibility, a husband who, when she shouted, 'I don't need to be provided for! I'm a lawyer! I make two hundred and fifty thousand dollars a year! I need to be loved!' had silently picked up the baby and smelled the baby's sweet hair, and had taken the baby for a crawl in the hotel corridor, and afterwards washed the baby's filthy hands and soft filthy knees, and thought about what his wife had said, and saw the truth in her words and an opening, and decided to make another attempt at kindness, and at nine o'clock, with the baby finally drowsy in his cot, came with a full heart back to his wife to find her asleep, as usual, and beyond waking.

In short, I fought off the impulse to tell Rachel to go fuck herself. I produced some remark about Jake which we both might cling to, and for a minute or two we did this, and then I went back to my son.

It had become my habit, during my stays in London, to take many photographs of him. On the flights back, I examined these so-called Kodak moments as the jet crossed the Arctic emptiness at a terrific altitude and suffused me with a terrestrial's nervousness not much allayed by the flight information monitor and its figure of an aircraft millimetrically bleeding a red trail as it crept upon the void. Once home, I tossed the packets of photos into a cardboard box that held all my photographs, including black-and-white shots dating back to the mysterious blankness of the sixties and seventies and showing a boy with blond hair poised to blow out candles at birthday parties. I never went through the box properly, had no idea what to do with any of these so-called mementos. There were, I knew, people who organised such things into files and folders, catalogued hundreds of examples of their kids' schoolwork and paintings, created veritable museums. I envied them – envied them for their faith in that future day when one might pull down albums and scrapbooks and in the space of an afternoon repossess one's life. So when the cardboard box began to overflow, I ran it over to the office of Chuck Ramkissoon's mistress and commissioned her to put the pictures of Jake into some kind of order. The pictures of Rachel I couldn't face.

'Sure,' Eliza said. 'You have anything special in mind?'

'Just do what you do,' I said, getting to my feet.

'That's what I like,' Eliza said. 'Creative leeway. Lets me look at the pictures, look at the client . . .' She gave me a confidential glance and reached into a shelf. 'I'll show you what I'm talking about.'

I sat down once again and followed her fingers as they turned stiff brown pages. Between these were semi-transparent leaves, the slenderest of mists that lifted to reveal an earlier Eliza with bell-bottoms and a ball of curling hair and a hippie (her word) husband. This man, the first husband, transported sets for a ballet company, and the two of them travelled round the country in a tractor-trailer: she pointed out the tractor-trailer and, standing rigidly in snow, a dog. 'We got a dog in Billings, Montana, and we named him Billings,' Eliza explained. She left the doomed transporter of ballet sets (he was afterwards shot dead in Rhododendron, Oregon) and took up with another, even more itinerant, man – a preacher who was also, she learned too late, a drug addict. This brought us to the second volume, which began with scenes from a Las Vegas wedding. Eliza and the preacher, a hat-wearing, ferociously bearded ringer for Father Abraham of Father Abraham and the Smurfs, ended up in New Mexico, near the Sangre de Cristo Mountains, and became the caretakers of a ranch next to D. H. Lawrence's old property. 'It was intense,' Eliza said. 'I painted – I was going through this Georgia O'Keeffe thing, I guess – and he took drugs. It killed him in the end. Look at him here, just a week before he died.' The eyes of the second husband regarded me from a drawn face. 'I guess I'm bad luck,' Eliza said. She opened a third album. This was devoted to her romance with Chuck: here they were at a charity cycle ride; at the top of a mountain, with backpacks; at Niagara Falls. I counted three winters. 'That's my apartment,' Eliza said. 'It's like a gypsy home, only neat and beautifully arranged. Basically I'm very bohemian.'

'Yes, I can see that,' I said.

Eliza put away the albums. 'People want a story,' she said. 'They like a story.'

I was thinking of the miserable apprehension we have of even those existences that matter most to us. To witness a life, even in love – even with a camera – was to witness a monstrous crime without noticing the particulars required for justice.

'A story,' I said suddenly. 'Yes. That's what I need.'

I wasn't kidding.

Exiting, I took the ten steps to Chuck's suite. A young South Asian guy answered the door.

'No Chuck?' I said.

'He's out,' he said, standing guard by the door. This was, I guessed, Chuck's director of operations. The air behind him carried a film of cigarette smoke.

'Tell him Hans dropped by,' I said, surprised at my disappointment. 'Just to say hello.'

Yes, I wanted to see Chuck Ramkissoon. Who else was left?

It's the case that a person's premature death brings him into view. His tale has come to a sudden end and becomes intelligible – or, more accurately, invites special attention. Some years ago, word reached me that a former football teammate at HBS, a kid I'd played with in a succession of junior teams from ages eight to fifteen but whom I hadn't given a thought to since, had suffered a fatal heart attack. He was thirty-two years old and died while watching television in his home in Dordrecht. His name was Hubert and the main fact about him was that he'd been a very small, gifted *laatste man* – last man, or sweeper – who skipped around tacklers with speedy twinkling steps. You couldn't take the ball off him. He had a craggy smile and closely cut hair, and he liked to horse around in the showers with towels and shampoo. Hubert! Longing for information, I made a couple of calls to The Hague. I learned the following: he had gone on playing football at HBS, for a range of senior teams, until the age of twenty-seven, at which point he found a job in Dordrecht as an IT consultant. He stayed in touch with one or two fellows from the club but had not been seen around. He lived alone. At the time of his death he hadn't been watching television but, to be exact, a video.

For months I was haunted by this summary. I still think of Hubert sometimes, and still find it unbearable that he died by himself; although for all I know he remained until the very last the same happy fellow he'd been in the days I knew him. Knowledge, here, is a relative matter. I never once ran into Hubert outside the bounds of sports. This circumscription applied to almost all of my football-playing friends, even though I knew their fathers and rode to matches in their fathers' cars and received words of encouragement, even love, from their fathers, cries from the touchlines that I can still hear.

Goed zo, Hans! Goed zo, jongen!

My point, I suppose, is the self-evident one that Hubert came to preoccupy me in a way and to a degree he would not have if he'd lived. But with Hubert, all thoughts soon come to a stop – not only for lack of information but also for lack of weight. Not so with Chuck. He is, in memory, weighty. But what is the meaning of this weight? What am I supposed to do with it?

I can see him now, waiting for me on the wooden steps of his porch. He is wearing a cap from his collection of caps, and shorts from his collection of shiny athletic shorts, and a T-shirt from his collection of T-shirts. Chuck covered up his extreme industry with a wardrobe suggestive of extreme leisure.

'So,' he says, 'what's the story?'

'There is no story,' I say, sitting next to him.

174

He looks at me with a cocked head, as if I've thrown down a challenge. 'There's always a story,' he says. Whereupon he feels for the buzzing phone at his breast.

He told his own story constantly, and the autobiography might succinctly, and clankingly, have been titled *Chuck Ramkissoon: Yank*. His legend was transparently derived from the local one of rags and riches. He couldn't afford the luxury of knowingness. 'Blood, sweat and tears,' Churchillian Chuck told me more than once. 'A fat coolie from the bush. No job, no money, no rights.' Arriving in the United States with his wife, Anne – it was 1975, they were twenty-five and just married – he started working on the first day of his supposed honeymoon. 'I had a cousin – actually, the friend of a cousin – taking care of me. Painting, plastering, demolition, cement work, roofing, you name it, I did it. I'd come home to Brownsville with this white face and grit on my hands. I couldn't wash it out, you know. For years my hands were always dirty. Then I got my big break. It was my wife, actually, who got it for me.' I'd nod my head, encouraging him, relaxing already at the prospect of another of his lulling monologues. 'She was a babysitter for this high-end Manhattan couple. They needed work done to their summer place on the Island. I gained their confidence and I took the job. It was my first job as chief contractor. Then I did their new apartment on Beach Street. Soon everybody else in the building wanted me as well. They liked me. It's a people business, Hans. I ran a team of Bangladeshi cement guys. I had Irish painters – well, the main guy was Irish, a terrific guy, his men were Guatemalans – I had Russian plasterers, I had Italian roofers, I had Grenadan carpenters. All from Brooklyn. Everybody was happy. I made real money for the first time in my life. This was around the time I got my citizenship and could finally crawl out from under my rock. Well, let me tell you, even through the property crash I was busy. That's when I decided to buy and fix up buildings on my own account – in '92. I knew prices would come back. I knew there was money to be made. I foresaw the Brooklyn boom, Hans. I saw it as clearly as you see me now. I focused on Williamsburg, which was full of the kind of run-down commercial buildings I wanted, buildings with high-profit potential. But they were owned by Jews. I had no access. Nobody wants a black landlord in the neighbourhood. So I hooked up with Abelsky. I met him at the Russian baths, this big fat guy who never stopped moaning.' Chuck started laughing. 'You know what we call a guy like that in Trinidad? We call him a pawmewan. A poor-me, self-pitying guy. The guy was unbearable. A disaster area. Nobody at the baths wanted to talk to him. Nobody wanted to whack him with the twigs. "Come on, guys, give me a break. Dimitri, I'm begging you. Boris – come on, Boris. Please. Just a few whacks." No. They wouldn't go near him.' Chuck howled happily. 'I'm telling you, those

Russian guys preferred my company. And believe me, they weren't happy having me around. Anyhow, I look at this guy, this pariah, and I say to myself, Here's a guy who's so desperate he'd work with a coolie. So I befriend him. That's why I went to the baths in the first place, to meet Jews. Where else was I going to meet them? Remember – think fantastic.' We'd be driving, and he'd be upright in the passenger seat now, stiff with pride. 'So I set up a real-estate company with Abelsky and I cut him in for twenty-five points to be my frontman. Of course, I took care of everything. Abelsky's job was to stay in the background and act like a big shot too busy to handle the details. And listen to him today: he actually thinks he is a big shot! When all he's ever done is lend me his Jewish name! Which isn't even that Jewish!' Chuck, not amused, said, 'Our sushi business? Abelsky & Co. The real-estate company? Abelsky Real Estate Corporation. We made money, of course. We still own three buildings, in prime locations. We have six people at Avenue K and we're looking to hire two more.' Chuck waggled a finger. 'But this cricket thing, this is a different deal. This is the big time. I don't need Abelsky for this. I don't want him involved. What does Abelsky know about the cricket market? No, this is my project, this has got my name on it.'

It made me uneasy, this kind of talk, and I was capable of experiencing a Samaritan urge to save him. It was a fleeting urge. I had troubles of my own, and

Chuck's companionship functioned as an asylum. And if it happened one night, this taking of his shelter, it happened the night of the 2003 Annual Gala of the Association of New York Cricket Leagues, held at the Elegant Antun's, Springfield Boulevard, Queens.

I found myself, that Friday night in late May, travelling with a clueless but cooperative Kyrgyz limousine driver. On the Long Island Expressway I guided him past the red neon signs of Lefrak City and a certain Eden Hotel, past Utopia Parkway, and then, following instructions I'd been given, down the turn-off at exit 27. There we instantly became confused by a succession of signposts placed in accordance with a bizarre New York convention that struck me again and again, namely, that all directions to motorists should be so located and termed as to disorient everyone except the traveller who already knows his way. Propelled into a Nassau County nowhere, we made our way back to Queens and finally ran into Hillside Avenue, from where the route was more or less clear. I was dropped off in front of a free-standing house-like structure. Its edges, arranged in a confusion of gables and recessed facades, were outlined by strings of fairy lights, and its walls were coated with a pale substance that looked like icing Hansel's dipping finger might scoop. It was ten o'clock. I stepped past two long-coated bouncers and entered the Elegant Antun's.

A group of teenagers came laughing out of double doors straight ahead and for an instant I peeped at a whirling bride. My own function was on the floor above. Ahead of me on the staircase walked an immense fellow in cream shoes, a cream suit and a cream bowler hat. He was accompanied by a pair of six-foot women in vivid long sparkling dresses and tall heels. The women's bared shoulders were broad and powerful and the laces crossing their backs were pulled tight by very black muscles that shifted with each climbing step. 'These Jamaican women,' someone would later confide to me, 'they look like they just run over from Belmont.'

It was, as they say, a big night. A table had been set aside for the umpiring fraternity, which had arrived in white dinner jackets and sat together like a conclave of ship's stewards. A Brooklyn assemblywoman was present, as were representatives of the parks department and, we were assured, the Mayor's Office – this last-mentioned an individual with a developing moustache who seemed barely out of his teens and, I heard, was later seen throwing up in the men's room. Air Jamaica was in attendance, and Red Stripe, and other supportive corporations. But mostly the diners were cricket men and their women – players and officers of the American Cricket League, the Bangladeshi Cricket League, the Brooklyn Cricket League, the Commonwealth Cricket League, the Eastern America Cricket Association, and the Nassau New York Cricket League; of the New York Cricket League, the STAR Cricket League, the New Jersey Cricket League, the Garden State

Cricket League and the Washington Cricket League; of the Connecticut Cricket League and the Massachusetts State Cricket League; of my very own New York Metropolitan and District Cricket Association; and, by particular invitation, Mr Chuck Ramkissoon, whose guest I was.

I made my entry just in time to hear a voice announce, 'Please stand for the national hymn,' and every person rose for a recording of 'The Star-Spangled Banner'. Immediately afterwards the master of ceremonies solemnly proposed a prayer for 'our troops abroad, who are tonight putting their lives at risk for our freedom', and people were silent for a few seconds before sitting down for dinner.

I remained standing, however, unable to find my table. Then, out of a corner, I saw Chuck's waving arm.

I joined my party just as a waitress with a badge stating ASK ME ABOUT NEW YEAR'S EVE took orders for chicken or baked salmon and, depending on the answer, placed a red or blue gambling chip next to the orderer's plate. Chuck, in black tie, introduced me – 'Hans van den Broek, of M—— Bank' – to a smiling Indian businessman named Prashanth Ramachandran, and to Dr Flavian Seem, a retired Sri Lankan pathologist who was, Chuck informed me as we ordered cocktails at the open bar, the manager of the angel fund backing his venture. There were two Guyanese brothers (importers of burnt sugar, almond essence, sorrel syrup and, they were very pleased to tell me, baby Edam cheese) and their wives, but the most arresting presence at our table was an elegant young woman in a silver frock who, if I am not mistaken, was named Avalon. She had come with Chuck and, despite being five inches taller than him and at least twenty years younger, she communicated an unaccountable pleasure in his and his guests' company. The penny only dropped when Chuck explained that Avalon was, as he put it, 'the top girl at Mahogany Classic Escorts. You ever use them?'

'I might start,' I said.

'You should,' Chuck said. 'These are girls with refinement, from the islands. College graduates, nurses. Not your American rubbish.'

By this point it was midnight and we were sitting half drunk at our table watching Avalon dancing with an ecstatically immobile Dr Seem. The dance floor was crowded. Everybody had been liberated from an hour of presentations during which colossal trophies mounted with golden batting and bowling cricketers and forming a divine throng on the high table were gradually dispersed to the centurions and hat-trickers and champions and other winners seated at the lower tables, so that wherever one looked, as one digested chicken or salmon, golden little chaps brazenly swiped at invisible balls or precariously tiptoed on one foot as they toppled into the act of bowling. The more I drank, the more entranced I became by the parallel world of these figurines, whose shimmering devotion to their cricketing business grew more poignant by the minute. I must have made a forlorn impression, because a stranger who claimed to recognise me kindly sat down next to me and, having ascertained that I'd lived in London, reminisced at length about his years in Tooting.

Avalon was now dancing with Chuck. Dr Seem, sitting next to me, said, 'Are you a scientist?'

He appeared satisfied when I told him I wasn't. 'I have devoted my life to scientific study,' he told me. He was slender and fine-fingered like so many Sri Lankans, and he delicately spread open a hand on the tablecloth. 'I'm trained to see things as they are. To understand the biological realities. When I look at this' – he showed me the dancers – 'I see the biological reality.'

'Which is what?' I asked, reflecting that I was possibly the only person contained by the apparent world who was unable to see through it.

'Deception,' Seem said. 'Deception dictated by nature. Our dancing lady friend, for example,' Seem said, referring to Avalon. 'False!' he madly cried. 'False!'

He stood up and went to get himself another drink. I gazed at the dancers and recalled Rachel's complaint that I never danced. That was long ago. We had returned from some party. Jake, maybe six months old, was sleeping in his cot next to our bed.

'I'm not the dancing kind,' I said. 'You've always known that.'

'You danced at our wedding,' she answered immediately. 'You were fine. You did that little shuffle thing with your feet.'

She looked stricken; and I suppose, since I am now fully aware, thanks to our figuratively speaking marriage counsellor, that the steamboat of marriage must be fed incessantly with the coals of communication, that I should have explained to my wife that I came from Holland, where I rarely saw dancing, and indeed that I'd been a little amazed to see how young Englishmen threw themselves around to music, dancing even with other men, and that this abandon was alien to me and that, perhaps, she might for this reason wish to bear with me. But I said nothing, thinking the matter inconsequential. It would certainly have astonished me to learn that years later I would look back on this episode and ask myself, as I did at the Elegant Antun's, if it represented a so-called fork in the road – which in turn led me to drunkenly wonder if the course of a relationship of love was truly explicable in terms of right turns and wrong turns, and if so whether it was possible to backtrack to that split where it all went wrong, or if in fact it was the case that we are all doomed to walk in a forest in which all paths lead one equally astray, there being no end to the forest, an enquiry whose very uselessness led to another spasm of wayward contemplation that ended only when I noticed Chuck leading a hobbled Dr Seem back into the chair next to mine.

'Hamstring,' Dr Seem said. He flexed his leg then sadly put it down. 'For ten years this is giving me a problem. Ten years.'

'A bad situation,' Chuck said.

Seem gave a hand a bitter twirl. 'My dancing days are finished now.'

'Nonsense,' Chuck said. 'You sit down, take a little rest, maybe a little drink, and watch, in five minutes you'll be up on your feet.' Chuck gave me a severe look. 'Hans – your turn. Look at Avalon. She's tired of old men. Go.'

I responded automatically – biologically, Dr Seem might say. I danced with Avalon.

That is, I clumsily moved around in her vicinity, glimpsing in the grins of those nearby the encouragement usually reserved for children. I was the only white person present, and reinforcing a stereotype. Avalon herself politely smiled and laughed and gave no sign of noticing my lumbersomeness, and then, out of pity or professionalism, she turned her back to me and lightly gyrated her ass against my thighs in rhythm with the rapid jingling soca that now replaced the American pop, the DJ shouting, 'All you wine! Wine that boom-boom! Wine!' and all the middle-aged women started to back their handsome asses into their middle-aged men with an air of great seriousness, as if an especially grave phase of the evening had been entered. Maybe it had. A rapt Chuck quickly walked onto the dance floor, his black face blackened still further by pursed black lips and half-sealed black eyelids. He approached without hesitation a woman in her fifties and instantly they began to shimmy in tandem next to me and Avalon. The soca tinkled and blared. Solidarity with my small round Trinidadian counterpart surged through me. Emboldened, I gave in to the situation and its happiness – gave in to the song, to the rums and the Coca-Colas, to Avalon's smooth skilful butt, to the hilarity of remarks made by Dr Flavian Seem and Prashanth Ramachandran, to the suggestion that we go on, after the gala, to some further place; and to the crush of hips and legs in Chuck's stretch limo; and to the idea that we swing by, since we're all dressed up, the all fours club down on Utica on the far side of Great Eastern Parkway, where the speechless all fours players have been playing all day and signal to partners by picking their ears and rubbing their noses, their women hanging around drinking and eating and very ready to go home; and to persuading some characters from the all fours club to come out and fête with us at the limo driver's place down on Remsen and Avenue A; and to stopping on the way there at Ali's Roti Shop for roti and doubles, and stopping at Thrifty Beverages to load up with beer and four bottles of rum, and, because there is no limit to our hunger, stopping also at Kshaunté Restaurant and Bakery to order a delivery of tripe and beans, patties and curry goat; and to the invitation, once inside the home of the limo driver, who is named Proverbs, to join in a card game called wapi; and to losing nearly two hundred dollars playing wapi; and to the truth of the remarks 'Boy, it have a good wapi there tonight' and 'Mankind does be serious about the wapi game, boy'; and to an ephemeral mouth belonging to a girl with a diploma in life-saving; and to six laughing pairs of hands that picked up my wrecked body and dropped it on a couch; and to water splashed on my face at six in the morning; and finally to the proposition, made by Chuck as we walked behind a gang of boisterous Hasidic boys in the first warmth of the weekend, that we sweat it all off at a *banya* just a few blocks from his house.

'Half an hour in the sauna,' Chuck argued, 'and you'll be like a new man.'

A yellow cab came freakishly into view.

The Russian baths were in a blockish cement building next door to a gas station on Coney Island Avenue. To get to the locker room you walked through a large open area with two pools – one a jacuzzi trembling with warm currents, the other a cold pool into which an attendant was dumping ice. Structural columns were decorated with oval plaster mouldings of Hellenic figures, and on the largest wall was a mural in which Greek maidens of antiquity struck beautiful poses by an immense waterfall that poured into a green valley. None of this, so far as I could see, bore any relation to the customers of the spa, a handful of pale-skinned men who sat in apparent exhaustion on plastic chairs.

We emerged from the locker room with rented towels tied around our waists. 'Where shall we go?' Chuck said. There were Russian, Turkish and American options. Chuck showed me the Turkish bath first. Save for an ill-looking man who sat by a bucket of water, it was empty. Next was the Russian sauna, where one man was slapping another with a bouquet of oak leaves. 'It's still early,' Chuck said.

The American steam room was the place to be. At least six others were present. They wore cone-like hats and poured water into the ovens in defiance of a sign specifically forbidding this. I sat down next to a fellow in soaked underpants.

The heat was extreme. I sweated heavily and without pleasure. I was about to suggest to Chuck that we leave when an unusual-looking man came in. He was fat, and yet great folds of excess skin wilted from his stomach and back and limbs. He looked unstuffed, an abandoned work of taxidermy.

Chuck said, 'Mikhail! Come, sit down.'

Mike Abelsky joined us with a great sigh. He said to me, in a strong accent that was part Brooklyn and part Moldova, 'You're the Dutch guy. I heard about you. You,' he said, pointing at Chuck, 'I wanna talk to.'

'We're taking a bath,' Chuck said. 'Relax.'

'Relax? I got my wife's relatives living at my house and you want me to relax?' Abelsky placed a cone on his head. 'I don't wanna sleep in other people's houses and I don't want other people to sleep in my house. I wanna walk around in my house in my underpants. Now I gotta wear pyjamas: I don't wanna wear pyjamas. I don't wanna put on the T-shirt. When I go to the bathroom, I wanna sit with my newspaper. What do I get? Somebody banging on the door, "I wanna shower." What the fuck do they wanna take a shower for? Let them take a shower in their house!' Abelsky looked at me without interest. 'I only understand one relative in the world,' he stated. 'It's the parents. The rest, they're only interested in using you.'

'You're looking well,' Chuck said.

'I look like shit,' Abelsky said. 'But I gotta do the reduction operation if I want to live. Now I can't eat shit. Look at this,' he said. He pinched his loose breast tissue with disgust. 'I'm like an old woman.' He looked at me again. 'Once I was a wrestler.'

'Oh?'

'Yeah, in the Russian Army. Also at home, with my brothers. I beat the shit out of them.' All this was said humourlessly. 'The only guy I didn't beat up was my father, out of respect. For money I let him beat *me* up.'

My hangover was getting to me. I didn't understand what he was talking about.

'I used to take beatings for my brothers,' Abelsky

explained. He rubbed his neck and examined the sweat on his hand. 'If my big brother scratched the car, he paid me to take the beating. My father was aware about what was going on, but still he would beat me. He used to beat the shit out of me. I laughed in his face. He couldn't get to me. He could beat me and beat me, but still I would laugh. What did I care? I was rich.' He added bitterly, 'That was Moldova. A nickel makes you a big shot. You wanna be rich in this country, you gotta win the Mega.'

'Tell him what the Mega is,' Chuck said. I understood what he was up to: he wanted me to see the kind of man he had to deal with. It's possible, too, that he wanted to show me off to Abelsky – indeed that the whole encounter had been orchestrated. Chuck had this idea I was a catch.

'You don't know what is the Mega? Are you kidding me? It starts with ten million. The jackpot – my God, the jackpot Mega is two hundred and ten million. I play it, sure I do, why not? My grandfather used to say, A dollar and a dream, that's all you need. Right off the bat I won two thousand bucks. Since then, my number never came up again. I play my car number, and I play my month and day of being birthed. They make it harder and harder. It used to be played only once a day. Now they play twice a day. Most of the time the winners come from Idaho, Kentucky. The potato cities win. Sure, sometimes we win right here in New York. One guy from Honduras won a hundred and five million with a ticket he bought on 5th

Street in Brighton Beach. I only want five million, that's all. My wife said, What would you do? I said, I tell you what I would do. First off, I buy each of my daughters a house. Then I give them five hundred thousand each, cash. They can use it for the college money for their kids. Then I'd buy a condo in Miami. I figure that would leave me with a million to live on. On top of what I got already. That's reasonable. I wouldn't go crazy.'

This went on for ten boiling minutes. When Chuck excused himself for a moment, one of the other men made a remark to Abelsky in Russian.

Abelsky looked the man in the eye and said something the gist of which even I understood. There was an exodus, and suddenly Abelsky and I were alone in the American steam room.

'What happened?' I said.

Abelsky was muttering into the steam. In a low, white-man-to-white-man voice, he said, 'They got a problem here with the Pakistan people. They come in, spoil things for everybody. It's a problem, sure. This is a fucking Russian baths. They should make their own baths. But when I went to the hospital' – he was leaning towards me now, pointing a thumb at the door – 'it's this Paki from the islands who visits me every day. *This* guy handles the health insurance company, tells my wife it's going to be OK. When I get to be fifty, *he* gives me a wine crate out of Moldova. It tastes like shit, OK, but it tastes like my homeland. These guys'

– he gestured again at the door, this time dismissively – 'I don't see anywhere. These guys? One hundred per cent assholes. I say fuck them. Fuck them where they breathe.'

Chuck returned and the three of us stewed and steamed a while longer.

'That's it,' Chuck said. 'Let's get going.'

After a shower, it was back out to Coney Island Avenue. I was ready to go home.

Chuck said, 'Here's what we're going to do. You're going to practise-drive in my car, and then you're going to use it in the test.'

In Ramkissoonian fashion, the assertion had come out of the blue, or almost so: a cloudlet of recollection brought back a conversation, the previous evening, about my misadventure in Red Hook.

I said, 'Chuck, that's crazy. Anyway, I can't practise unless I'm with a qualified driver.'

'I'm a qualified driver,' Chuck said. 'I'll go with you. Look,' he said, 'we'll make some arrangement. Hans, no more discussion. This is going to happen. Right now.'

'Now?' I suppose this was the moment I understood his modus operandi: wrong-foot the world. Run rings around it.

'No time like the present,' Chuck advised. 'Unless you have something better to do.'

While Chuck walked home to fetch his car, I went to a diner and ordered a coffee. I hadn't yet finished it when he came into the diner, rattled keys, tossed me a catch. 'Let's go,' he said.

The Cadillac was illegally parked on the far side of the road. I slid onto the cracked leather of the driver's seat, adjusted the seat and the mirror, and started the engine.

'Where to?' I said.

'Bald Eagle Field,' Chuck said, rubbing his hands. 'We've got work to do.'

We travelled the length of Coney Island Avenue, that low-slung, scruffily commercial thoroughfare that stands in almost surreal contrast to the tranquil residential blocks it traverses, a shoddily bustling strip of vehicles double-parked in front of gas stations, synagogues, mosques, beauty salons, bank branches, restaurants, funeral homes, auto body shops, supermarkets, assorted small businesses proclaiming provenances from Pakistan, Tajikistan, Ethiopia, Turkey, Saudi Arabia, Russia, Armenia, Ghana, the Jewry, Christendom, Islam: it was on Coney Island Avenue, on a subsequent occasion, that Chuck and I came upon a bunch of South African Jews, in full sectarian regalia, watching televised cricket with a couple of Rastafarians in the front office of a Pakistani-run lumber yard. This miscellany was initially undetectable by me. It was Chuck, over the course of subsequent instructional drives, who pointed everything out to me and made me see something of the real Brooklyn, as he called it.

After Coney Island Avenue there was Belt Parkway, and then there was Flatbush Avenue, and then there was Floyd Bennett Field – in early summer, a sub-Saharan flat of shrubs, scattered trees, and hot, weedy concrete runways. Save for a kite-flyer and his son, Chuck and I were the only ones there. We drove over tarmac past the last hangar. We stopped at signs stating PRIVATE PROPERTY and NO ENTRY and KEEP OFF.

I couldn't believe it. In front of me was a bright green field.

'Jesus,' I said, 'you did it.'

A man was seated on a roller that inched across the centre of the field. 'Come,' Chuck said. 'Let's talk to Tony.'

We removed our shoes and socks. We were still wearing our party gear from the night before.

The grass was soft beneath our feet. 'He says he used to be a groundsman at Sabina Park,' Chuck said, nodding towards Tony. 'But of course there's a world of difference between Jamaica and what you have here.'

We reached the square. Chuck fell to his knees and spread his hands on the shortened grass like a hallower.

Tony, a small, scrawny fellow in his late fifties, dismounted from the roller and slowly approached us. He wore a filthy T-shirt and jeans and, I'd find out, like Pigpen went round in a haze of gasoline, rum and machinery. He slept and ate out here, in the converted shipping container that sat at the far side of the ground and housed Chuck's equipment. He kept a gun in that container to ensure what Chuck called 'the safety of all concerned'.

'Lord, what a way it hot,' Tony said to Chuck. He removed his cap and wiped his sweating face and gave me a blank look. 'Who this?'

I was introduced. Tony said something to Chuck that I simply could not understand. From Chuck's reply I gathered they were talking about the mower, which sat fifty feet away. 'Nothing no happen to it, boss, it good,' Tony said. He made another indecipherable remark and then grew animated as he elaborated about some 'idiot thing' that had happened in connection with kids who'd been 'frigging around' on the field.

The three of us looked at the square. 'We roll it and roll it,' Chuck said. 'Crosswise, like a star. That way it's perfectly level.' Chuck said, 'Looking good, right, Tony?'

Tony spat agreeably and went back to the roller and fired it up.

'Now comes the fun part,' Chuck said.

We mowed the outfield. We took turns driving a light-weight fairway mower with an eighty-inch cut and fast eleven-blade reels. Chuck liked to stripe the grass with dark green and pale green rings. You started with a perimeter run and then, looping back, made circle after circle, each one smaller than the last, each one with a common centre. They would be soon gone, but no matter. What was important was the rhythm of cutting, and the smell of the cutting, and the satisfaction of time passed fruitfully on the field with a gargling diesel engine, and the glory and suspensefulness of the enterprise. There was to be no cricket played on this field that summer or even the next. And in any case you never really know how a grass pitch will turn out, not even a minute before start of play. You do not know whether a twenty-two-yard strip of turf, often cut so closely as to appear grass-less, will deliver a quick or slow or high or low bounce, whether a spinning ball will deviate upon bouncing and if so to what degree and with what speed. You do not know if it will be a featherbed, or a dog, or a slow-and low-bouncing pitch dispiriting equally to batsman and bowler. Even after you've begun to play on it, you do not know what it holds in store. The nature of earth, like the nature of air, is subject to change: wickets have their own weather and are given to deterioration and change as a match progresses. Cracks open in the ground, ground moisture rises and falls, the surface is disturbed or compacted. Shots that can be played one day cannot safely be played on another. In baseball, essentially an aerial game, conditions are very similar from game to game, from ballpark to ballpark: other things being equal (for example, altitude), to throw a slider at Stadium A differs little from throwing a slider at Stadium B. In earthly cricket, however, conditions may be dissimilar from day to day and from ground to ground. Sydney

Cricket Ground favours spin, Headingley, in Leeds, seam bowling. This differentness is not only a question of differing grass batting surfaces. There is the additional question of the varying atmospheric conditions – humidity and cloud cover, in particular – that obtain from time to time and from place to place and can dramatically affect what happens to a cricket ball as it travels from bowler to batsman. Likewise, soft and hard outfields will respectively preserve and roughen a ball. For all of its apparent artificiality, cricket is a sport in nature.

Which may be why it calls almost for a naturalist's attentiveness: the ability to locate, in a mostly static herd of white-clothed men, the significant action. It's a question of looking. One contradiction of the sport is that its doings simultaneously concern a vast round acreage and a batter's tiny field of action. Baseball also demands a dilation and contraction of focus, but the task is made simpler by the diamond, which acts as a perceptual funnel, and the single batter, whose position enables us to readily imagine the tiny box of the strike zone. The uninitiated onlooker at a cricket game is by contrast puzzled by the alternation of two batsmen and two bowlers and two sets of stumps – a dual duel – and the strange activity that occurs after every six balls, when the fielders stroll, for chaotic seconds, into positions that imperfectly mirror the positions just abandoned. It can take a while before the puzzle is sufficiently solved, particularly for the American viewer. I can't count the number of times I, in New York, fruitlessly tried to explain to a baffled passer-by the basics of the game taking place in front of him, a failure of explanation and comprehension that soon irritated me and led me to give up.

After an hour or so, Tony reclaimed the mower. Chuck got a couple of Cokes from the cooler in the equipment container and we sat down on the grass. It was on this first afternoon at Bald Eagle Field, with Tony transformed by distance into a species of half-man, half-mower, and my skin reddening in the heat and wind, that Chuck told me that he was from the village of Las Lomas #2, which is in the countryside of Trinidad not far from the international airport, and – here was the point of his recollection – grew up in a shack next to the village's recreation ground. That ground was a scruffy, dusty, typical affair. On two sides were domestic gardens, with chickens and roosters and chained dogs and latrines, and bordering the remainder were cashew fields and cassava gardens. On all sides there were trees: coconut trees, a devil's ear tree, a tamarind tree.

Chuck interposed, 'They said the branch of the tamarind is the cure for human stupidity. Why? Because your schoolteacher whacked you with it.'

I took a swig of Coke. 'So that's where I went wrong,' I said.

When Chuck was still a kid, Las Lomas Cricket Club

decided to plough up the old recreation ground and build a real cricket field. He recalled that it took four years of ploughing and digging and rolling and hauling and seeding to get the field truly flat and grassed; and after that came the struggle to drain and maintain it, with limited success: the wicket, made of black earth, was very slow, and balls pitching on it were given to popping up. Trinidad is a jungle island, he reminded me. The rains are heavy and things grow almost unstoppably. Grazing animals – donkeys, cattle – have to be kept off the grass. It took work and money to fight these forces, and some of the villagers resented it. 'That's Trinidad for you,' Chuck declared darkly. 'It's just full of people against this, against that. Negativity is a national disease. I'll tell you something true: they never call a glass half full. Really! They *always* call it half empty.'

Chuck's father, I learned, was dead against the cricket club – so opposed to it that he wouldn't let his two young sons set foot on the field; and so Chuck never truly played the game. Chuck remembered himself and his brother pressed against the fence at the back of his house, watching the groundsman scything the outfield on Saturday mornings, and the butterflies and ground birds going about in the cuttings, and bright creases being painted onto the black wicket, and the stumps going into the soil of the wicket, and the players taking the field, and the radiance of the players on the field, and his father dragging the two boys away from the fence and putting cutlasses in their hands and sending them off to work in the cane field – the same cane field, Chuck told me, in the shed of which he listened to the BBC for the first time: the ball-by-ball commentary on the West Indies' tour of India. When the West Indians went to Australia under the great Frank Worrell, in 1960–61, Chuck took to sneaking out of the house in the middle of the night to join his next-door neighbour in listening to the Test match broadcasts. The eleven-year-old boy and the ancient man sat next to each other in the near-darkness, drinking coffee as the voices of the commentators, travelling in waves over the Pacific Ocean, strengthened and weakened out of a red Philips radio. You got your sense of the wider world in this way. You heard about Sydney and Calcutta and Birmingham. It was from cricket commentators like John Arlott, Chuck Ramkissoon told me, that he learned to mimic and finally perfect 'grammatical English', learned words like 'injudicious' and 'gorgeous' and 'circumspect': and he'd always whisper a running commentary to himself, he said, whenever he was able to escape from his father and watch a cricket game.

The discussion (or rather, Chuck's disquisition) ended with the subject of grass: the pure ryegrass that grew in the outfield, and the special blend – seven parts chewings fescue to three parts bentgrass – that grew on the square. He told me about thatch and aeration and watering. He told me about the pH of the loam, about how you could feel the ground binding under the rollers, about rolling the outfield in the dryness of spring, and about the layer of gritty earth underneath the square's surface layer. He told me about the soil samples he'd sent to a pair of turf experts at SUNY and the advice they'd given him. He drew my attention to the dangers of soil compaction and earthworms and dollar spot, to the necessity of brushing the dew from the square to prevent the rise of fungi, to the very faint lipstick stain a cricket ball leaves on a track that has been perfectly prepared. Considered, too, was the depth and density of grass roots and the crucial disproportionality of a blade of millimetres-high wicket grass travelling six inches underground, and of course we talked of the constant battle to defeat moss and bluegrass and clover and the other weeds. Grassy ground is a devil to control and left alone will grow motley and wild.

Once a weekend, then, Chuck became my driving mentor, as he put it – thereby casting me as poor Telemachus – and in return I became his assistant groundskeeper, because our motorised promenades invariably ended with a stint of cutting or rolling or watering his cricket field. He and I came to pass many hours together in that car, far more than were necessary to warm me up for a driving test. What respite it was, after the working week, to catch the Q train at Union Square and to alight miles from Manhattan at Cortelyou Road station, with its pavilion suspended over always-gleaming tracks, and to stroll along Cortelyou Road into the pooled green shadows of Rugby Road. From the corner, it was thirty steps to the Ramkissoon place. The Cadillac would be waiting in the drive, and Chuck himself as often as not would be parked on the porch, making calls. Then off we went on our little odyssey. As I chauffeured him around the neighbourhood, crouching conscientiously to a halt at every junction, I became familiar with the topical sights: the chiming, ceaselessly peregrinating ice-cream truck, driven by a Turk; the Muslim funeral home on Albemarle Road out of which watchful African American men spilled in sunglasses and black suits; the Hispanic gardeners working on the malls; the firehouse on Cortelyou that slowly gorged on reversing fire trucks; the devout Jewish boulevardiers on Ocean Parkway; the sticks of light that collected in the trees as though part of the general increase. Lush Flatbush . . .

The first time I travelled there on my own, I became lost. Panicking, I'd gotten off the train a couple of stops too soon. Instead of the suburban sights I was expecting, I was faced with a roaring street and scenes from the African wild: the wall surrounding the subway station hosted a tattered painting of Kilimanjaro, snow-capped and circled by clouds. In the foreground were enormous leaves and bushes and fronds, and in the middle distance

– the perspectives had been mishandled, so that distance clumsily equated to size – one made out a rhinoceros accompanied by her calf. A wild ass ran across the plain. A lion, its face ravaged by holes in the plaster, stood on top of a pile of boulders. On the right-hand side of the station gates was a still larger mural in which a flowery and green rainforest was prominent. I saw a snarling leopard; a vulture; a monkey dangling from a tree by its tail; some tiny, presumably far-off, scampering giraffes; a herd of wildebeest under pale skies; a study of a humming-bird inserting its beak into a flower. A tusked elephant was headed for Prospect Park. A flock of flamingoes flew south to Flatbush.

'You're up by the zoo,' Chuck told me when I rang him. 'Walk down Flatbush to the big church. I'll meet you there.'

I had never been to this section of Flatbush Avenue. Every second premises, it seemed, was devoted to the beau-tification, one might even say veneration, of those bodily parts that continue to thrive after death: there were hair palaces, nail palaces, barbershops, African hair-braiding specialists, wig and hairpiece suppliers, beauty parlours, unisex hairdressers. West Indian enterprise dominated. The food outlets – delicatessens, pie shops, bakeries, the very occasional restaurant – were almost exclusively Caribbean, and the music coming out of one hole-in-the-wall store was dance reggae. Presently the towers of Erasmus Hall High School came fabulously into view, promising Trebizond or Tashkent; and then I saw the leaning wooden white spire of the old Reformed Protestant Dutch church. Chuck was waiting for me by the church entrance, a phone pressed to his ear. When he was done talking, he took my arm and said, 'Let me show you something, my friend.'

He led me into the graveyard at the rear of the church. Blurred ancient headstones, crumbling and toppling, filled the muddy yard. These, he told me, were the graves of Brooklyn's original settlers and their descendants. 'This entire region,' Chuck said, 'everything for miles and miles around, all of it was Dutch farmland. Until just two hundred years ago. Your people.' The word 'Yankee' itself, I was informed, came from that simplest of Dutch names – Jan.

He thought I'd be thrilled. But it struck me as a baffling little drama, this neglected smattering of pale Dutch farming folk who had, I learned from my friend, cleared dense hickory and oak forests, and repelled the Canarsie and Rockaway Indians, and developed the pasturelands of Vlackebos and Midwout and Amersfoort, and worshipped at this old village church, built in 1796 with predecessors going back to 1654. We walked among the headstones. A few names had not yet been completely effaced: Jansen, van Dam, de Jong . . . I practically heard clogs ringing on the flagstones. But then what? What was one supposed to do with such information? I had no idea what to feel or what to think, no idea, in short, of what I might do to discharge the obligation of remembrance that fixed itself to one in this anomalous place, which offered so little shade from the incomprehensible rays of the past. Also, it had quite recently struck me with force that I did not want to join the New York dead. I associated this multitude with the vast burying grounds that may be glimpsed from the expressways of Queens, in particular that shabbily crowded graveyard with the monuments and tombs rising, as thousands of motorists are daily made to contemplate, in a necropolitan replica of the Manhattan skyline in the background. A quality of abnormal neglect and dismalness attached to this proliferation of urban graves, and each time I hastened by, invariably on my way into the city from JFK, I was reminded of the tradition of oblivion in force in this city – in which, howling ambulances aside, I went for years without ever seeing a sign of funerary activity. (The moment came, as everybody knows, when that changed.)

Evidently Chuck was having related thoughts. Walking down Church Avenue he said to me, 'Seriously, Hans, have you made plans for your funeral?'

From anybody else, the enquiry would have struck me as bizarre.

'No,' I said.

'I have made plans,' Chuck affirmed.

We turned off Church, and in an instant that raucous Caribbean boulevard, with its 99-Cent stores and discount clothing outlets and solo sellers of cocoa butter and its grocery stores displaying yams and green bananas and plantains and cassava and sweet potatoes, had given way to a neighbourhood unlike any other I'd seen in New York. Huge old houses – Victorians, I learned to call them – rose on both sides of a grassy mall, each building of a unique character. There was a plantation house with huge neoclassical columns. There was a Germanic place with dark green window frames inhabited, to all appearances, by an evil doctor from a Hitchcock movie. There was a sprawling yellow manor with countless yellow-brick chimneys and, startlingly, there was a Japanese-style mansion with upturned eaves and a cherry tree in photogenic blossom. But most striking of all was the quiet. New York City was here as still as The Hague.

Chuck's place was on a slightly less grand block. 'This is it,' he said, and for a moment I thought we were entering a vinyl-coated two-family house with a bricked-up porch and a front window conspicuously covered by an Old Glory that almost thoroughly obstructed any view of the outside world. But Chuck's house was one lot farther along and more substantial. It had a wooden wrap-around porch, six bedrooms, nicely painted clapboard and a little tower.

Chuck led me directly to the garden and sat me down

in a wicker armchair while he went indoors. Manhattan seemed far away. Lilacs bloomed, a cardinal flashed through the trees, and a serpentine hose lying in Chuck's flower beds dribbled water out of the hundreds of holes in its coils. The day itself was perforated by the rattle of a woodpecker.

I jumped out of my chair. Squatting next to my foot was the most enormous and repulsive frog I had ever seen.

Chuck, returning at that moment from the house, shouted out happily. He bent down and picked up the monstrous fat torso and the long, uncannily flippered legs; it seemed, in fact, as if he grasped a tiny, rotund frogman. 'This is an American bullfrog,' Chuck said. 'It'll eat just about anything. Snakes, birds, fish . . .' I followed him to the plastic fence that marked the border with the property containing the vinyl house. 'There's a pond back there. This guy must have escaped.' Lodged in the fence, I saw, were the corpses of other neighbourhood frogs that had died trying to migrate into the garden with the water. Chuck dropped the bullfrog where he belonged.

I was thinking about telling Chuck the only frog story I knew – about the annual shutdown of the Duinlaan, which ran in sight of my house, to enable the safe crossing of the little frogs of The Hague – when Anne Ramkissoon appeared at the back door. She was an African Caribbean woman of around fifty, markedly paler than Chuck, with very short hair. She wore a shapeless green sweatshirt, jeans and white training shoes. She smiled shyly as Chuck made the introductions.

'My dear,' Chuck said, 'Hans and I were just admiring a bullfrog.'

Anne said, 'Would you please not talk about that? We eating just now.'

'It's true,' Chuck admitted. 'Frogs are disgusting. Even in Trinidad we draw the line at eating frogs.'

'Some people eat frog,' Anne corrected him. 'Mountain chicken, they call it.'

'I heard that but I never saw it,' Chuck said. 'And in Trinidad, boy, we eat just about any kind of wild meat. Lappe, agouti, manicou, turtle, iguana – we hunt them and we eat them with curry, to cut the gamy taste. Curried iguana with coconut milk? Mmm.'

We went indoors and sat at the kitchen table. Anne began pouring coffee.

I made conversation. 'How do you hunt an iguana?' I asked.

'Iguana,' Chuck said thoughtfully. 'Well, some people might spear them, even shoot them, but we used to climb trees and just shake them down from the branches. You see, the iguana comes out in the morning sun and bakes itself on the branch of a tree. That's your chance. One guy shakes the branch, and the other guy grabs the iguana after it's fallen down. I tell you, you have to be quick, because an iguana is a rapid animal. My brother Roop's specialty was hunting iguana.'

He was on his feet now, pressing halves of oranges on a manual juicer. 'Roop was totally fearless – and agile? My God, he could climb anything. That maple tree outside? He would have found a way up. They used to call him the monkey of Las Lomas. I used to be very proud of his nickname,' Chuck said. 'It made him seem famous. Then one day my father heard me using it and he gave me a mighty lick. "Never call your brother that nigger name again."' Chuck handed out glasses of orange juice. 'He died hunting iguana – Roop. He was fourteen – or fifteen, was it?' Anne said quietly, 'Fifteen.' 'Fifteen,' Chuck said. 'That's right. I was twelve. One day he and some friends saw the green lizard up in a silk cotton tree. Now the silk cotton is the biggest, most charismatic tree in the forest, this real giant reaching way up above all the others into the sky. You know the one I mean, don't you? Most Trinidad people believe spirits live in the silk cotton. Nobody in his right mind would think of chopping one down. Just climbing a silk cotton is wrong – and they're practically impossible to climb, by the way: huge bare trunks and branches covered with wild pines that'll tear you to pieces. But Roop went right ahead. He went up this one tree and hopped over onto the silk cotton tree. He started to crawl on his belly towards the iguana, crawling along a big branch. There was a terrible explosion – like the world had exploded. They found my brother's body on the ground. He had stopped breathing. Smoke was coming off his skin. When the old people in the village heard about it, of course, they said it was the spirits that lived in the tree. But it was lightning. My brother was killed by lightning.'

I glanced at Anne. She was drinking her coffee and watching her husband.

Chuck said, 'I admired him so much. You know how, when you're a kid, you have heroes? Well, he was my hero. My brother Roop.' He noisily stirred his coffee.

Anne came to us with a dish loaded with an exotic pink mush. 'Saltfish,' Chuck said, rather pleased. 'You eat it with bread. Go on. I got it this morning at Conrad's. That's the best place for saltfish and bake.'

While Chuck and I ate breakfast, Anne chopped up a chicken with a cleaver, making great slamming noises. I asked her what she was cooking. 'Stew chicken,' she said. 'I chop it like this and season it. Garlic and onion. Thyme. Chive. Fitweed.'

'Tell Hans about the noise when you put it in the caramel,' Chuck said.

Anne tittered.

'Shoowaaa!' Chuck howled. 'The chicken goes, Shoowaaa!'

Their laughter filled the kitchen.

'That stew chicken, Hans?' Chuck said. 'It isn't for you,

and it sure isn't for me. It's for the bishop.' The bishop was the minister at Anne's church in Crown Heights. His birthday was coming up and his devotees were getting ready for a week of celebrations. 'Appreciation week, they call it,' Chuck said. He snorted. 'He should be doing the appreciating. Four daughters in private colleges, all paid for by his followers.'

'He's a good guy,' Anne said firmly. 'You can call him any time, day or night. And he'll bury anyone, even a stranger. You don't get that at the Tabernacle. Our bishop say, It not my church, it God's. Everybody welcome.'

'Well,' Chuck said, 'that's something I want to talk to you about. Anne? Listen to me. Are you listening? I'm going to tell you something important. Listen to me now.' 'I'm listening,' Anne said. She was covering a bowl of curried rice with cling wrap. 'Put that down for a moment,' Chuck said. Without hurrying, Anne placed the bowl in the refrigerator. 'Yes?' she said, now moving to the sink. Chuck said, 'I want to rest here. In Brooklyn. Not Trinidad, not Long Island, not Queens.' Anne did not react. 'Did you hear me? In Brooklyn. A cremation, and then an inter-ment of the ashes. Actual burial, I'm saying. No colum-barium, no urn garden. I want a real headstone, rising from real turf, with an appropriate inscription. Not just, "Chuck Ramkissoon, born 1950, died" – whenever – "2050."' He looked at me as if he'd just had a brainwave. 'Why not? Why not die a centurion?'

Anne was rinsing dishes.

'Will you respect my wishes?' Chuck said to her.

She remained impassive. I later heard, in the course of some discussion or other, that Anne had already arranged to be buried in Trinidad with her three unmarried sisters. A plot had been bought outside San Juan, their home town. The four women had even agreed on the outfits each would wear in her coffin. How Chuck was supposed to fit into this underground sorority was unclear.

'Anyhow, you heard me make my declaration with Hans as my witness,' Chuck said. 'I'll put it in writing, so there'll be no confusion.'

Anne said provocatively, 'The graveyard in the city all full up. It full up in Brooklyn, it full up in Queens. You want to be buried in this country, you be buried in Jersey.'

'Who told you that?' Chuck cried. 'There's space at Green-Wood Cemetery. I know this for a fact. I made enquiries.'

Anne said nothing.

'What is it? You think I should spend all eternity in Jersey?'

Anne started laughing. 'I just thinking of them parrot. You and them parrot.'

I said, 'Parrots?'

Chuck, smiling at his wife and shaking his head, didn't reply immediately. 'There are parrots at the cemetery,' he said. 'Monk parakeets. You sometimes see them around here in the summer – small green birds. Actually, you hear them,' Chuck said. 'Squawking in the trees. It's quite unmistakable.'

I must have looked doubtful, because Chuck insisted, 'There's another colony a few blocks from here, at Brooklyn College, and another one down in Marine Park. Years, they've been here. Why not? You get wild turkeys in Staten Island and the Bronx. Falcons and red-tailed hawks on the Upper East Side. Raccoons in Prospect Park. I'm telling you, one day, and it won't be long now, you're going to have bears, beavers, wolves inside the city limits. Remember what I said.' Chuck, wiping his mouth, added, 'Anyhow, you'll see the parrots for yourself.'

Anne said, 'He don't want to be tramping round a graveyard.'

'It's not a graveyard,' Chuck said. 'It's a historic cemetery.'

We got up and went out for a drive.

That is, I drove and Chuck talked – incessantly, indefatigably, virtuosically. If he wasn't talking to me he was talking on the phone. An intercontinental cast of characters passed through the old Cadillac. From Bangalore there came calls from a man named Nandavanam, who, in association with the Mr Ramachandran I'd met at Antun's, apparently was in the process of finalising a million-dollar sponsorship deal with an Indian corporation. From Hillside, Queens, there was George el-Faizy, an Alexandrian Copt who had produced preliminary drawings of the arena and the rehabilitated hangars for next to no money and still drove a taxi four days a week and indeed had first met Chuck when the latter had hopped into the said taxi on Third Avenue. And, from a private jet toing and froing between Los Angeles and London, there was Faruk Patel, the guru on whose top-secret multimillion-dollar participation the further expansion of the cricket venture depended. Even I had heard of Faruk, author of *Wandering in the Light* and other money-spinning multimedia mumbo-jumbo about staving off death and disease by accepting our oneness with the cosmos. I couldn't quite believe Chuck had this mogul on the line (and in fact Chuck usually spoke to Faruk's associates); but he had, because it was Chuck Ramkissoon who'd found out that beneath the mystical Californian quackery was a cricket nut with millions of dollars to play with, and who'd tracked down Faruk in Beverly Hills and cornered him and sold him on the idea of the Cricket World Cup coming to New York City and extracted from him a letter of comfort which he proudly showed me. And then there were strictly local characters – lawyers and realtors and painters and roofers and fishmongers and rabbis and secretaries and expediters. There was an official from the Bureau for Immigrant Sports and a man at Accenture and Dr Flavian Seem of the angel fund. He, Chuck, talked all these people into being – and, if necessary, non-being: when Abelsky

213

called, which he repeatedly did, Chuck invariably ignored the call. 'I've made this man this rich,' he once said, 'and this is what I have to put up with. You know when I met him he was driving a limousine? A bum from Moldova who couldn't wipe his own caca-hole.' If his phone, instead of buzzing, gurgled a few bars of '*Für Elise*', he rarely answered, because this was Eliza's ringtone. 'Limits,' he told me. 'These things must have limits. But not business. Limits in business are limitations.' He liked nothing better than to put bare feet on the dashboard and hit me with an aphorism. Or a fact. Chuck was a know-it-all on everything from South African grass varieties to industrial paints. His pedagogic streak could be gratuitous: he wouldn't hesitate, for example, to inform me about Holland's history of flooding, or to draw my attention to the importance of some pipeline under construction. Best of all, though, he loved to give speeches. I began to understand how he'd been able to extemporise an oration that first day we met: because he was constantly shaping monologues from his ideas and memories and fact-findings as if at any moment he might be called upon to address the joint houses of Congress. As early as June he told me of his preparations for his December presentation to the National Park Service in support of his application to build the cricket arena (Phase Two of his great scheme, Phase Three being the operation of the facility). The precise content was top secret. 'I can't tell you anything about it,' he said, 'except that it's going to be dynamite.' Dynamite? Clueless Chuck! He never quite believed that people would sooner not have their understanding of the world blown up, not even by Chuck Ramkissoon.

'What were his politics?' Rachel asks one day.

When we have this exchange, she is going through a phase of eating sticks of celery, and she crunches on just such a stick. I wait for her to finish crunching, and then I think carefully, because on this kind of subject, indeed on almost every subject, my wife is invariably on the money. It is my favourite of all her traits.

'We didn't really talk about politics,' I say. I decide against mentioning the pointed, possibly opportunistic, remarks he made at that fateful first cricket match, because he never said anything similar again – which didn't matter to me. The decisive item, if I'm going to be honest about this, was that Chuck was making a go of things. The sushi, the mistress, the marriage, the real-estate dealings and, almost inconceivably, Bald Eagle Field: it was all happening in front of my eyes. While the country floundered in Iraq, Chuck was running. That was political enough for me, a man having trouble putting one foot in front of the other.

'So what did you talk about?'

'Cricket things,' I say.

Rachel says, 'What about us? Did you talk about us?'

'Once or twice,' I say. 'But not really, no.'

'That's just weird,' Rachel says.

'No it isn't,' I say. I'm tempted to point out that our dealings, however unusual and close, were the dealings of businessmen. My ease with this state of affairs no doubt reveals a shortcoming on my part, but it's the same quality that enables me to thrive at work, where so many of the brisk, tough, successful men I meet are secretly sick to their stomachs about their quarterlies, are being eaten alive by bosses and clients and all-seeing wives and judgemental offspring, and are, in sum, desperate to be taken at face value and very happy to reciprocate the courtesy. This chronic and, I think, peculiarly male strain of humiliation explains the slight affection that bonds so many of us, but such affection depends on a certain reserve. Chuck observed the code, and so did I; neither pressed the other on delicate subjects.

I refrained, in particular, from asking him about the one category of telephone communications I didn't understand, incoming calls arriving on a separate phone (Chuck carried a mysterious second) and eliciting the tersest of responses from Chuck; calls which I soon had reason to connect to unexplained stops we made in the nether regions of Brooklyn.

Because from the beginning he ran so-called errands. Thus, without explanation, Chuck directed me, his driver, to addresses in Midwood and East Flatbush and Little Pakistan in Kensington, a couple of times taking us even as far as Brighton Beach. What happened, when we arrived,

216

was always the same. 'Pull over right here,' Chuck would say. He'd trot into a building and come back out within five minutes. 'Drive on,' he'd say, slamming the passenger door. And then he'd start talking again.

It wasn't until late July that he decided to give me a clue about what was going on.

He took a call on his mystery phone; said, 'OK, understood;' and then turned to me. 'Chinatown.'

'Chinatown?'

'Brooklyn Chinatown,' he said, very pleased to have confused me.

I wasn't aware of any Chinese quarter in Brooklyn. But it existed, I discovered, in a neighbourhood where you might look up and see, beyond rooftops dipped westward, the Verrazano Bridge. We stopped in front of a grimly ordinary Chinese restaurant. 'Some early lunch?' Chuck said.

We took a seat at the window of the restaurant's miserable room. There were no other customers. A busboy was sweeping last night's noodles into a pan.

'My father would never have been comfortable in a spot like this,' Chuck observed.

'Oh?' There was no sign of a waiter.

'He never went into a café except to do business, and he never did business unless there was a getaway. Look.' Chuck pointed over my shoulder. 'No rear exit. Somebody comes in through the front door, you're trapped.'

I wondered what he was talking about.

'That would have been my father's first thought: How do I get out of here?'

Before I could respond, two men, Chinese or perhaps Korean, entered the restaurant. Chuck approached them and shook their hands, and the three men sat down at the back of the restaurant, outside my earshot. They spoke for a minute or so in a friendly way, with much grinning. Chuck wrote something on a slip of paper, tore the slip into two stubs, and presented a stub to the men. One of them passed him a packed envelope.

'Well?' I said to Chuck in the car. We'd skipped lunch. 'What was that all about?'

'I was taking an order for food,' he said preposterously. 'What else would I be doing?'

'Chinese restaurants order sushi now?'

'Fish,' Chuck said. 'Everybody needs fish. Now drive on.'

In my flat-footed way, I have since figured it all out. By bringing me into the restaurant, by telling me about his father and making me view his transaction with the Chinese/Koreans and spinning me a yarn, Chuck was putting me on notice. On notice of what? Of the fact that something fishy was afoot. That I had the option of discontinuing our association. He guessed I wouldn't. He guessed I'd continue to see him as I wanted to see him, that I'd offer him the winking eye you might offer your ham-handed conjurer uncle.

Rachel, whom I sometimes suspect of having mind-reading powers, is of course on to this. 'You never really wanted to know him,' she remarks, still crunching on her celery. 'You were just happy to play with him. Same thing with America. You're like a child. You don't look beneath the surface.'

My reaction to her remark is to think, Look beneath Chuck's surface? For what?

In a spirit of legalistic fairness, Rachel continues, 'Although I suppose in Chuck's case you'd say, how could you be expected to know him? You were two completely different people from different backgrounds. You had nothing important in common.'

Before I can take issue with this, she points a celery stick at me and says, more amused than anything, 'Basically, you didn't take him seriously.'

She has accused me of exoticising Chuck Ramkissoon, of giving him a pass, of failing to grant him a respectful measure of distrust, of perpetrating a white man's infantilising elevation of a black man.

'That's just wrong,' I say, vehement. 'He was a good friend. We had a lot in common. I took him very seriously.'

With no trace of harshness, she laughs. Suddenly she looks up: she thinks she has heard a cry coming from upstairs, and she stops chewing and listens. And there is Jake's cry again – 'Water, please!' – and off she goes.

At the foot of the stairs, though, she turns to take a parting shot. 'You know why you two got on so well? Pedestal.'

I have to smile at this, because it's a Juliet Schwarz joke. Dr Schwarz is our marriage counsellor. Rachel and I saw her once a week for the first year of our reunion and still see her once a month at her office in Belsize Park, even though I happily find myself at an ever-growing loss as to what to talk about. Dr Schwarz is a great believer in the idea of couples as mutual esteemers above all else. 'This is your husband!' she once shouted to Rachel. 'Pedestal!' she shouted, raising a horizontal arm. 'Pedestal!'

At first, Rachel did not take to this kind of advice. She called Juliet Schwarz old-fashioned and bossy and biased in my favour. She questioned her doctorate. But evidently she listened to her, because one day I came home to find a sizeable block of limestone in the hallway.

'What's this?'

'A plinth,' Rachel said.

'A plinth?'

'It's for you.'

'You bought me a plinth?'

'Pedestal!' Rachel roared. 'Pedestal!'

To revert: it's true that I did not make enquiries into the deeper goings-on of Chuck Ramkissoon. It's also true that Chuck was a friend, not an anthropological curiosity.

In any case, there was no need for me to conduct

enquiries. Chuck was only too happy to make disclosures about himself.

He decided, for example, to let me in on his little racket.

I was rolling the outfield one hot Sunday morning when a man approached. He was an ordinary fellow in his forties, black, in sneakers and a T-shirt, and he stood around looking ill at ease. I dismounted the roller and went to him.

'Chuck there?' he said.

I took him to the hangar where Chuck was taking photographs and measurements. We couldn't see him and were about to step out when his voice called from somewhere, 'Nelson!'

They shook hands. Chuck said, 'I got it right here, boy,' and from a buttock pocket he extracted a wad of bills. I watched him count off a bunch and hand them to Nelson with a great smile. Nelson was smiling, too. Chuck walked him to his car. There was a brief chat, and then the car pulled quickly away.

'Well, he seems pretty happy,' I said.

'He should be,' Chuck said.

Tony wasn't around. It was just Chuck and me on that field. We climbed onto the roller, an ancient, peeling piece of equipment that moved on two drums filled with water. Chuck took the seat and I stood next to him on a small metal platform. The engine roared and we began to crawl towards the container shed.

Chuck shouted, 'You a gambling man, Hans?' When I shook my head, he said, 'Not even scratchies?'

'Maybe once or twice,' I said. I remembered rubbing a coin on a grid of silver boxes, hoping for the same dollar number to reveal itself three times in the gashes in the silver. It hadn't, and I hadn't cared; but the business had been sufficiently gripping to provide a clue as to why the hard-up half of New York was addicted to the experience – this being the impression I gained practically every time I had reason to step into a deli.

Presently the roller eased into the shed. We started chaining it up. Chuck said, 'How about weh-weh? You ever heard of that?' Chuck and I sat down on the two chairs he kept handy. We each opened a soda and drank thirstily. 'It's an old Trinidad game,' Chuck said. The weh-weh man, also known as the banker, he explained, wrote down a number from one to thirty-six on a piece of paper, folded the paper and deposited it at an accessible location – a shop, say, or a bar, or a street corner. 'My father was a weh-weh man,' Chuck said. 'He liked to pick a spot by the river. It used to be popular, that river. Maybe it still is. People would go up there to the basins where you could dive, places full of millions fish. You went up there, you cooked by the river. There was catfish, cray-fish in the water, but people hardly fished. You went there to lime. One time,' Chuck digressed, 'my brother Roop went off and stole a duck late, late at night. We took the duck to the river, slaughtered it, cut its head off. I remember Roop holding it up by the foot and letting the blood run off. Then we plucked it and cooked it. A white duck,' Chuck recalled. 'Nobody can lay claim to a white duck.'

Once the winning number, or mark, was chosen, Chuck resumed, the runners would go out and collect the bets – which in those days might range from fifty cents to fifty TT dollars. At a fixed hour, the banker revealed, or 'burst', the mark. 'Remember that guy with me at the restaurant in Manhattan? You were with the food critic.'

'McGarrell,' I said.

'That's right,' Chuck said. 'You remember his name. Anyhow, that's how I know McGarrell. He came running down to our house to place a bet for his father. Everybody played weh-weh, even though it was illegal. I'm talking about the countryside here, miles away from Port-of-Spain or any other big town. Even my father played sometimes. Listen to this: one afternoon, it was raining heavily and we were all at home, sitting on the gallery. A one-eyed frog comes out of the rain, hopping up the step of the gallery. My father jumped.' Chuck leaped sideways, pointing at the ground. '"Look that the frog! This is a mark for the weh-weh, boy." He put his hand in his pocket and gave me seventy-five cents. "Put all this on crapaud," he said. And of course crapaud won.'

You chose your numbers, Chuck told me, according to

what you saw around you or, especially, what you saw in your dreams. There was an art to remembering your dreams, and some people were fanatical about it. 'They wake up in the middle of the night and write it down, quick, before it's gone.' If you saw a priest or a pundit, you played parson man, number five; or if you saw a knife or a cutlass or broken glass, anything that cut, you played centipede, number one. 'Men would lie down just to dream for weh-weh,' Chuck Ramkissoon said. 'More you sleep, more you dream, my father used to say.'

Where was he going with this?

Chuck said, 'After my brother died, I helped out my father a lot. I was his right-hand man. He worked in the fields, you know. The weh-weh was a sideshow. But it was where most of the money came from. People trusted him. They liked him. I learned a lot just watching him talk to them, handle them. Deo Ramkissoon.'

Chuck stood up and searched around for something. He said, 'When I first began to save some money, I began to ask myself, What if I could set up a little weh-weh game here? People like to play, it reminds them of the old country. So I did. Small bets, very small bets, just for fun. I *made* it fun,' Chuck said. He told me that he devised an elaborate sign system tailored just for Brooklyn, with numbers corresponding to sights and scenes that daily surrounded the gamblers: a Haitian, cops making an arrest, a street fair, a game of cricket or baseball, an airplane, a graveyard, a drug dealer, a synagogue, 'every kind of thing you see around here. People came to me with their dreams and I translated the dreams into numbers. People love that kind of thing. After a while,' Chuck said, 'I figured out I could afford to take bigger bets. But I didn't want to get into trouble. I stopped the small-time game and restricted myself to more serious customers. A boutique lottery, I call it. Very discreet, very select.' He wiped his hands clean of all dirt. 'It isn't just Trinis playing any more. I get Jamaicans, Chinese. A lot of Chinese. When Abelsky joined me, the Jews became involved. They play five, ten, twenty thousand. Big bucks. It's me they trust, not Abelsky,' Chuck said. 'It's my game. I'm the banker. I burst the mark.'

'Why would people want to play?' I said. It felt strange asking him this question, since there were plenty of other things that needed saying. 'Why not just play the regular lottery? Or go to Atlantic City?'

'I give better odds,' Chuck said. He pulled out an old cricket bat and leaned it against his chair. 'I provide a door-to-door service. It makes it more special. You know, people are desperate for something special.'

I understood, now, the point of my driving lessons. It gave Chuck a measure of cover, maybe even prestige, to have a respectable-looking white man chauffeuring him while he ran around collecting bets all over Brooklyn. Apparently it had not bothered him that he was putting me at risk of arrest and imprisonment.

'Door-to-door service,' I said. 'Nice going, Chuck. You really had me there.'

He laughed. 'Come on, you were never in any danger of anything.' He bent down with a groan and picked up a box of old cricket balls.

We walked together to the field's centre. This was how we ended each of our sessions of groundsmanship: by whacking a dozen balls to the edge of the field and studying the consistency of each sector of the field. We were making progress. The outfield was getting quicker and truer. In accordance with our routine, I took the bat and with one-handed underarm strokes scattered the balls in every direction. We circled the field together, picking up the balls dotted around the field like markers of hours. Neither of us spoke then, or ever again, about his lottery.

Afterwards, as was usual, Chuck drove me to wherever it was I was playing that day – Baisley Pond Park, perhaps, or Fort Tilden Park, or Kissena Corridor Park, or Sound View Park. Our field and those fields were in one continuum of heat and greenness.

I strained the summer through a strainer that allowed only the collection of cricket. Everything else ran away. I cut back on my trips to England, inventing excuses that were easily accepted by Rachel. Whenever possible I took my lunch in Bryant Park, because in Bryant Park I could lie down on grass and inhale the scent of cricket, and look up at the sky and see a cricketer's blue sky, and close my eyes and feel on my skin the heat that coats a fielder. Not once did I think about the park as the place, say, where my wife and I watched an open-air screening of *North by Northwest* with a cashmere blanket spread out beneath us, and the tiny baby asleep on the blanket, and wine, and food bought on the hoof at a Fifth Avenue deli, penned in by summer foliage and fine heaps of man-made lights and, as darkness fell and Cary Grant wandered into the Plaza, only the boldest and most select stars.

Work, too, went down the drain. I remember one weighty evening in El Paso. My hosts had gone to a lot of trouble. Nobody expressly said so, but a big brokerage deal was on the line. When the client asked me to stay for an extra day, I almost laughed. The next day was a Saturday. There was a cricket field to be tended in the morning and a cricket match to be played in the afternoon.

Nobody understands better than I that this was a strange and irresponsible direction in which to take one's life. But it is what happened.

That season, 2003, I invariably played both days of the weekend – played in more matches, it may be, than anyone else at my club. My status grew with my visibility. I was offered, and I accepted, a position on the club's fund-raising committee and immediately raised a record-shattering five thousand dollars by writing a cheque I pretended to have squeezed out of some crazy Indian guys at work. There were Indian guys at work but they weren't crazy, and even if they had been crazy I wouldn't have involved them in this part of my life, whose separateness was part of its preciousness. I became so embedded in the proceedings of the club, so transparently upstanding and unavoidable a presence, that by the end of the summer I had come under consideration – so I was told – for the position of suitor to one of the Guyanese member's nieces. 'Why not?' my informant said. 'We know you.' He was kidding, yes, but also paying me a compliment.

Of course, he didn't know me, just as I didn't know him. It was rare for club members to have dealings that went beyond the game we played. We didn't want to have any such dealings. When I accidentally ran into one of the guys working a till at a gas station on 14th Street, there was awkwardness beneath the slapping of hands.

Beneath that, though, one might find kindness. One day our leg-spinner, Shiv, turned up drunk for a match. In a colloquy with the captain he revealed that his wife of ten years had left him for another man. We made sure that someone was with him in his empty house that night and all the nights until the following Saturday. That Wednesday I left work and rode a PATH train to Jersey City and from there rode a money-up-front taxi to Shiv's house. Another guy from the club was already on the spot, cooking up a curry. The three of us ate together. When the cook went home to his family, I stayed on with Shiv. We watched television.

At a certain moment I asked Shiv if I could crash at his place. 'I'm too tired to head back,' I said. He nodded, looking away. He knew what I was offering.

I sometimes wondered why the respect of these men mattered so much to me – mattered more, at the time, than anyone else's respect. After that night with Shiv, I thought I had the answer to my question: these people, who in themselves were no better or worse than average, mattered because they happened to be the ones, should anything happen to me, whom I could prevail on to look after me as Shiv had been looked after. It was only after the fact that I figured out they'd already been looking after me.

Chuck merged, in my mind, with these other West Indians and Asians I played with, and I suppose their innocence became confused with his innocence, and his numbers game with the one we played on a field. There was a physical merger, too. Chuck loved to watch cricket and watched us whenever he could, keeping an eye on play as he made phone calls. Now that he'd quit umpiring, he became a follower of the team and assumed the right of a follower to give advice. One afternoon, after I'd struggled as usual to hit the ball through the outfield, he said to me, 'Hans, you've got to hit the thing in the air. How else are you going to get runs? This is America. Hit the ball in the air, man.'

I tore open my pads' Velcro straps and tossed the pads into my bag. 'It's not how I bat,' I said.

The last league game of the season was played on August's first Sunday. It was hot, we were playing Cosmos CC, and we batted second. Four wickets fell and I was the next man in. I pulled a plastic chair into the shade of a tree and sat alone, bare-headed and sweating. I fell into that state of self-absorption that afflicts the waiting batsman as he studies the bowling for signs of cunning and untoward movement and, trying to recall what it means to bat, trying to make knowledge out of memory, replays in his mind bygone shots splendid and shaming. The latter predominated: in spite of the many matches I'd played that season, I'd never found myself in that numinous state of efficiency we evoke with a single casual word, form. There was a handful of shots I could look back on with pleasure – a certain flick off the legs, a drive that streaked through extra cover for four – but the rest, all the wafts and dishonourable pokes and thick and thin edges, was rubbish beneath recollection.

And on this day, when we were chasing almost two hundred and fifty runs, a big target that required quick scoring on an outfield made especially sluggish by a wet summer, I was once again confronted by the seemingly irresolvable conflict between, on the one hand, my sense of an innings as a chanceless progression of orthodox shots – impossible under local conditions – and, on the other hand, the indigenous notion of batting as a gamble of hitting out. There are hornier dilemmas a man can face; but there was more to batting than the issue of scoring runs. There was the issue of self-measurement. For what was an innings if not a singular opportunity to face down, by dint of effort and skill and self-mastery, the variable world?

A cry went up in the field. A stump lay stricken on the ground. I lowered my helmet over my head and walked out.

'Go deep, Hans! Go deep!' somebody shouted from the boundary as I chalked my guard on the mat. The voice was Chuck's. 'Go deep!' he shouted again, demonstrating the shot with a swinging arm.

I took stock of my situation. There was the usual plotting afoot between the bowler and his captain, who was making adjustments to his field, moving one fellow a few paces to his right, bringing another in to a close catching position. Finally the traps were set and the wicketkeeper slapped his gloves and crouched behind the stumps. I settled into my stance.

The bowler, a specialist in fizzing Chinamen and thus a very rare specimen, ran up and turned his arm. I blocked the first two balls.

'Do it now!' Chuck called. 'Do it now, Hans!'

When the third ball came looping down towards my legs, something unprecedented happened. Following the spin, I executed an unsightly, crooked heave: the ball flew high into the trees, for six. A huge cheer went up. The next ball, I repeated the stroke with a still freer swing. The ball flew even higher, clearing the sweetgums: there were shouts of 'Watch it!' and 'Heads!' as it bounced wildly in the tennis courts. I thought I was dreaming. What happened after that – I was soon out, and in the end we were defeated – ultimately didn't count. What counted, after my disappointment about the match result had waned and the last beers had been drunk and the extra-hot Sri Lankan chicken curry had been finished and the matting had been rolled back up and stuffed into its box and I found myself, once again, in the privacy of my ferry ride, what counted was that I'd done it. I'd hit the ball in the air like an American cricketer; and I'd done so without injury to my sense of myself. On the contrary, I felt great. And Chuck had seen it happen and, as much as he could have, had prompted it.

All of which may explain why I began to dream in all seriousness of a stadium, and black and brown and even a few white faces crowded in bleachers, and Chuck and me laughing over drinks in the members' enclosure and waving to people we know, and stiff flags on the pavilion roof, and fresh white sightscreens, and the captains in blazers looking up at a quarter spinning in the air, and a stadium-wide flutter of expectancy as the two umpires walk onto the turf square and its omelette-coloured batting track, whereupon, with clouds scrambling in from the west, there is a roar as the cricket stars trot down the pavilion steps onto this impossible grass field in America, and everything is suddenly clear, and I am at last naturalised.

I'm still working at M——. It was surprisingly uncomplicated to arrange for a transfer to London and to start up again, this time in a corner office that permits me, depending on which way I spin my chair, to admire St Paul's Cathedral or the Gherkin.

Of course, it felt strange to be back. In the first week I was sitting at one of the long tables that litter the bank's cafeteria – we lunch in rows, like monks – when I noticed a familiar-seeming face a few spots away. I was almost through with my lunch before I realised, with a little shock, that this was the same SVP who'd ominously stepped into my cubicle half a decade before.

I felt a strong impulse to approach him, say something about our shared exilic lot. But what to say, exactly? I was thinking it over when he got up and left.

Since then I've seen him around quite regularly – he's

with the M & A crowd and every now and then puts his name to a fairness opinion – but in two years I have not spoken to him. I still haven't figured out what there might be to say.

My work these days is directed at the activity in and around the Caspian Sea: on the map on my office wall, black stars stand for Astrakhan and Aktau and Ashgabat. Last year, the bank ordered a promising young analyst, Cardozo, to fly over and help me grow the operation. Cardozo, from New York out of Parsippany, New Jersey, loves it here. He has a flat in Chelsea and a girlfriend from Worcestershire who has forgiven him his exotic name. He wears pink shirts with pink silk cufflinks. He twirls a tightly furled brolly on sunny days. His pinstripes grow bolder and bolder. I wouldn't be amazed to see a signet ring turn up on his pinkie.

I understand something about what's going on with Cardozo, because when I arrived in London in my twenties I too felt like a performing extra. There was something marvellous about the thousands of men in dark suits daily swarming down Lombard Street – I even remember a bowler hat – and something decidedly romantic about the leftover twinkle of empire that went from Threadneedle Street to the Aldwych to Piccadilly and, like tardy starlight, perpetrated a deception of time. At Eaton Place, in drizzle, I half expected to run into Richard Bellamy, MP; and when I say that in Berkeley

Square I once listened for a nightingale, I'm not joking.

But nobody here holds on to such notions for very long. The rain soon becomes emblematic. The double-deckers lose their elephants' charm. London is what it is. In spite of a fresh emphasis on architecture and an influx of can-do Polish plumbers, in spite, too, of the Manhattanish importance lately attached to coffee and sushi and farmers' markets, in spite even of the disturbance of 7/7 – a frightening but not a disorienting occurrence, it turns out – Londoners remain in the business of rowing their boats gently down the stream. Unchanged, accordingly, is the general down-the-hatch, who-are-we-fooling light-heartedness that's aimed at shrinking the significance of our attainments and our doom, and contributes, I've speculated, to the bizarrely premature crystallisation of lives here, where men and women past the age of forty, in some cases even the age of thirty, may easily be regarded as over the hill and entitled to an essentially retrospective idea of themselves; whereas in New York selfhood's hill always seemed to lie ahead and to promise a glimpse of further, higher peaks: that you might have no climbing boots to hand was beside the point. As to what this point actually was, I can only say that it involved wistfulness. An example: one lunchtime, Cardozo, mulling over popping the question to his Worcestershire girlfriend, points out a beautiful woman in the street. 'I'll no longer be able to go up to her and ask her out,' he says, sounding dazed. Plainly the logical response is to enquire of Cardozo exactly when was the last time (a) he asked out a girl on the street, and (b) she said yes, and (c) he and she went on to greater things; and in this way bring home to him that he's being a dummy. I say no such thing, however. We are in the realm not of logic but of wistfulness, and I must maintain that wistfulness is a respectable, serious condition. How, otherwise, to account for much of one's life?

On a recent Friday, Cardozo and I knock off work early and walk in the direction of the river. It is an English summer's evening of the best sort, in which the day cloudlessly slips past nine o'clock and the price of a barrel of oil, scandalously ticking over in the seventies, seems to have not the slightest bearing on the world. The lanes south of Ludgate Hill are crowded with happy gangs of drinkers, and at Blackfriars we decide to stop for a quick one. An interval of this kind is most natural in this unwieldy city, where to be in one's home is, in terms of society, more or less to be like the fellow washed up on the little island with the single palm tree.

Cardozo and I take our drinks outside and stand around in the sunlight and the fumes. We get on very well. He coins flattering, if ridiculous, professional nicknames for me (the Dopester, the Ax) and in return I clue him in on the little tricks that go into holding oneself out as an augur in the matter of world affairs, which more than ever is

what our line of work requires. I seem to have an apti-
tude for the act: voice a first-hand opinion about the
kebabs of Baku and people will buy almost anything you
follow up with; and if, at a dinner party, I talk about West
Texas intermediate crude or the disgustingness of the
Volga, or drop the name Turkmenbashy (the man, I add
at that moment, who renamed January after himself), even
my wife's ears will prick up. But there is usually no call
for my show of expertise. At the said dinner party – and
so much, in this city, revolves around these drinky, smoky,
chronic get-togethers of friends who have known one
another since university, if not school, days – the talk
invariably concerns itself with ancient running jokes or
the doings of old so-and-so, whom everybody except me
knows, and I'm only able to chime in when the topic
switches to, say, the traffic, which everybody bitterly agrees
is worse than ever and not at all relieved by the private
buses that have been released like cattle onto the London
streets or indeed by the congestion charge, and then of
course there is the galling and wondrous fact that one's
taxi home will cost more than a flight to Italy – an obser-
vation that quickly leads to the subject of holidays.
Nowadays I spend a lot of time discussing *gîtes*, and *plages*,
and ruins. I don't remember anyone in New York talking
about his vacation for longer than a minute.

This is not to say that there's anything wrong with
weighing the felicities of Brittany against those of

Normandy. But in London, it must be recognised, escape – to the country, to warmer climes, to the pub – is a great, bittersweet theme. Sometimes this results in a discussion of New York City, in which case I'm quite happy to listen to somebody report excitedly on the Chrysler Building or the jazz riches of the Village or the distinctive largeness of experience that a simple walk down a Manhattan street can summon. Here, too, my opinion is rarely sought. Although it's not a secret that I lived for some time in the city in question, I'm not accorded any unusual authority. This isn't because I've been back for a while but, rather, because I'm precluded by nationality from commenting on any place other than Holland – one of those parochialisms, I am pissed off to rediscover, that remind me that as a foreign person I'm essentially of some mildly buffoonish interest to the English and deprived, certainly, of the nativity New York encourages even its most fleeting visitor to imagine for himself. And it's true: my secret, almost shameful feeling is that I *am* out of New York – that New York interposed itself, once and for all, between me and all other places of origin. It may be that this is what I like best about Cardozo, that he accords me the status of fellow émigré. 'Pedro,' he murmurs as he reads the baseball reports in the *Herald Tribune*, rightly trusting that he need say nothing more.

Not that long ago, at yet another gathering of familiars, our host, an old friend of Rachel's named Matt, makes some remarks about Tony Blair and his cata-strophic association with George W. Bush, whom Matt describes as the embodiment of a distinctly American strain of stupidity and fear. On this side of the Atlantic, this is a commonplace judgement, so commonplace, in fact, as to be of no real interest; but then the conversa-tion strays in a direction that's rare these days, to the events synonymous with September 11th 2001. 'Not such a big deal,' Matt suggests, 'when you think of everything that's happened since.'

He is referring to the numbers of Iraqi dead, and as a matter of arithmetic I understand his argument, indeed must admit it. He refers also to the dark amazement with which he and, if my impression is correct, most of the rest of the world have followed the various doings of this American administration, and on this score I again have not the slightest urge to contradict him. I speak up nonetheless.

'I think it was a big deal,' I say, interrupting whatever somebody is saying.

Matt looks at me for the first time that evening. It's an awkward moment, because I look right back at him.

Rachel says unexpectedly, 'He was there, Matt.'

Out of the best of intentions and acting as my loyal wife and Englisher, she wants to accord me a privileged standing – that of survivor and eyewitness. I'd feel dishonest to accept it. I've heard it said that the indiscriminate nature of the attack transformed all of us on that island into victims of attempted murder, but I'm not at all sure that geographic proximity to the catastrophe confers this status on me or anybody else. Let's not forget that when it all happened I was in a rubbernecker in Midtown, watching the same television images I'd have watched in Madagascar. I knew only three of the dead, and then only slightly (though well enough, in one case, to recognise his widow and his son playing in the sandpit at Bleecker Playground). And while it's true that my family was displaced for a while, so what? If ever, out of a wish to appear more interesting or simply to make conversation, I'm tempted to place myself closer to those events – and, perhaps because I work in the financial world and am easily to be imagined in a high tower, some people have assumed I was closer to them – I only have to think of the waving little figures who were visible for a while and then not.

I say, 'That's not my point. I'm just saying, it was a big deal.'

'Well, of course,' Matt says, his tone marking me out as a nitpicker. 'I'm not arguing with that.'

'Good,' I say, with as much abruptness as the situation allows. 'So we're in agreement.'

Matt makes a pleasantly concessionary face. Someone else picks up the chatter and everything goes back to normal. However, I notice Matt leaning over and muttering out of

241

the corner of his mouth to his neighbour, who mutters back. There is a secretive exchange of smiles.

For some reason, I'm filled with rage.

I lean over to Rachel. I gesture with my eyes, Let's go.

Rachel has not followed what has happened. She looks surprised when I stand up and put on my jacket. It's a surprise for all, since we have not finished our roast chicken.

'Come on, Hans, sit down,' Matt says. 'Rachel, talk to him.'

Rachel looks at her old friend and then at me. She stands up. 'Oh, piss off, Matt,' she says, and waves goodbye to everyone. It is quite a shocking moment, in the scheme of things, and of course exhilarating. When we step out together into the wet street, holding hands, there is a tang of glory in the air.

Gratifyingly, Rachel doesn't ask me what exactly transpired. But in the taxi home, there's an epilogue of sorts: my wife, mooning out of the window at rainy Regent's Park, says, 'God, do you remember those sirens?' and, still looking away, she reaches for my hand and squeezes it.

Strange, how such a moment grows in value over a marriage's course. We gratefully pocket each of them, these sidewalk pennies, and run with them to the bank as if creditors were banging on the door. Which they are, one comes to realise.

Which brings me back to Blackfriars: Cardozo wishes

to have that most British conversation about getting away to foreign parts, or so it seems as we discuss his imminent romantic weekend in Lisbon, where Cardozo's ancestors lived and, according to Cardozo legend, in their capacity as mastic importers ran into Columbus himself. Then, with shadows creeping towards us from across the street, Cardozo says, 'I'm going to ask Pippa to marry me. In Lisbon.'

I raise my glass of black beer. 'That's wonderful,' I say.

Toasting Cardozo's matrimonial future, we each take a sip and renew our watch over the vehicles grunting towards Blackfriars Bridge. There are pedestrians to keep an eye on, too, hundreds of them, all trotting downhill to the train station.

'Any advice?' Cardozo says. I see that he is wearing a candid expression.

'About what?' I ask.

'All of it. The whole marriage deal.'

He's not an idiot, Cardozo. He's heard through the grapevine that my wife and I have been round the old block, and he thinks that maybe I can be the Dopester in this regard, too – in the matter, that is, of what lies round the old corner.

I wrinkle my mouth and give my head a wobble of difficulty. I am able to say, 'You're sure this is what you want?'

'Pretty sure,' Cardozo admits.

'Well, I was pretty sure, too,' I say.

Cardozo looks at me as if I've said something important. 'But what about now?' he presses. 'What do you think now?'

I feel a great responsibility towards my enquirer, who is twenty-nine years old but gives the impression at this moment of being a very young man indeed. I recall Socrates' unhelpful advice to his young friend – 'By all means, get married. For either you will end up happy, or you will become a philosopher' – and feel that I, by contrast, ought to be able to pass on a practical tip or two of the sort that I myself might have benefited from, the kind of lowdown you would readily give to a voyager bound for a corner of, say, the Congo that you've visited yourself and about whose drinking water and mosquitoes you have gained some costly knowledge. But of course things are more complicated than that, and the notion of married life as analogous to life in the Congo is simply unintelligent. This particular voyager, Cardozo, will be setting forth from Lisbon, a city which, perhaps because I have never been there, I have always associated with departures into the ocean and dreadful and beautiful extra-European adventures. So I am full of goodwill for my youngish mariner friend, but I have nothing precise to tell him – by which I mean, nothing that might not be construed as discouraging. And this is the one thing I feel sure about, that I am under a duty to not discourage; and

I am visited by a shiver, because it seems I have truly crossed into what one might call the largely exemplary stage of life, which may be a slightly tragic term for adulthood, and I must make an effort, on the sunny and shadowy pavement, to not feel a little sorry for myself as I inwardly wave Cardozo bon voyage.

Meanwhile he is still expecting me to speak. So I speak. I say, 'What do I think now? I think I have no regrets. None at all.'

Cardozo, I see, is considering this statement very seriously. I take the opportunity to finish my beer and make my move. We split, Cardozo heading for the tube to Sloane Square, I going on foot to Waterloo Bridge and from there to the London Eye, where on this fine July evening I have arranged to meet my son and my wife.

One Sunday morning, back in June, Rachel calls down from the storage room. She has been performing a thorough cleaning. If in doubt, throw it out, is Rachel's slogan in such situations.

I go up to her. 'I found this,' she says. In one hand she is holding my bat. 'Do you still need this? And what about this thing?' In her other hand is my cricket bag, which she has pulled out of the storage room.

I take the bat from her. It's still marked by New York dirt.

'Are you going to play this year?'

'I don't think so,' I say, licking my finger and rubbing at the dirt, which continues to stick. I haven't played since my return to England. It would feel unnatural, is my feeling, to separate myself from my family in order to spend an afternoon with understated teammates and cups of tea and something essentially nostalgic at stake; yet to throw out this odd paddle would also go against nature, even though its wood, faintly striped by a dozen grains, is now swollen with age and cannot have a sweet spot to speak of.

However, once I hold a bat in my hands I have trouble putting it down. I'm still carrying it when I step into my bedroom to check on Jake. He's underneath our duvet, in the spot where most mornings I wake up to find, pressed against me, the following bundle: boy, bear, blanket. He is watching *Jurassic Park* for the thousandth time.

We watch half a scene together. Then, with no particular purpose in mind, I ask him a question.

'Do you know what this is?'

He looks up. 'A cricket bat.'

I hesitate. I am recalling how I became hooked on the game: alone, with my own eyes. Until the age of nine I was merely a footballer and the summer sport a rumour not worth verifying. Then one day I was walking in the woods by my club and through the trees came the white flashes of boys mysteriously organised in a green space.

It occurs to me that Jake's situation is different. He has a father, after all. There is no need for him to walk alone in the woods.

I say, 'Do you want me to teach you how to play?'

He is drowsily following a rampaging tyrannosaurus. 'OK.'

'This year, or next year?' He is only six. When he plays football he is still dreamy in the extreme and only kicks at the ball if woken up by a shout. It is like Ferdinand the Bull and the flowers.

There's a pause. He turns to look at me. 'Next year,' he says.

I feel unexpectedly glad. There's no rush. It's only a game, after all. 'Fine,' I say.

Rachel's voice climbs to me from afar. 'Tea?'

I actually flinch. It comes to me, this question, as the pure echo of an identical offer she voiced three years ago.

'Tea?' Rachel asked.

This was in London, in her parents' kitchen. I sat at the dining table with my son and his grandparents. Yes, please, I called back, gratified and a little puzzled by her kindliness.

For during the first week of that summer holiday – this was in early August 2003 – Rachel had been in a politic mood. She was considerate and attentive and low-key and, like her parents, powerfully exercised by my preferences. Everybody was making an effort for Hans: and unwarrantedly and (in retrospect) suspiciously so, because, as previously noted, I'd been an absentee for much of that summer.

The tea was poured. I engaged Jake in conversation.

'Who's your best friend at camp?' I said. 'Cato?' I had heard all about Cato. I imagined him grave and severe, like Cato Uticensis.

Jake shook his head. 'Martin is my friend.'

'Right,' I said. This was a new name. 'Does Martin like Gordon the Express? How about Diesel?'

My son nodded emphatically. 'Well that's good,' I said. 'He sounds like a very nice boy.' I looked at Rachel. 'Martin?'

She sprang from her chair in tears and ran up the stairs. I had no idea what was happening. 'You'd better go up,' Mrs Bolton told me, exchanging furious glances with her husband.

My wife was lying face down on her bed.

'I'm sorry,' she said. 'I should have told you. That was awful. I'm so sorry.'

I fell into a chair. 'How long?' I said.

She sniffed. 'About six months.'

I came out with, 'So it's serious.'

She gave a small shrug. 'It might be.' She quickly went on, 'It's the only reason I introduced him to Jake. I wouldn't have, otherwise. Darling, I've got to move on. You've got to move on. We can't go on like this, waiting for something to happen. Nothing's going to happen. You know that.'

'I know shit, apparently.' I'd thought myself prepared for this eventuality; more accurately, thought myself no longer in possession of the emotion required truly to care.

Now Rachel was sitting up on her bed and looking down at the quilt. She had been growing her hair steadily since her return to London, and a glossy ponytail flopped down over a shoulder.

When she started to speak, I cut her off. 'Let me think,' I said.

I closed my eyes. There was nothing to think except that she was not in the wrong; that another man had her love; that she was at this very moment undoubtedly wishing me very far away; and that my son would soon have another father.

'Who is he?' I said.

She gave me a name. She told me, without my asking, that he was a chef.

'I'll leave tomorrow,' I said, and Rachel gave a horrible little nod.

I brushed Jake's teeth with his dinosaur-themed toothbrush. I read him a story – at his insistence, *Where the Wild Things Are*, even though it frightened him a little, this story of a boy whose bedroom is overtaken by a forest – and calibrated his bedroom's dimmer switch according to his instructions. 'More light,' a voice softly commanded

249

from his bedding, and I gave him more light. Rachel stood at the door, arms folded. Later, as I packed my belongings in the adjoining room, I heard a childish squeal of protest. 'What's going on?' I said. 'Nothing,' Rachel said. 'He's just making a fuss.' I saw that she had completely lowered the dimmer. I restored the light in a rage. 'I won't have my son sleeping in the dark,' I said to Rachel in a near-shout. 'Jake,' I said, 'from now you sleep with the light on, if that's what you want. Daddy says so. OK?' He widened his eyes in assent. 'OK,' I said. Trembling, I kissed him. 'Goodnight, my boy,' I said.

He and I spent most of the following morning in the garden. For a while we played hide-and-seek, the ultimate object of which, of course, is not to remain concealed but to be found: 'I'm here, Daddy,' my son cried out from behind the tree he always hid behind. Then, in furtherance of his obsession with space, the two of us searched the garden for his plastic planets and his plastic golden sun, balloons I'd blown into being earlier in the week. We found all of them except the runt world, Pluto, which once missing became my son's favourite. I was craning into a hedge when I was joined by Charles Bolton. He kept me company for a minute or two, filling his pipe with tobacco while I, on my hands and knees, kept my head in the bushes. When I got up, clapping the dirt off my hands, my father-in-law stood there like perspicacity made flesh. He removed the pipe from his mouth.

'Some lunch before you go?' he said.

Rachel insisted on driving me to Heathrow. We sat together in silence. I did not think that it fell to me to talk.

Somewhere near Hounslow, she began to say things. She gave assurances about my place in my son's life and about my place in her life. She told me of the agony in which she, too, found herself. She said something important about the need to reimagine our lives. (What this meant, I had no idea. How do you reimagine your life?) Each of her soothing utterances battered me more grievously than the last – as if I were travelling in a perverse ambulance whose function was to collect a healthy man and steadily damage him in readiness for the hospital at which a final and terrible injury would be inflicted. I stepped out at Terminal 3 and leaned my head into the car. 'Goodbye,' I said, and it came out more dramatically than I'd intended. But it seemed finally to have ended, our paired adventure unto death, a truth at once undermined and supported by the bewildering ordinariness of what was left to me: an encounter with the woman at the check-in desk; a drink of water in a travellers' lounge; an airplane seat.

An hour before landing, a stewardess came by with a basket of Snickers bars. I took one. It was cold and solid, and when I took my first bite I felt a painless crunch and the presence of something foreign in my mouth. I spat into my napkin. In my hand, protruding from brown gunk, was a tooth – an incisor, or three-quarters of one, dull and filthy.

Dazed, I called over an attendant.

'I found a tooth in my chocolate bar,' I said.

She looked at my napkin with open fascination. 'Wow . . .' Then she said carefully, 'Are you sure it's not yours?'

My tongue lodged itself in an unfamiliar space.

'Shit,' I said.

The tooth was greying in my pocket when I arrived back at the hotel. My first impression, on entering the lobby, was that the Chelsea had been invaded by theatre-goers and lady golfers from the Midwest. It turned out that these sporty-looking men and women in Bermuda shorts and baseball caps were from the FBI and were here to arrest the drug dealer from the tenth floor. All of this was explained to me by the angel. I had barely seen him all summer, but here he was in his favourite chair. It was not a reassuring sight. His wings were tipped with dirt and his toenails had grown long and yellow. Something about his person – his feathers, or perhaps his feet – reeked. Sitting in the neighbouring armchair was a small, dark-haired woman in her sixties. With her careful coiffure and chic gold bracelet and Gucci handbag, I took her to be one of those unfortunates who check into the Hotel Chelsea in the mistaken belief that it is a normal estab-lishment with normal amenities. 'This is my mother,' the angel said, flopping a wrist in her direction. I shook Mrs Taspinar's hand. 'How do you do,' I said with as much conventionality as I could muster, as if an ostentatious show of *comme il faut* might minimise her son's aberrancy and the dark, inordinately troubling gap in my smile and the collapse of law and order betokened by the detectives surrounding us and, this particular slope being a slippery one, the hellishness of the world.

She smiled up at me and made a remark in Turkish to her son.

'My mother is here to take me home,' the angel said. He was worrying the hem of his wedding dress as he watched the federal agents. 'She thinks I should return to Istanbul and find a wife there. Maybe become a doctor. Or work in computers.'

The angel's mother gave an excruciated laugh. 'Have you been to Istanbul?' she asked me in a feminine, slightly lilting voice.

'No,' I said. 'I hear it's a wonderful city.' I felt terribly sorry for her.

'It is,' she said. 'It is quite beautiful. Like San Francisco, with many hills and bridges.'

A moment followed in which the angel and his mother and I made a dumbstruck triangle.

'Well, I must go,' I said, picking up my travel bag. 'It was very nice meeting you.'

At that moment there was a commotion by the front

desk. A bunch of feds were spilling out of an elevator, and in their midst, head lowered and wrists bound by a plastic loop, was the ginger-bearded man who so loved horses.

'Hang in there, Tommy,' somebody called out to him. There was a Laurel and Hardy moment as men took turns squeezing through the glass doors, and then the ginger-bearded man was gone. He left no dog behind him. Evidently the date hadn't worked out.

The next day, a Thursday, I asked the guys at the front desk about the in-house dentist. 'He's good,' I was told.

By lunchtime, a fake new tooth, as discoloured as its neighbours, had materialised over the chip in my lower gum. The dentist, masked and gloved, hovered in and out of his little floodlight for the best part of an hour. It was unexpectedly reassuring to receive his deepest considera-tion. He nattered about his salmon-fishing vacations in Ireland, which by coincidence had been precisely the pastime of my Dutch former dentist and led me to wonder if there was a connection between angling and tinkering with teeth. Certainly he seemed as happy as a fisher, this New York practitioner, and why not? One of the great consolations of work must be its abbreviation of the world's area, and it follows that it must be especially consoling to have one's field of vision reduced to the space of a mouth. At any rate, I was very envious.

And I didn't want to go into work. Perhaps operating under an oral inspiration, I decided instead to fix my bathtub's drain, which for weeks had been almost fully blocked. I walked to a hardware store and bought a state-of-the-art plunger and attacked the drain like a maniac: instead of shrivelling in minute increments, the bathwater now escaped in a tiny silver twister. This failed to satisfy me. I called in one of the hotel handymen. After sombrely assessing the problem, he returned with a snake, that is, a length of wire he slithered into the depths of the hole in order to extract whatever might be down there. At that moment, the bathroom fell dark.

We went out into the hallway, where the fuses were located, and it became apparent that all the lighting in the hotel had failed. It turned out that the whole of the city – indeed most of north-east America, from Toronto to Buffalo to Cleveland to Detroit – had mislaid its power. We did not learn this until some while later; our immediate sense was that more disastrous violence had been perpetrated on the city. I joined the people collected in the hallways, which were lighted only by the distant brown skylight above the staircase, and somebody speculated authoritatively that the Indian Point power station had been hit and shut down. I thought about packing a bag at once and trying to escape the island on foot, or by boat, or running over to the 30th Street heliport and paying whatever it took to clamber into a chopper, Saigon style. Instead, I found myself at a tenth-floor window surveying the panicked, immobilised traffic on West 23rd Street with the apartment's tenant, a pretty, conventional-looking woman in her thirties named Jennifer. Presently Jennifer said, 'There's only one thing to do in a situation like this, and that's drown our sorrows.' She brought out a bottle of coldish white wine and for an hour we watched the confusion on the street. 'I'm leaving this city,' she declared at one point. 'This is it. This is the final straw.' Then the good news reached us that in fact no disaster had occurred, and Jennifer said, 'There's only one thing to do in a situation like this, and that's celebrate.' She produced another bottle of wine.

Stillness came over New York. Seventh Avenue was crowded with people trudging quietly homeward, and in the heat many of the pilgrims removed their jackets and even their shirts, so that a spectacle of mass near-nakedness presented itself to us. Jennifer spent a lot of time trying to contact her boyfriend. The phone systems were overloaded and she couldn't get through. She was worried for him because, she intimated, there was something clueless about this man, whom she'd met, she said, at the auction house where she worked: he came in one day and gave her instructions to sell a diamond ring returned to him by his ex-fiancée. 'I got him fifteen thousand bucks,' Jennifer said brazenly. Meanwhile her heart had been quite taken by this forlorn client. She learned that he'd accepted an offer from business school at Case Western over an offer from Harvard because his then-fiancée – the woman for whom he'd bought the ring – had told him that Case Western was where she was herself bound; but then she accepted an offer from another school, leaving him high and dry in Ohio. 'He didn't take the hint,' Jennifer said. 'But I guess hints don't really cut it, do they?' It was only after he'd started at Case Western, Jennifer related, that he discovered that his fiancée was seeing another man. This was why she worried for him, Jennifer said, because he was someone capable of getting the wrong end of the stick.

'You know the kind of guy I'm talking about?' she said.

'I think I do,' I said.

Somebody knocked on the door and declared that a party had gotten under way on the roof. So up we went. There was quite a gathering. People were setting up tables and chairs and candles and getting ready for the spectacle of nightfall. A man smoking a joint predicted that the city would go to hell. 'I think you're completely underestimating the situation,' he told me, even though I hadn't voiced an estimate of any kind. 'Basically we're going back to a time before artificial light. Every nut out there is going to be acting under cover of darkness. You know what cover of darkness means? Do you have any idea at all?' This fellow, who had long grey hair but otherwise looked, I swear, exactly like the sexagenarian Frank Sinatra, had read a book about the history of artificial illumination and told me that throughout human time light had been associated with optimism and progress, and with good reason. Nightfall, in the days before street lighting, marked the emergence of an untoward alternative world, a world of horrors and delights whose existence revealed all too troublingly the correspondence between luminance and codes of human behaviour, a world whose occupants, removed from the scrutiny afforded by lamps and fires, engaged in conduct the moral dimension of which was as imperceptible as they themselves were. Such, he said, would be the effect of the power outage. 'It's going to be a mess,' he predicted. 'Turn off the lights, people turn into wolves.'

He was a plausible guy, as far as rooftop buttonholers go. But in fact, as everybody knows, the blackout gave rise to an outbreak of civic responsibility. From the Bronx to Staten Island, citizens appointed themselves traffic cops, gave rides to strangers, housed and fed the stranded. It also transpired that the upheaval provoked a huge number of romantic encounters, a collective surge of passion not seen, I read somewhere, since the 'we're-all-going-to-die sex' in which, apparently, everybody had indulged in the second half of September two years previously – an analysis I found a little hard to accept, since it was my understanding that all sex, indeed all human activity, fell into this category. What was certainly true was that, once the sun had sunk and the strawberry clouds blazing over the bay had disappeared, a terrific dark came upon New

York. The physical elements of the city, unlit save for a very few office blocks, acted as intensifiers of the night, raising and spreading an extreme, corporeal obscurity that was only minimally disturbed by the roaming, ever less numerous automobiles. There were just a few glimmerings in the low hills of New Jersey. The sky itself looked like an imperfectly electrified settlement.

The roof party grew more and more raucous as the entire population of the building, it seemed, rose upward to laugh in the warm night. Jennifer the auctioneer's boyfriend finally turned up, as did, with midnight approaching, the angel, his mother in tow – literally so, for she clung to a strap that formed part of her son's outfit. He seemed in very good spirits and wore his black wings in honour, he said, of this special occasion. We exchanged a few words before I lost sight of him. There was more drink and talk. Someone croakily sang a song. Someone else explained that the boundary between the moon's bright and dark portions was called the terminator. A hand grabbed my arm.

It was the angel's mother, in a state of hysteria. Gasping, she dragged me to the south perimeter of the roof, which was bordered by a ledge only four feet high. She was screaming and sobbing now. A crowd had gathered at the parapet, on which a few candles flickered. 'The angel jumped,' somebody said. I held the angel's mother in my arms and looked down into a zone where, in daylight, one might have seen the gardens of the houses on 22nd Street. Now there was nothing to be seen. The angel's mother had caught her breath and was screaming. I shouted out, 'Did anybody see him?' and a futile buzz went around. I instructed the angel's mother to follow me, but she couldn't walk, so I picked her up and piggybacked her indoors. She moaned and weakly punched my shoulders as I steadily marched down the candlelit marble staircase, our merged shadow abhorrently stretching and shrinking on the walls. In the lobby I asked, 'Did anybody see the angel leave?' and Guillermo at the front desk shook his head. Mrs Taspinar dropped to her feet and ran out screaming, Mehmet, Mehmet, and I hurriedly followed, catching up with her in front of El Quijote restaurant. She kept screaming, Mehmet, Mehmet. At exactly this moment I heard hooves. I turned towards two stamping horses. Lights came nearer and from their sources emanated a pair of cops who slowly dismounted and began asking questions, and then we heard a voice crying out, and Mrs Taspinar stopped screaming, and the voice called out again, and she and the flashlights went in the direction of the voice, and there, in the play of the flashlights, was the angel, waving over the crenellated gable of the synagogue that adjoined the hotel. The cops looked up. One of them yelled, 'Get down, sir! Get down right now!' The angel retreated, obediently it seemed, and his mother collapsed again, as behind me the horses strained and twitched in a condition of near-matterlessness. I went back into the hotel and Guillermo told me how to get onto the roof of the synagogue. I took his flashlight and ran up several floors and made my way onto the fire escape. Below was the blackbird body, in the cleft between the hotel and the steeply pitching roof of the temple.

'Your mother's looking for you,' I said.

A cigarette ember brightened his mouth. 'You should come down,' he said. He was lying on his back. 'It's very comfortable.'

I lowered a leg and very slowly transferred my body onto the synagogue roof. Taking care to leave a good distance between me and the angel, I lay down on the warm, sloping tiles with my arms and legs spread out in an X.

'Uh, Hans,' the angel said.

'What?' I said.

'Could you turn off that light?'

I pressed the flashlight's rubber button. I was looking upward. Everything blacked out except stars and a memory of stars.

I was twelve. I was on a summer holiday with my mother and old friends of hers – Floris and Denise Wassenaar, a married couple. We travelled along the south coast of Italy. We drove from place to place, stayed in cheap hotels and took in sights, an itinerary banged together, from my youthful perspective, with a heavy hammer of boredom. Then, over dinner one night, Floris announced he'd organised a spear-fishing expedition. 'Just for the men,' he said, ganging up with me. 'The women will stay on land, where it's safe.'

We went out on a wooden motorboat – Floris and I and a local man with dense white body hair. The two men were armed with full-sized spearguns. I was given a smaller speargun requiring only boyish strength to pull back the rubber catapult that fired the spear. For hours the boat bumbled parallel to the shore. We passed two or three headlands and came to a stretch of the coast that was mountainous and truly wild, with no roads for many miles inland. We moored in the beryl of a small bay. There was a beach with white pebbles. A pine forest grew right down to the beach. This was where we would fish and spend the night.

I had never snorkelled before. It was astounding to discover how a simple glass mask made clear and magni-fied a blue-green water-world and its frightening inhab-itants: when a ray glided towards me, I scrambled ashore, flippers and all. Snorkelling was hard. Gianni, the Italian, and pale and enormous Floris seemed to be able to hold their breath forever – you needed to, to find the big fish; the big fish lurked in shadows beneath rocks and had to be staked out – but with my small lungs I could only dive for a short while, and shallowly. It hurt my ears to go down deep. As the day wore on, however, a predatory boldness overtook me. A whippersnapper Neptune, I lorded it over the grassy, glistening inlet, sending my matte iron thunderbolt through startled groups of small silver and brown fishes. I grew fierce and began to hunt with intent. Stalking one particular fish, I followed the rocks out of the little bay. The fish twisted into a crevice, and I dived after it. Then I became aware that the water had become cold and dark.

I was swimming at the foot of a mountain. From thousands of feet in the air the mountain plunged directly into the water and sank into an endless dimness beneath me.

Like a chump in a horror movie, I slowly turned round. Confronting me was the vast green gloom of the open sea.

In a panic I bolted back to the cove.

'Catch anything?' Floris asked. I shook my head shamefully. 'No problem, *jongen*,' Floris said. 'Gianni and I got lucky.'

The killed fish was cooked over a campfire and seasoned with thyme growing wild in the pine forest. Afterwards it was time to sleep. The men lay down under the pines. The most comfortable sleeping berth, in the boat, was reserved for me.

What happened next, on the little wooden boat, was what came back to me on the synagogue roof – and what I once told Rachel about, with the result that she fell in love with me.

She revealed this in the week after Jake was born. We were up in the middle of the night. Jake was having trouble falling asleep. I held him in my arms.

'Do you want to know exactly when I fell in love with you?' Rachel said.

'Yes,' I said. I wanted to know about the moment my wife fell in love with me.

'In that hotel in Cornwall. The Something Inn.'

'The Shipwrecker's Arms,' I said. I could not forget that name and what it called before the imagination: treacherous lights on the land, the salvage of goods at the expense of the drowned.

My wife, on the point of sleep, murmured, 'Remember when you told me about being in that boat at night, when you were little? That's when I fell in love with you. When you told me that story. At that exact moment.'

A small anchor fixed the boat to the bed of the cove. I lay on my side and closed my eyes. The rocking of the boat by the waves was soothing but unknown. The men on the shore were asleep. Not the twelve-year-old, though. He shifted and lay on his back and decided to look up at the sky. What he saw took him by surprise. He was basically a city kid. He had never really seen the night sky for what it is. As he stared up at millions of stars, he was filled with a dread he had never known before.

I was just a boy, I said to my wife in a hotel room in Cornwall. I was just a boy on a boat in the universe.

The angel was gone. Discounting the moon, discounting the Milky Way, I was alone. My hands searched out the surface of the roof. Rachel, I said to myself. I cried out softly, Rachel!

I did not see Mehmet Taspinar again. He left in the morning with his mother. His vacated room was cleaned up and rented out that very day to two rich girls freshly enrolled at NYU.

In my last American August one thunderstorm followed another: I can still picture a suddenly green, almost undersea atmosphere, and hailstones hopping like dice on asphalt, and streams criss-crossing Chelsea, and huge photographical flashes visiting my apartment. It's hard to believe, from my Englander's perspective, in those subtropical weeks, when the humid air could be so blurred with reverberated light as to leave me with a mild case of colour blindness. Everyone scurried in the shadowed fraction of the city. Few things were more wonderful than hopping into a cold summer cab.

With all that rain and heat, Brooklyn almost returned to the wild. Pools welled up in basements, weeds overran planted things. Mosquitoes, fizzing and ravenous and bearing the West Nile virus, emptied the gardens and porches at twilight. A block over from the Ramkissoon home, on Marlborough Road, a tree knocked down by lightning flattened an old lady, killing her.

And the grass on Chuck's cricket field kept on growing. Chuck reported this fact to me a week or so after my return from England. 'Mowing time,' he said.

I wasn't in the mood. Despair busies one, and my weekend was spoken for: I was going to lie down on the floor of my apartment in the draught of the air-conditioner and spend two days and nights travelling a circuit of regret, self-pity and jealousy. I was obsessed, needless to say, with Rachel's lover – Martin Casey, the chef. A definite article is appropriate because Martin Casey was sufficiently well known that Vinay, whom I rang in LA in the hope of inside information, immediately said, 'Sure, Martin Casey.'

'You've heard of him?'

I'd Googled the name and found out that it belonged to the proprietor-chef of a gastropub, the Hungry Dog, in Clerkenwell, which was round the corner from Rachel's office (and where, I surmised, they'd met). But I had not been able to get a clear picture of his standing.

'The guy specialises in boiled potatoes and turnips and beetroots,' Vinay told me. 'Old English vegetable ingredients. Very interesting.' He said pompously, 'I'd classify him as a cook, not a chef.'

No doubt, I thought, he was also an expert in reviving Anglo-Saxon erotic traditions. A sensualist who embodied a classic yet contemporary approach to carnal pleasure.

I told Vinay the score.

'Oh, fuck that,' he said.

'Yeah,' I said.

'Jesus. Martin Casey.'

'Yep,' I said, feeling brave.

Vinay, excited, said, 'The dude's short. He's a fucking dwarf, Hans. You're going to blow him out of the fucking water.'

It was good of Vinay to say this, but Vinay, in spite of his own six feet, had a terrible record with women and was, I knew for a fact, a bonehead about anything he couldn't eat or drink. Moreover there was nothing dwarfish about the Casey I'd uncovered online, a healthily tubby, attractive man in his forties with ruffled black hair and, in one photograph, a crew of fantastically good- and talented-looking sous-chefs who stood ranged behind him like merry pirates.

I told Chuck I couldn't make it. 'I've got stuff to take care of,' I said.

'OK,' he said with a surprising readiness.

The following Sunday morning, at eleven o'clock, the house phone rang. It was you-know-who, calling up from the lobby.

'I told you, I can't do this,' I said. 'I've got a plane to catch.'

'What time?'

'Five,' I said reluctantly.

'No problem. I've cancelled the mowing – too wet. I've got a special programme. You'll be home by two, at the latest.'

'Listen, Chuck, I don't want to,' I said.

'I'm parked outside,' he said. 'Get down here.'

This time Chuck drove. It was a fine day. The East River from the Brooklyn Bridge was a pure stroke of blue.

I thought of my mother, whom I thought of whenever I crossed that bridge.

Two weeks after Jake was born, she made her first and last visit to America. It had taken a number of carefully suggestive calls on my part to persuade her to make the trip, which loomed, as it did for many of her generation, as a voyage of terrific proportions. From the moment she arrived, she seemed downcast and preoccupied in a way that struck me as uncharacteristic, although I could not be sure, since I had not seen my mother in three years. To divert her, I proposed a bicycle ride; and once mounted on a rented bicycle she rode strongly enough, certainly for a woman of sixty-six. We rode to Brooklyn. We admired the brownstones of Brooklyn Heights ('If I lived here, this is where I would live,' said my mother), and after eating a bagel with smoked salmon ('So this is the famous bagel') we set off on the return journey. It was a cloudy morning in late September. A slight wind was in our faces as we crept up the incline of Brooklyn Bridge. A third of the way across, we stopped. We stood next to each other, bicycles at our side, and somewhat formally observed the sights. A mist had thickened over New York Bay. I explained to my mother that the island directly ahead was Governors Island, and that beyond it, lost in silver murk, was Staten Island. My mother asked about the docking facilities that were just visible in the distance, and I identified New Jersey for her.

My mother said, 'And there you have the . . .' Annoyed, she searched for the name. 'The Statue of Liberty,' I said. 'We can go there, if you like.' My mother nodded. 'Yes,' she said. 'We must do that.' After a moment or two, she said, 'Let's go on,' and we climbed back on our bicycles and continued up the bridge. We went forward side by side. My mother pushed the pedals steadily. She was tall and big and white-haired. Her skin wore a raw, slightly meaty flush. She was dressed in that combination of dark blue raincoat and college scarf and leather loafers that is, in my mind, the immemorial uniform of the bourgeoises of The Hague. Beyond the crest of the bridge we started the downhill glide into Manhattan. From the deck beneath us came the rhythmic chuckling of car tyres. At the foot of the bridge, by City Hall, we entered the traffic; my mother followed me cautiously, a sweat of concentration gathering on her face. On Broadway she abruptly pulled over and stepped off her ride, and when I asked her if she was all right, she merely nodded her head and walked on, pushing her bicycle alongside her. This was exactly how she'd accompanied me when, as a fourteen-

year-old, I delivered the *NRC Handelsblad* in the Boom-
and Bloemenbuurt – the Tree and Flower District. On
my first day on the job, she escorted me through the
opening section of my round, going with me to
Aronskelkweg, Arabislaan and Margrietstraat until she
was satisfied that I knew what I was doing. The challenge
was to not get lost: I carried a piece of paper on which
were sequentially set out the addresses of the drops, the
sequence prescribing a route that, if transcribed onto a
map, would resemble one of those densely marked puzzle
mazes that pencilling small children produce. Mama led
the way. 'I'm going back now,' she said after an hour. 'Can
you finish on your own?' I could, although it must be
said that I was an unsystematic paperboy who generated
many complaints. My overseer, a semi-retiree who took
great pleasure in handing over my weekly envelope of
cash, was forced to take me aside and explain that these
complaints – *klachten* – were no joke and that I had to
take my work seriously. 'Have you ever read the newspaper?' he asked me. I gave no answer. 'You should. You'd
learn a lot, and you'd understand why people get upset
if they don't receive it.' On Saturdays, when sports
commitments prevented me from working, my mother
substituted for me. She would cycle down to the newspaper depot, load up the heavy black saddlebag, and set
off. I took this for granted, of course. My assumption was
that it was the job of parents to do such things and that

my mother was secretly overjoyed to fill in for me, even though this could require her to wander in the rain and cold for over two hours and certainly to humbly accept a lower station in life.

It was in the course of the paper round that she met her gentleman friend Jeroen. 'I was very curious,' Jeroen told me at the reception he hosted after the cremation. 'Who was this woman who delivered the paper every Saturday? It was so mysterious. Don't forget, she wasn't much older than you are now. And so beautiful: tall, blonde, athletic. Always well dressed. My type of woman. But coming to my door with the newspaper? This was intriguing.' We were in Jeroen's flat in Waldeck, on the fifth floor of the notoriously long apartment block known to all as the Wall of China. It was just us two; everybody else had gone home. He unsteadily poured another shot of jenever. 'After a few weeks of watching her come and go, I decide to make my move.' Jeroen lit a cigarette. 'You don't mind me telling you this, do you?'

'No,' I said, although naturally enough I was hoping he would skip certain details.

'So here's what I do,' Jeroen said, a wide yellow-and-brown smile in his cadaverous face. Within three months he, too, would be dead. 'I dress in my best clothes. Sports jacket, shirt, tie. I polish my best shoes. I put a goddamned handkerchief in my breast pocket. Then I wait. At four o'clock, I hear the garden gate open. It's Miriam. Just as she comes to the door, I open it. "Thank you," I say. She just smiles and goes back to her bicycle. I run after her and open the gate. I'm on my way out, you see, that's my story. I don't want her to think I'm ambushing her. I introduce myself. "And your name is . . . ?" Miriam van den Broek, she says, getting on her bicycle. And then she rides off.' Jeroen laughed and adjusted his spectacles. 'Perfect, I thought. She's reserved but friendly. Like you,' he said, pointing his cigarette at me. 'You see, with reserved people, it's simple: you have to be direct. So the next week, I'm waiting for her again. I've had a haircut. I've brushed my teeth. Here she comes, up the garden path. I open the door and accept the newspaper. "Would you like to go for dinner?" I say. I'm not messing around, you see. I'm too old for that, and I'm guessing she is, too. This is what I've learned on the subject of women: never delay. The more quickly you act, the greater the chance of success. She smiles and walks back to her bicycle. Then she stands there, like this, like a schoolgirl.' Jeroen sprang up and stood upright, his blue, frozen-looking hands gripping invisible handlebars. '"Why not?" she says. Why not. I'll never forget it.' A convulsion of coughing overtook him, and he lowered himself into a chair. 'The rest you know,' he said, exhausted. Which I didn't, in point of fact. I had very little idea about what passed between them. I didn't know, for example, why five years later he and my mother had put an end to things.

She had regained enough energy, on our return to Tribeca, to ask immediately if she might take the baby for a walk.

'Are you sure?' Rachel said.

'We'll just go around the block,' my mother said. 'Come, Jake,' she said, lifting the baby into the stroller.

After an hour or so they had not returned. This was worrying. Rachel said that I should go out and look for them.

I found my mother a couple of blocks away, looking distressed.

'What happened?'

'I got lost,' she said. 'I don't know how.'

'All these buildings look the same,' I said, and I accepted her arm in mine and pushed the stroller home.

Now Chuck was driving us through Brooklyn. I heard myself tell him, 'My wife is seeing another guy.'

He showed no surprise, even though it was the first time I'd raised directly the subject of my marriage. After a moment, he said, 'What do you want to do about it?'

'What can I do?' I said hopelessly.

He gave his head a categorical shake. 'Not *can* do: first figure out what you *want* to do. It's project management 101: establish objectives, then establish means of achieving objectives.' He glanced at me. 'Do you want her back?'

I said, 'Let's say I do.'

'OK,' he said. 'Then you should go back to London. Right away. It's a no-brainer.'

I thought, No-brainer? What would happen in London? A seduction with flowers? A ravishment? Then what?

'Otherwise,' Chuck, growing emphatic, said, 'you're in danger of having regrets. My bottom line is, no regrets.'

This was on Atlantic Avenue, by Cobble Hill, in traffic.

'It wouldn't be the same,' I said.

'It's never the same,' Chuck said. 'Even if everything goes well it's never the same. Right?' He tapped my knee. 'Let me tell you something: these things have a funny way of working out. You know the best thing that happened to me and Anne? Eliza.'

I wanted to talk about my situation, not Chuck's. I also wanted something other than the usual from him.

He concentrated on overtaking a bus. Chuck was a speedy, dodgy driver. 'Anne and me,' he continued, 'we've known each other since we were babies. She's been with me through thick and thin. When we were living in Brownsville with Mike Tyson beating up people on the streets, she didn't complain once. So we're together for life. But my theory is, I need two women.' He wore the most solemn expression. 'One to take care of family and home, one to make me feel alive. It's too much to ask one woman to do both.'

'That's very big of you,' I said.

He gave a snort of amusement. 'Listen, what can I tell

you? After a certain point, their agenda changes. It's all about kids and housekeeping and what have you. With Anne, it's that damn church. We're the romantic sex, you know,' he said, fighting a burp. 'Men. We're interested in passion, glory. Women,' Chuck declared with a finger in the air, 'are responsible for the survival of the world; men are responsible for its glories.' He turned the Cadillac south, onto Fifth Avenue.

We drove through Park Slope. A plotter's grin formed on his face. We took a sharp turn, passed under a huge pair of arches, and halted at a prospect of grass and tombstones.

He had brought me to Green-Wood Cemetery.

'Look up there,' Chuck said, opening his door.

He was pointing back at the entrance gate, a mass of flying buttresses and spires and quatrefoils and pointed arches that looked as if it might have been removed in the dead of night from one of Cologne Cathedral's more obscure nooks. In and around the tallest of the trio of spires were birds' nests. They were messy, elaborately twiggy affairs. One nest was situated above the clock, another higher up, above the discoloured green bell that tolled, presumably, at funerals. The branches littered a stone facade crowded with sculptures of angels and incidents from the gospels: a resurrected Jesus Christ prompted Roman soldiers to cover their faces with their hands. Come forth, a second Jesus exhorted Lazarus.

'Parakeet nests,' Chuck said.

I looked more carefully.

'They come out in the evening,' Chuck assured me. 'You see them walking around here, pecking for food.' As we waited for a parrot to show, he told me about the other birds – American woodcocks and Chinese geese and turkey vultures and grey catbirds and boat-tailed grackles – that he and his buddies had sighted among the sepulchres of Green-Wood during his birding days.

I was half listening, at best. It had turned into a freakishly transparent morning free of clouds or natural inconsonance of any sort. Huge trees grew nearby, and their leaves intercepted the sunlight very precisely, so that the shadows of the leaves seemed vital and creaturely as they stirred on the ground – an inkling of some supernature, to a sensibility open to such things.

There still was no sign of parrots. Chuck said, 'This is by the by. There's something else I want to show you.'

We followed a roaming lane through a spread of hills and lawns: evidently directness is undesirable in a graveyard. 'This is like a Hall of Fame for retailers,' Chuck said. 'There are Tiffanys here. You have the Brooks brothers. You have Steinway. Mr Pfizer. Mr F.A.O. Schwarz. Wesson, the rifle guy, is out here.' The Cadillac was now travelling in what seemed like circles. A gravedigger wandered by with a shovel.

'OK,' Chuck said, stopping. He opened the glove

compartment and pulled out a camera. 'Right here. I think this is it.'

I followed him off the path. Walking over burned grass we went past an obelisk, past an angel guarding a plot with outspread wings, past the graves of ex-individuals named Felimi, Ritzheimer, Peterson, Pyatt, Beckmann, Kloodt, Hazzell. We stopped at an angular column several feet high and topped by a globe – an oversized baseball, judging from its meandering seam. The column bore an inscription:

In Memoriam Henry Chadwick
Father of Baseball

'Do you know about Chadwick?' Chuck said. 'He wrote the first Rules of Baseball.' Chadwick, Chuck said with that explanatory fluency of his, was the English immigrant and Brooklyn man who as a cricket reporter for the *Times* inaugurated baseball coverage in that newspaper and went on to popularise and modernise the sport of baseball. 'What's interesting about this guy,' Chuck said, wiping a handkerchief across his mouth, 'is he was a cricket nut, too. He didn't think it was America's fate, or America's national character, or what have you, to play baseball. He played cricket *and* baseball. They were totally compatible as far as he was concerned. He didn't see them as a fork in the road. He was like Yogi Berra,'

Chuck said not at all humorously. 'When he came to a fork in the road, he took it.'

I'd heard the Yogi Berra line a million times before. My attention was given over to the small square stone in the grass – a maverick slab of crazy paving, one might have thought – on which Chuck had carelessly placed a foot. It was a gravestone. A word was engraved on it:

DAISY

Chuck handed me his camera and stood next to Chadwick's tomb with hands clasped behind his back. I took the picture – took several, at his insistence – and returned the camera to him. 'Very good,' Chuck said, studying the picture viewer. He would post the images on his forthcoming website, newyorkcc.com, and, he said, deploy them in the slide show he was preparing for his great presentation to the National Park Service.

He started to say something on this subject when his second phone rang. He took the call beyond my earshot, dangling a flip-flop from one foot. When he snapped shut his phone, he said, 'So here's my thinking, Hans.' His hands were in the pockets of his shorts and he was looking at Chadwick's grave. 'I'm thinking a cricket club might not be big enough. To get the attention of the NPS, I mean. It might seem exclusive; small-time. People might feel it has nothing to do with them.' He quickly said, as if I might interrupt him, 'But they'd be wrong. And that's what I've got to make them see. This isn't just a sports club. It's bigger than that. My own feeling – and listen to me on this before you say anything, Hans, this is something I've been thinking about a lot – my own feeling is that the US is not complete, the US has not fulfilled its destiny, it's not fully civilised, until it has embraced the game of cricket.' He turned to face me. 'Do you know the story of the Trobriand islanders?'

'Of course,' I said. 'It's all people talk about.'

'Trobriand Island is part of Papua New Guinea,' Chuck said professorially. 'When the British missionaries arrived there, the native tribes were constantly fighting and killing each other – had been for thousands of years. So what did the missionaries do? They taught them cricket. They took these Stone Age guys and gave them cricket bats and cricket balls and taught them a game with rules and umpires. You ask people to agree to complicated rules and regulations? That's like a crash course in democracy. Plus – and this is key – the game forced them to share a field for days with their enemies, forced them to provide hospitality and places to sleep. Hans, that kind of close-ness changes the way you think about somebody. No other sport makes this happen.'

'What are you saying?' I said. 'Americans are savages?'

'No,' Chuck said. 'I'm saying that people, all people, Americans, whoever, are at their most civilised when they're playing cricket. What's the first thing that happens when Pakistan and India make peace? They play a cricket match. Cricket is instructive, Hans. It has a moral angle. I really believe this. Everybody who plays the game benefits from it. So I say, why not Americans?' He was almost grim with conviction. In a confidential tone, he said, 'Americans cannot really see the world. They think they can, but they can't. I don't need to tell you that. Look at the problems we're having. It's a mess, and it's going to get worse. I say, we want to have something in common with Hindus and Muslims? Chuck Ramkissoon is going to make it happen. With the New York Cricket Club, we could start a whole new chapter in US history. Why not? Why not say so if it's true? Why hold back? I'm going to open our eyes. And that's what I have to tell the Park Service. I have to. If I tell them I'm going to build a playground for minorities, they're going to blow me away. But if I tell them we're starting something big, tell them we're bringing back an ancient national sport, with new leagues, new franchises, new horizons . . .' He faltered. 'Anyhow, that's what I'm doing here, Hans. That's why I'm ready to do what it takes to make this happen.'

I didn't immediately dwell on his final statement. I was too taken aback by the Napoleonic excess of the peroration, the dramatisation as much as the content of which had disturbed me: the man had set up a graveside address, for God's sake. He had premeditated the moment, rehearsed it in his mind, and seen fit to act it out. It was flattering, in a way, that he'd gone to such trouble; but he'd lost me, and I felt I had to speak up. I had to warn him.

I said, 'Chuck, get real. People don't operate on that level. They're going to find it very hard to respond to that kind of thinking.'

'We'll see,' he said, laughing and looking at his watch. 'I believe they will.'

Let's remember I was in a bad mood. I said, 'There's a difference between grandiosity and thinking big.'

I might as well have punched him on the nose, because for the only time in our acquaintance he looked at me with hurt surprise. He began to say something and decided against it.

I could see what had happened. I had knocked him off his pedestal. I had called into question his exercise of the New Yorker's ultimate privilege: of holding yourself out in a way that, back home, would be taken as a misrepresentation.

I said, 'That came out wrong. I meant to say . . .'

He waved me down good-naturedly. 'I understand exactly. No problem.' He was smiling, of that I'm sure. 'We'd better go. It's getting hot out here.'

We left the cemetery. My strong inclination was to catch a train back to Manhattan, but Chuck drove directly onto the BQE and said something about running late and having to see quickly to a business matter. It's clear to me, now, that he'd already decided on the form of his retribution.

After twenty minutes we came to a stop somewhere in Williamsburg.

'This shouldn't take long,' Chuck said. He went briskly into the nearest building.

I waited in the car. After ten minutes, Chuck had not returned. I stepped outside and looked about me in that state of prepossession almost any unfamiliar New York place was capable of bringing about in me, even a place like this section of Metropolitan Avenue, where trucks gasped and groaned past commercial buildings of no note. Chuck had entered one of these, a two-storey effort in brick with a signboard proclaiming the presence of the FOCUS LANGUAGE SCHOOL. The school, which seemed closed or dormant, was situated above an open warehouse. Inside the warehouse, a solitary Chinese man sat on a pile of pallets and smoked a cigarette as he contemplated cardboard boxes marked HANDLE WITH CHUTION. I passed a quarter of an hour on the roaring sidewalk. Still no Chuck. A pair of Coke-drinking cops walked by. The Chinese man rolled down the warehouse door, exposing a blaze of graffiti. I decided to buy a bottle of water in the deli across the street.

I was coming out of the deli when Abelsky, in Judaic white shirt and black trousers, waddled by. To be accurate:

I saw a baseball bat first, carried in a man's hand. Only then was I moved to recognise Abelsky. He went to the language-school building and pressed the doorbell. The door opened, and Abelsky went in.

I drank from my water bottle and waited. It's true to say, I had an uneasy feeling. After another ten minutes, I telephoned Chuck.

'Is this going to take much longer?'

He said, 'No, we're pretty much done here. Why don't I buzz you in? We're having coffee.'

I walked up a staircase covered by a new grey carpet. There was a landing that led into a tiny hallway lined with bulletin boards and posters. I remember a photograph of grinning students bunched together with their thumbs up, and a classic snap of downtown Manhattan with the legend, for the benefit of the passing Martian, NEW YORK.

Abelsky's voice came from a room at the rear of the building – DIRECTOR, the sign on the door stated. Abelsky was standing to one side of the room, pouring himself a cup of coffee from a coffee beaker. He'd shrunk further since the time I'd met him at the baths, and the effect was to make him even more shapeless.

Chuck was sitting behind the desk, rocking on a leather chair. He raised a hand in greeting.

The office, a windowless box, was more or less destroyed. A filing cabinet had been upended and its contents were strewn everywhere. A framed map of the

United States lay on the floor, its glass in pieces. Somebody had smashed a potted plant against the photocopying machine.

'You got NutraSweet?' Abelsky yelled out to no one that I could see. 'I gotta have NutraSweet.'

Chuck said, 'Hans, you remember Mike.'

Abelsky remarked, 'Would you believe this mess? Look at it.'

A toilet flushed, and moments later the flusher, a man in his thirties, came in. He had splashed water on his face, but there were traces of soil around his ears and in his hair, which was of the pale, almost colourless, Russian variety. His blue shirt was filthy.

'You got NutraSweet?' Abelsky repeated.

The man said nothing.

Abelsky took a mouthful of coffee then spat it back into the cup. 'Without NutraSweet, it tastes like shit,' he said. He put the coffee down on the leather desktop. 'That OK there? I don't wanna make a ring.'

The man wiped a hand across his mouth.

Abelsky said fussily, 'You're the director here. You should respect your office, make an example.'

The baseball bat was resting against a wall. It was stained with dirt.

'Jesus Christ,' I said. I walked out and walked down the street for all of fifty yards, at which point I realised I didn't have the strength to continue.

Thus, on that cool and beautiful August day, I crossed the street and sat down in the green light of a phantasmal little park at the junction of Metropolitan and Orient. The shadows in this little park were just like the shadows I'd been seeing all day, otherworldly in their clearness. A very old, very small man, sitting like a gnome in the green light, regarded me from a nearby bench. A furious bird screeched in the trees.

I slapped at my ankle. A red smudge took the place of a mosquito.

The furious bird screeched again. The sound came from a different place. Maybe there were two birds, I thought stupidly, two birds answering each other with these screeches.

Now the meaning of what I'd seen – Chuck and Abelsky had terrorised some unfortunate, smashed up his office, shoved his face in the dirt of a flowerpot, threatened him with worse for all I knew – arrived as a pure nauseant. I almost threw up then and there, at the feet of the gnome. I dropped my head between my knees, sucking in air. It took an effort of will to get up and go onward to a subway stop. Violence produces reactions of this kind, apparently.

Back at the hotel, I took a shower, packed a bag and got into a car to La Guardia. I woke up in a hotel room in Scottsdale, Arizona.

My work, that morning, went passably – I was a panellist in a conference discussion with the could-mean-anything title 'Oil Consumption: The Shifting Paradigm' – and, better still, finished well ahead of schedule. But when three hedge fund guys from Milwaukee discovered I had a few hours to kill before going home, they insisted to my stupefaction that we all drive out to a nearby casino and hit the tables and maybe even get a little fucked up.

'Great idea,' I said, and somebody slapped me on the back.

And so I went into a cactus-filled desert with three bald-headed buddies who each wore a complimentary conference baseball cap. On our way out we passed through downtown Phoenix. It was seemingly an uninhabited place given over to multilevel garages that, with their stacked lateral voids, almost duplicated the office blocks and their bands of tinted glass. The general vacancy was relieved by the slow and for some reason distinctly sinister movement of automobiles from street to street, as if these machines' careful, orderly roaming was a charade whose purpose was to obscure the fact that the city had been forsaken; and all the while the radio ceaselessly reported crashes and emergencies in the streets around us. It was one of those occasions on which the disunion between one's interior and external states reaches almost absolute proportions, and even as I smiled and nodded and knocked my can of Bud Light against another's, I had fallen into the most horrible misery. I escaped into sleep.

'Lunchtime,' a voice announced.

We had pulled over onto dirt. Nearby, two white-haired Indian women tended a barbecue pit beneath an awning that raggedly extended from a breezeblock hut. ('What are these guys? Apaches? I bet you they're Apaches,' the fellow next to me said.) One of my hosts, Schulz, presented me with a Diet Coke and two slices of bread filled with chunks of fatty meat. 'They're calling it mutton,' Schulz said.

The eatery abutted a ridge. On the far side of the ridge lay a flat sea of dust and rock. In the sky above it, a single cavaliering cloud trailed a tattered blue cloak of rain. Highlands showed in the extreme distance. Closer by, black heaps of volcanic rock protruded from the reddish waste. A ubiquitous grey-blue scrub gave everything a pixellated finish, as if this land were a vast malfunctioning television. 'The Wild West,' Schulz said thoughtfully as he wandered off to absorb the view from atop a nearby boulder. I saw that each of my other *compañeros* had likewise assumed a solitary station on the ridge, so that the four of us stood in a row and squinted into the desert like existentialist gunslingers. It was undoubtedly a moment of reckoning, a rare and altogether golden opportunity for a Milwaukeean or Hollander of conscience to consider certain awesome drifts of history and geology and philosophy, and I'm sure I wasn't the only one to feel lessened by the immensity of the undertaking and by the poverty of the associations one brought to bear on the instant, which in my case included recollections, for the first time in years, of Lucky Luke, the cartoon-strip cowboy who often rode amongst buttes and drew a pistol faster than his own shadow. It briefly entranced me, that remembered seminal image, on the back cover of all the Lucky Luke books, of the yellow-shirted, white-hatted cowboy plugging a hole in the belly of his dark counterpart. To gun down one's shadow . . . The exploit struck me, chewing mutton under the sun, as possessing a tantalising metaphysical significance; and it isn't an overstatement, I believe, to say that this train of thought, though of course inconclusive and soon reduced to nothing more than nostalgia for the adventure books of my childhood, offered me sanctuary: for where else, outside of reverie's holy space, was I to find it?

We went back to the air-conditioned car, and soon afterwards the casino appeared ahead of us in clear light. It assumed the form, as we drew nearer, of a gigantic adobe-like structure vaguely evocative of the great edifices of native civilisations. The interior of this spurious pueblo, accessible only via a series of ramps helpful to gamblers in wheelchairs, was given over to a trashy iconography of ice cream, coronets and slot-machine personalities: the Frog Prince, Austin Powers, Wild Thing, Evel Knievel, Sphinx and others, entities whose baroque electronic vigour served only to accentuate the limpness and solitude of the figures expressionlessly tending to them. While each of my friends ventured forth with hundreds of dollars in chips, I accepted a drink from a waitress and sat at a table in that specifically bloodless clamour of piped music and quarters jingling down chutes and bleeping and burping machines of chance. For the sake of appearances I summoned the will to approach a roulette table.

I stood with the onlookers and followed the play for a few spins of the wheel. I began wishing luck on a friendly-looking moustachioed man in a Hawaiian shirt. He was losing; and whom should I recognise in this man's expression but Jeroen, who wore exactly the same hopeful, slightly perspiring face as he slid chips onto the baize of the roulette table and watched the leaping ball fasten to a niche in the wheel: there it coasted, in giddy circles, until the number slowed into terminal focus. Likewise here, where the croupier, a tiny bow-tied woman, coolly raked the scattered hopes of the gamblers into a single horrible hillock. Jeroen, in the days when he was in the picture, would drop by on St Nicholas' Day with a cash gift for me, gaily coloured guilder bills that no longer circulate, and after the holiday dinner he would always ask me, a young teenager, to accompany him to the casino at the Kurhaus in Scheveningen. He made no bones about his need, as he put it, to play; nor did he hide his desperation for company of any sort. So I would head out with him in his cigarette-strewn Peugeot 504, where he would offer up anecdotes about his early childhood in Java. Jeroen seemed always to lose. *Pech*, he'd say as we stepped out into Scheveningen's salty air hundreds of guilders poorer – rotten luck. He'd light a Marlboro and give a rich, glamorous cough. In those days Jeroen had sought out my company. Now I sought out his.

I think it's customary, in the kind of narrative to which this segment of my life appears to lend itself, to invoke the proverb of rock bottom – the profundity of woe, the depth of shit, from which the sufferer can go nowhere but to higher, more sweetly scented places. In terms of objective calamities, of course, The Adversity of Hans van den Broek, as such a tale might be called, amounts to not very much. But it's also true that the casino floor felt to me like an ocean bottom. In my blackness I wasn't to know that I lay only, and exactly, one fathom below the surface, one fathom, I've heard it said, being the reach of a pair of outstretched arms.

Then and there, amongst the blushing slots, I underwent a swerve in orientation – as though I'd been affected by the abrupt consensus of movement that redirects flocking birds. I decided to move back to London.

At our very first meeting, Juliet Schwarz turned to Rachel and asked if she loved me and, if yes, what it was about me that she loved. Objection! I felt like shouting to this rotten, risky, terrifying interrogation.

'"Love",' Rachel desperately replied, 'is such an omnibus word.'

Here was an irony of our continental separation (undertaken, remember, in the hope of clarification): it had made things less clear than ever. By and large, we separators succeeded only in separating our feelings from any meaning we could give them. That was my experience, if you want to talk about experience. I had no way of knowing if what I felt, brooding in New York City, was love's abstract or love's miserable leftover. The idea of love was itself separated from meaning. Love? Rachel had got it right. Love was an omnibus thronged by a rabble.

And yet we again climbed aboard, she and I.

What happened – what set us on the road to Dr Schwarz and, by means of said bus, the place we are now – was that she and Jake suddenly moved out of Martin Casey's Farringdon loft, where they'd lived only four months.

This was November 2004. I'd been back in England for exactly a year – had, as a matter of fact, just rented a place in the Angel so as to be within strolling distance of my son.

'You've left him?' I said.

'I'd rather not talk about it,' Rachel said.

A few days later, she called me again. Martin would not be joining her and Jake on their Christmas trip to India; accordingly there was a vacancy, accordingly Rachel wondered if I could fill in. There was no question of cancelling the holiday. Jake had already packed his bag and notified Father Christmas of his Indian whereabouts by postcard to the North Pole. 'I can't disappoint him,' Rachel said.

I bought a ticket within the hour.

We flew to Colombo and thence, as travellers used to say, to the Keralan city of Trivandrum, which on a map can be found almost at the very tip of India. I was worried about Jake catching a strange Indian disease; however, once we were established in a simple family hotel colonised by darting caramel lizards and surrounded by coconut trees filled, incongruously to my mind, with crows, I was quite content. This was at a seaside place. There was a lot to look at. Women wrapped in bright lengths of cloth walked up and down the beach balancing bunched red bananas on their heads and offering coconuts and mangoes and papayas. Tug-of-war teams of fishermen tugged fishing nets onto the beach. Tourists from northern parts of India ambled along the margin of the sea. Foreigners lounged on sunbeds, magnanimously ignoring the sand-coloured dogs dozing beneath them. Lifeguards, tiny slender men in blue shirts and blue shorts, attentively inspected the Arabian Sea and from time to time blew on whistles and waved swimmers away from dangerous waters; and indeed on one occasion an Italian yoga instructor, a long-limbed male, became stuck in a web of currents and had to be rescued by a lifeguard who skimmed over the water like an insect flying to the rescue of a spider.

And there was Rachel to look at – in particular, Rachel's back, which I'd forgotten was spotted with unusually large, lovely freckles, as if she were part Dalmatian. Most afternoons we re-located by motor rickshaw to the swimming pool of a luxury hotel, and as we zipped through the coconut groves that covered the entire coastal region and gave one the false impression of a jungle, I'd peek over at my wife, think about offering a rupee for her thoughts, and think again. Very often during those rickshaw rides her eyes would be closed. She slept indiscriminately: on the beach, by the pool, in her room. It seemed as if she were trying to sleep her way through the holiday – even through Christmas morning, with Jake tearing open the gifts Father Christmas had left for him on my balcony. On somebody's recommendation, I went with my son to a nearby fishing village for a Church of India Christmas service. The church, by far the proudest building in the locality, sat on the top of a hill. It had a tall creamy tower and a cave-like interior painted in pinks and blues. Other than the floor, there was nowhere to sit. From time to time a crow flapped in to join the congregation, perched on a ceiling beam, and flapped out again. All proceedings were spoken in Malayalam, a chattering language filled with buzzing and drilling sounds – until, at the conclusion of the service, the children's choir suddenly struck up a rendition of 'Jingle Bells' and the words 'snow' and 'sleigh' flew up into the heat.

I wanted to tell Rachel all about it; but when we returned, at noon, she was still in bed.

Occasionally she was communicative. The poverty troubled her, she said – as did her perception that I, by contrast, was not at all troubled. When I haggled, pro forma, with a lungi salesman, she broke in, 'Oh, for God's sake, just pay him what he's asking for.' It was I who had to deal with the fruit hawkers, because Rachel could not bear to look into their mouths, abounding in rotted black teeth, or their eyes, abounding in unthinkable need. She half apologised one evening. 'I'm sorry. I just find it oppressive being an *economy*. The nanny' – we'd hired an English-speaking Assamese woman to babysit Jake for a few hours every morning – 'the drivers, the waiters, the deck-chair boys, all these people selling stuff on the beach . . . I mean, every stupid spending decision we make has a huge impact on their lives.' We were sharing a nightcap bottle of Kingfisher on the balcony of her hotel room. Jake was asleep in my room. Before us, at eye level, were palm fronds. Between the fronds, on the sky-black sea, fishing boats lined up dozens of lights. Rachel swallowed directly from the huge bottle. 'You don't seem at all bothered,' she said. 'You're just happy splashing in the water.'

That much was true. I was very taken by the waves,

which had a sweet, sickening taste and were ideal for body-surfing, an activity I'd never even known existed: you waited in waist-deep water for the large benign breaker that might carry you, coasting on your torso, all the way to frothing shallows. It's fair to say that I became a little obsessed. At lunch, invariably taken on the second floor of a restaurant overlooking the water, I'd interrupt Rachel's reading in order to say, Look, that's a great wave there.

Rachel said, funnily, 'You're becoming something of a wave bore, did you know that?'

One afternoon I approached the sea and saw that seaweed was washing ashore, and also that the sand was littered with triangles of purple matter which I took a moment to identify as fish. I walked on, into the sea. All kinds of things were floating in the water – coconut shells, a comb, a rotting flip-flop. A storm had done this. Seeing a white plastic bag ahead of me, I resolved to pick it up and throw it out onto the beach. It was not a plastic bag. It was a dog – a sizeable puppy, turning to pulp, drifting with its four legs dangling plumb. I withdrew to the land.

The next day, women wearing glum municipal jackets over their saris swept up the sand and disposed of the storm trash. The sea cleared up. When I re-entered the water in the afternoon, Rachel, as tiny and pale and skinny as I've seen her, came with me. 'All right,' she said, frowning and smiling at once, 'show me how it's done.'

'There's nothing to it,' I said. Along came a slightly

menacing wave, perfect for surfing. 'Here we go,' I said. 'You just push . . .'

I raised my arms, put my head down, and caught the wave. I surfaced twenty yards away, exhilarated.

Rachel hadn't moved. Rejoining her, I said, 'You'll catch the next one.'

'I think I'll swim for a while,' she said, and she floated away from me on her back and closed her eyes. She slept even in the ocean.

On the first day of 2005, I set off with the boy to the mountains. The driver of our mock Jeep took us through rice fields and thereafter, climbing up, up, up, successively through shadowy forests of rubber trees, and tea farms, and spice gardens. Jake sat between me and the driver, thrilled and talkative at first but eventually falling into silence and carsickness. The journey was slow, bumpy. It was evening by the time we'd checked into an old colonial hunting lodge.

That night, as my son slept amongst his new toys – these toys peopled his somnolent mutterings, as did dinosaurs and monkeys – I sat on the veranda and thought about his mother. 'No messages,' the hotel manager had volunteered before our departure earlier in the day. 'Messages?' I said, puzzled. Laughing, he replied, 'Your wife is always asking if I have received a message for her.' 'Have we?' 'Not yet,' the manager said. 'But if it comes, I will let you know immediately.'

In this way I received confirmation of my suspicion, which was that Martin had jilted Rachel.

I'd met him only once, on a damnably sunny day six months earlier. The encounter was a trap, because – and this had been my only sticking point in our parental cooperation – I'd refused to have any contact with him. Without prior consultation (Rachel said, 'You'd only have got yourself into a tizzy'), I found myself attending a barbecue held in the back garden of Grandma and Grandpa Bolton. While I skulked around, desperately prolonging my interactions with food and drink and pressing Charles Bolton for his views on the new rugby season, my rival made himself at home at the grill, making only the most modest, self-effacing, family-friendly fare. Jake appointed himself his sidekick and, wearing an apron that came down to his feet, waited for the word to turn a sausage. The gift I'd brought – one of the most prestigiously obscure, hard-to-find members of the Thomas the Tank Engine clan – lay unattended on the patio. I was conscious for the first time of a cuckold's prickling pair of horns.

As for Rachel, she was smiling, diplomatic, evasive, and always finding some reason to go indoors. She wore a long white skirt that blazed with roses. My impulse – albeit one secondary to the impulse to pick up the grilling contraption and throw it through the kitchen window – was to corner her, point out that this was torture, demand some consideration, and protest generally. But I had no confidence in my standing. I was an ex and bound, although I scarcely believed it, by the rules governing the conduct of exes.

My father-in-law went on indistinctly about rugby. 'Yes, I see,' I told him. What I was actually seeing was Martin's appeal for my wife. He was a doer. He didn't stand still. He ran around making things happen.

Very carefully holding a cup of water in two hands, my son inched up to his hero and poured the water over the coals.

'This is rather good,' Charles said cheerfully, placing his last spare rib on his plate. He moved away.

I sat down on the grass with, I counted, my fifth glass of the Hungry Dog's best Grüner Veltliner. Just as I'd decided to lie on my back and impersonate a dad grabbing forty deserved winks, Martin joined me.

He gave me a sheepish blokey smile and pulled a tuft of grass out of the lawn.

He said, 'Bit awkward, this.'

I didn't reply. We must have sat there for a full minute without a word passing between us. Jake ran over and leaped on Martin's back and began pawing at him.

'Don't tickle me, you little so-and-so,' Martin said, seizing him and pinning him down.

'Come play, come play,' Jake shouted.

'In a minute, I'm just talking to your dad, all right?

In a minute, Jake.' To me he said, 'I've got one of my own.'

I'd heard this already: a fifteen-year-old daughter by the first Mrs Casey. Rachel, if he married her, would be wife number three. This was my chink of light. I couldn't picture Rachel as a third wife.

'She's a good girl,' Martin said. 'I've got her working at the Dog.' He said clumsily, 'Business is good.'

Oh yeah? I wanted to say. Get back to me when you're grossing ten thousand dollars per working day, asshole.

'We're thinking of opening a place in your old neck of the woods,' Martin said. 'New York, I mean.'

'You should think about Flatbush,' I said. 'In Brooklyn. It's the hot neighbourhood. East Flatbush,' I added viciously.

'East Flatbush?'

'Very funny, Hans,' Rachel said.

The great moment had arrived. My wife had joined us in her flowery skirt. She lowered herself into a non-aligned space. It was quite the fête champêtre as the three of us sat together.

'Try the carrots,' Rachel said. I hadn't touched the food on my plate. 'They're very good.'

I didn't want to make trouble, but neither did I want to eat. 'Fuck the carrots,' I said.

The predictable silence followed. Martin rose to his feet. 'I'd better start cleaning up my mess,' he said.

Rachel and I watched him leave. 'Thanks for that,' Rachel said.

I said, 'This is my weekend with Jake. I'll spend it how I choose. This is the last time you do this.'

My wife got up and brushed cuttings of grass from her skirt. 'You're right,' she said, and she went over to Martin and kissed him on the cheek.

The kiss was an attempt, very possibly altruistic and certainly characteristic, to deal in truth.

Once, in the forthrightness of our earliest, most robust moments, she'd sought to belittle an old boyfriend by describing him as an 'expert'.

'What do you mean, "expert"?'

'Oh, you know, one of those men who prides himself on getting any woman to come like a porn star.'

'And did he?' I was scandalised.

She gave no reply, and I heard myself insisting.

Rachel said, 'Well, yes, but . . .'

'So I'm not an expert?'

We were in bed, as was practically obligatory at that time. She propped her head on her hand as she gave my question her consideration.

'No,' she said, looking me straight in the eye. 'But you're better. More passionate.'

She had decided that I could handle the truth, or that I *should* handle it. I did, just about. And though I cannot say it made me stronger, I have the comfort of knowing, with the benefit of hard-won hindsight, that something is going right if I am a little nervous as to what my wife may say next.

However, on my Indian mountaintop, stirring a gin and tonic and pondering like Menelaus and King Arthur and Karenin my errant heartbroken wife, a stupider and far less generous thought came to me: What goes around, comes around.

A monkey appeared. He was a grey-green, white-bellied, fluffy little fellow with a centre parting and a frankly displeased expression. He crouched on the paling of the veranda for a few seconds, stared at me with his furious red face, and rolled away like an old tennis ball into the darkened grounds.

The truth, since we were on the topic, my imaginary interlocutory wife and I, was that the Hans van den Broek drinking gin in the Western Ghats was not the same man as the New York Hans van den Broek. On an autumn morning a few months previously, I'd woken up with a whistle at my lips and a sense that I was . . . fine. The stock advice of the columnists in the women's magazines had been vindicated: time had healed my wounds. A gloss: time spent in London, my matter-of-fact city. A notable consequence was that I began to see other women. (With little ado a couple of dates were consummated: there was an actress and there was a personnel manager, both met in wine bars, both cheerful and game, and both, incredibly, makers of the statement, 'Well, that was jolly.') Another consequence, since we found ourselves in the realm of stock situations, was that I conceived of myself no longer as the idiomatic man who stands between the rock and the hard place but as the more happily placed idiomatic man who can take it or leave it: it, here, being my marriage.

Rachel and I hardly exchanged a word for the rest of the holiday.

After the holiday, one Sunday afternoon in February, I dropped Jake off at his grandparents' house. I was about to set off when his mother ran out to ask for a lift: her car was at the mechanic's and she needed to drop by at her office.

It had been a very long time since we'd been truly alone with each other: a month back, in India, there had been Jake or, in shadow form, the jilter. Rachel wore a blue coat and a blue scarf and blue jeans, a new combination. The situation was so thick with novelty that it felt natural to ask her straight out about Martin.

'He's fucking someone else,' Rachel said.

'Good,' I said. 'That means I can fuck you.'

She seemed to be searching for something in her coat pocket. 'OK,' she said.

We went to my flat. The arrangement repeated itself, about once a week, for two months. We fucked with the minimum of variety and history: our old bag of tricks belonged to those other lovers and those other bodies. I didn't kiss Rachel's mouth and she didn't kiss mine; but she smelled me, smelled my arms and hair and armpits. 'I've always liked your smell,' she stated in all neutrality. We hardly spoke, which worked in my favour. She remarked about Martin, 'He'd say things that were actually stupid. It almost made me puke.' There was a thoughtful silence, and then our first shared burst of laughter in years.

It wasn't long afterwards that we kissed. Rachel murmured mid-kiss, 'We should see a marriage counsellor.'

Six months later we bought a house in Highbury. Chastened by the price – 'Astronomical,' the estate agent admitted – I took it upon myself to wallpaper Jake's room and two guest rooms. I became an expert wallpaperer and as a consequence something of a ponderer: few activities, I discovered, are more conducive to reflection than the unscrolling and measuring of a length of wallpaper, the cutting of it and the painting of glue on it, and the gluing of the cut paper to a wall so as to produce a pattern. Of course, I also found myself patterning the events that had led to the mysterious and marvellous business of my putting up wallpaper while Rachel's voice sounded through a house that was ours.

It was not the case that I'd heroically bowled her over (my hope) or that she'd tragically decided to settle for a reliable man (my fear). She had stayed married to me, she stated in the presence of Juliet Schwarz, because she felt a responsibility to see me through life, and the responsibility felt like a happy one.

Juliet turned her head. 'Hans?'

I couldn't speak. My wife's words had overwhelmed me. She had put into words – indeed into reality – exactly how I felt.

'Yes,' I said. 'Same here.'

Though not exactly the same, I thought, stepping down from my stepladder and squinting at my handiwork. Rachel saw our reunion as a continuation. I felt differently: that she and I had gone our separate ways and subsequently had fallen for third parties to whom, fortuitously, we were already married.

Jake and I spent the second day of our Indian expedition at a nature reserve. There was a boat safari on a lake, and from the boat we saw elephants and deer and wild pigs. Best of all, there were monkeys everywhere; Jake was a monkey fanatic and believed he could speak the language of monkeys. There was also the wonderful knowledge that the hills around us held tigers. The next morning we left well before sunrise. There wasn't much going on, at this dark hour, aside from dogs skittering across the road. In the village, street lights shone and my son's head on my lap was a waxing and waning moon; but presently all wayside illumination came to an end.

The car and its dazzling forerunner went onward through the mountain forest. There, at the edge of the beam, I saw movement.

Men were walking by the side of the road. They were on their way to work. They walked not in groups but alone, in a broken single file. They were almost unnoticeable, and when they were noticeable it was only for an instant. Some of these men wore a shirt, some did not. Most wore a lungi arranged like a skirt. They were small and thin and poor and dark-skinned, with thin arms and thin legs. They were men walking in the forest and the darkness.

For some reason, I keep on seeing these men. I do not think of Chuck as one of them, even though, with his very dark skin, he could have been one of them. I think of Chuck as the Chuck I saw. But whenever I see these men I always end up seeing Chuck.

Marinello is the name of the ice-cream shop, or *ijssalon*, in The Hague where, after a shopping eternity at the Maison de Bonneterie, my mother would sweeten me with two scoops of chocolate ice cream. Marinello is also the name of the NYPD detective who telephones me about Chuck Ramkissoon. I've been trying to speak to him for a month. It's the end of April. I heard from the *Times* reporter in late March.

My first reaction, on this earlier occasion, is to fly to

New York for the funeral. But the telephone directories don't have a phone number for Anne Ramkissoon; only Abelsky's listed.

'When he disappears,' Abelsky says right off the bat, 'a guy says to me, Maybe he killed himself. I said, You idiot! Chuck isn't a suicide guy! This guy has more life inside him than ten people! Then they find him in the river with his hands tied up. I tell this schmuck, I tell him, You see? I was right.' Abelsky wheezily inhales. 'They never said what he died for.'

'I'm sorry?'

'What was the reason for death?' Abelsky asks scientifically. 'Drowning? Or was he killed before?'

I don't have an answer. Abelsky continues, 'When I get the news, I'm like a statue. He was a great employee. Full of ideas. Although I should have fired his ass a hundred times. I'm paying his salary and he sets up an office in the city? With no one else I would have allowed this! Nobody! Only Chuck!' Very reasonably he says, 'But we adapted already. You gotta adapt, to stay in business. You gotta move with the times.'

Abelsky, who tells me he doesn't know about the funeral, gives me Anne Ramkissoon's phone number.

'What's happening to her share of the business?' I ask.

There is a pause. 'The lawyers are investigating all of this. She will get what she is entitled, of course.'

'Yes, she will,' I say.

'Otherwise what?' Abelsky replies immediately. 'Otherwise what? What gave you the right to talk?'

I laugh at him, this shrunken businessman.

He says in a wounded voice, 'You think I killed him? You think I killed Chuck? What the hell!' he shouts. 'Because I'm a Russian, I kill him? Because I yell at the guy? Always we were fighting! From the beginning, when he told me how to sell kosher fish to the Jews. What a guy!' There is more coughing and wheezing. Abelsky doesn't sound good. 'Nobody knew Chuck then,' he says, all tender emotion now. 'He was a nobody. A nothing. But I saw something in this guy. He was a great guy, a terrific guy. If I find out the fuck who gone and did this, I'm going to kill him with my hands. That's a promise I make to his wife.' This calms him, apparently, because he says, 'I don't know what you know about Chuck. But if you know like I know, you wouldn't talk to me like this. But that's OK,' he says, releasing me from culpability. 'You only know what you know.'

I know that I last saw Chuck on Thanksgiving Day 2003. I'd rung him a few days before and told him, out of correctness more than anything else, that I was about to fly to England for good.

'Let's get together for the holiday,' Chuck said. 'We'll mark your departure.'

It was agreed. I imagined a lunch in Flatbush, with Anne serving up the turkey and my host lecturing us on the significance of the day of national gratitude. What in fact happened was that I received a call from Eliza. She said I was to meet her and Chuck at his office on 27th Street, whereupon we'd walk the few blocks to Herald Square and catch the tail end of the Macy's parade. The rest of the agenda, of Chuck's devising, remained undisclosed. When I responded to this last item with silence, Eliza said, 'Yeah, me too.'

Thanksgiving Day in New York, that year, was clear and windy. I walked through Chelsea's streets with an exodist's attentiveness. For the last time I took in the benign monumentalism of Seventh Avenue, and for the first time I noticed a row of small golden trees at the corner of Seventh and 25th Street.

On Fifth Avenue, Eliza was waiting for me outside the office building. 'He's saying meet him at Herald Square,' she said. 'I mean, can you think of anything crazier?'

It was a good question. Herald Square – or, rather, 32nd Street, where barriers and squad cars blocked further progress – was a scene of near-chaos. Spectators were massed on and around the ledges and windows of the skyscrapers, and on the street a great crowd, held back by cops and barricades, pushed and strained to see what was going on in the square. In this regard, I had no problem; I had the advantage of height. The parade seemed to have come to a halt. Ronald McDonald, thirty feet long, yellow-gloved, red-shoed, red-mouthed, red-haired, hovered and hovered over Herald Square, his right arm stuck in a terrible wave. Human Ronald McDonalds teemed beneath, holding the balloon ropes and gesturing and smiling at the multitudes. Immediately behind Old McDonald, as Jake used to call him, was a pink float on which princesses frantically gesticulated at us, and farther up, on Broadway, other airborne monsters could be made out – poor Charlie Brown poised to kick a football, and Chicken Little, and a giant foetus-like character, red-skulled and forward-leaning, who meant nothing to me. From behind a building, a marching band's trumpets and drums carried over to us in a splintered din.

'We're never going to find him,' Eliza wailed. 'Where is he?'

The parade at last lurched onward. Ronald McDonald turned the corner and flew into the gap of 34th Street.

I tapped Eliza's arm. 'Straight ahead,' I said.

Chuck was on the far side of 33rd Street, on the east side of the square, where a few members of the public had been allowed to gather. He was watching the parade. We pushed towards him. 'Hey!' Eliza shouted. 'We're over here!' Chuck turned to her voice and broke into a grin. 'Hey!' he shouted back faintly. 'I'm coming.'

We watched him approach a police officer and point in our direction. The officer shook her head. Chuck persisted, and we gave thumbs-ups to confirm his story. Still the police officer refused to let him cross. 'Get going,' a cop on our side of the street said. 'You got to keep moving. You too, ma'am.'

'We're just trying to hook up with that guy over there,' I explained.

'What guy?' the cop said.

'That guy, there. See? With the briefcase.' I was pointing.

'I don't see nobody with a briefcase,' the cop said, not even looking. 'You want to go north, you go up Ninth Avenue. East is all blocked.'

I phoned Chuck. 'The cop says we have to go up Ninth. But there's no way you'll be able to cross Broadway.'

'Don't worry about it,' Chuck said, giving me a salute. 'I'll figure it out. I'll see you at Ninth and 34th. Give me twenty minutes.'

So we headed west. At Seventh Avenue, in front of Penn Station, we ran into another crush of people. Evidently this was the parade's final stop. Bandsmen with huge drums wandered round, as did a pack of elves. I said sorry to a mermaid for stepping on her tail. Ronald McDonald was back, his giant rump tilted upwards as he was lowered for deflation. Eliza and I instinctively drew closer to the spectacle. It was sharply breezy now, and the midget Ronald McDonalds holding the vertical ropes worked hard to steady the balloon. We were on the point of walking on when there was a loud collect- ive gasp. I turned round just in time to see Ronald McDonald veering away and crashing into the barriers.

There were screams. A man in a doughnut costume was knocked over and at least two women fell as they tried to get out of the way. Ronald McDonald drew back. Then he again came forward enormously, head first, turning in the draught so that his rigid beckoning arm swung round in a slow haymaker that scattered a mesmerised shoal of bystanders and ultimately connected with a fellow trying to film the debacle with a cellphone. That man fell to the ground, as did the police officer next to him who was trying to apprehend the fantastic yolk-yellow mitt with his bare hands, this last fall provoking a ducking young officer to draw his gun and point it at the amok Ronald McDonald, which led to a fresh burst of screams and panicky running and mass diving onto the asphalt and Eliza grabbing my arm.

The gust of air subsided; Ronald McDonald's handlers reined him in.

Eliza said, 'Did that really happen?'

We laughed most of the way to Ninth Avenue.

Chuck was not to be found at the agreed place. Eliza asked me, 'So, did you like my albums?' I did, I told her. She'd done a good job. The story of my son, as she put it, was now gathered in a single leather-bound volume inscribed with his initials.

Eliza flexed a bicep triumphantly. 'What did I tell you?'

'You've got the knack,' I agreed. I didn't tell her that while her work gave me joy – who can resist images of

311

one's laughing child? – it also documented my son's never-ending, never truly acceptable self-cancellations. In the space of a few pages his winter self was crossed out by his summer self which in turn was crossed out by his next self. Told thus, the story of my son is one that begins continuously, until it stops. Is this really the only possible pagination of a life?

Chuck was late, then very late. We called him repeatedly, with no answer.

'OK, now I'm worried,' Eliza said. We'd been waiting almost an hour.

'He just got screwed up by the crowds,' I said, kissing Eliza goodbye. 'His phone battery probably died.'

That was Thursday. On Saturday, I called Chuck again; I still hadn't heard from him. 'Hey, it's me,' I asserted to the voicemail. 'I'm on the plane, just getting ready for take-off. Where are you? What the hell happened to you? Anyhow, take care. Bye.'

The aircraft went into reverse; taxied; rumbled innocently out of New York's clear sky.

It's not quite true to say that Chuck out of sight was Chuck out of mind. I did think about him. I concluded that his Thanksgiving no-show was merely the newest manifestation of his whimsicality and didn't hold it against him, just as I didn't hold it against him, or me, that in the end all I got out of him was an e-mail:

312

Good luck with everything! Sorry about
Thanksgiving. I got held up. Speak soon.

Chuck

We never spoke. Every once in a while, in the grip of affectionate curiosity, I'd search the Web for a mention of Chuck Ramkissoon. I found none – which told me that his cricket project was going nowhere. A pity, but there it was. There were other things to think about.

Then I'm told that his body has been found in the Gowanus Canal and that it was put there very soon after I left New York.

Immediately after talking to Abelsky, I ring Anne Ramkissoon's number. Another woman answers and it's a while before Anne comes to the phone. I am looking at St Paul's Cathedral. The afternoon is another dull one, with white clouds mottled by smaller grey clouds.

Anne accepts my condolences. 'Do you need any help with anything?' I say. 'Anything you need.'

'It all taken care of,' she says. 'I ready for this. The bishop taking care of everything.'

'And the funeral? I'd like to be there.'

She says squarely, 'My husband body going back to Trinidad. He going to rest with his people.'

I feel under an obligation to speak up. 'But Anne,' I say, 'you heard him. He wanted to be cremated, in Brooklyn.

I was there when he said it, remember? I was his witness.'

'You his witness?' Anne says. 'Everybody his witness. Everybody witness Chuck. I his wife. I waited for him for two years. Nobody else waiting; not you, not the police. I waiting.'

It has not occurred to me until this moment to think carefully about what it might mean to be the widow Ramkissoon.

'They bring my husband out of the Gowanus Canal,' she goes on. 'Who put him there? Not me. His witness put him there. Now I lost him,' she says. 'I have to live with this. You go back and live your life. What I do? Where I go?'

'I'm so sorry, Anne,' I say.

Do I need to declare to her, to all whom it may concern, that I am distraught? That, although I may not have missed him for two years, I now miss Chuck terribly? Do I declare that I loved Chuck? Is this what is required?

Or perhaps I should more concretely declare that, having spoken to Anne, I leave the office early, at three thirty, and walk all the way home, uphill and in light rain, and that in Highbury Fields I stand for twenty minutes in my raincoat, thinking about whether I should fly to Trinidad for the burial. That when I arrive home I touch Jake on the head and tell Paola, our nanny, that I'm going to my bedroom and should be left in peace. Perhaps I should declare that I call the New York Police

Department and am put through to a Detective Marinello who promises to call me back but doesn't. That when Rachel comes home from work she senses immediately that something is up, and that at nine o'clock we sit down together with a glass of wine. Perhaps I should declare that we proceed to talk about Chuck Ramkissoon and that thoughts of Chuck come to me at all hours in the months thereafter. What is the declaration that is in order here?

It doesn't take long to tell Rachel about the good times: how Chuck and I met in remarkable circumstances, how we stayed in touch, how we came to collaborate in heat and grass and fantasy. To all of this she listens quietly. It's when I tell her about the day of the parrots, as I mentally label the worst day, that she interrupts me.

'Go over that one more time,' she says, examining the shadow in the wine bottle and dispensing one half of the shadow into each of our glasses. 'Tell me exactly what you saw.'

My wife is a lawyer, I remember. 'I don't know what I saw,' I say. 'I just saw that this guy had been roughed up. And his office as well.'

'Why?'

I give her a blink. 'I don't know. They were into something. They had a real-estate business, so maybe . . .' I say, 'Chuck liked to diversify. He liked to get into all kinds of things. Things that were not necessarily . . .' As best and briefly as I can, I explain the weh-weh and, as I see it, my unwitting role in it.

Rachel can't quite believe what she hears. She purses her lips and leans on an elbow. 'It doesn't look very good, does it?' she decides to say. 'You drive him around while he runs his numbers game? What were you thinking?' She says, 'Darling, this man was a gangster. No wonder he ended up the way he did.'

Now on top of everything else I'm anxious as hell and running a hand through my hair, and my wife leans over to take this hand and hold it between hers. 'Oh, Hans, you silly goose,' she says. 'It'll be all right.' But she also says that she's calling a New York attorney first thing tomorrow. (Which she does. The attorney opines that as a practical matter I have nothing to fear and charges us two thousand dollars.)

When I go on with my account, Rachel interrupts me once again. She seems aghast. 'You continued to see him? After what happened?'

I recognise the accusation on the tip of her tongue: that I have a temperamental disposition to pardon that simplifies things for me and is certainly a symptom of moral laziness or some other important character weakness. And she'd be right, in general, because I'm a man to whom an apology of almost any kind is acceptable.

'Just hear me out,' I say.

In October – two months after what I'd thought had

been my last dealings with Chuck – my electronic diary gave me a week's notice of the personal day I'd set aside, back in the summer, for a driving test in Peekskill, a town upstate (the farther away from Red Hook the better, I reasoned). I confirmed the date. Why try out for an American driver's licence just before you're leaving the country? This is Rachel's question, too, and there's no answer I can give her.

I travelled in a rented car up the Saw Mill and Taconic parkways. My preparatory examination of the road map had turned up such place names as Yonkers, Cortlandt, Verplanck and, of course, Peekskill; and set against these Dutch places, in my mind, were the likes of Mohegan, Chappaqua, Ossining, Mohansic, for as I drove north through thickly wooded hills I superimposed on the landscape regressive images of Netherlanders and Indians, images arising not from mature historical reflection but from a child's irresponsibly cinematic sense of things, leading me to picture a bonneted girl in an ankle-length dress waiting in a log cabin for Sinterklaas, and redskins pushing through ferns, and little graveyards filled with Dutch names, and wolves and deer and bears in the forest, and skaters on a natural rink, and slaves singing in Dutch. Then out of nowhere came the loud blast of a horn – I'd swerved halfway into the next lane – and this dreaming came to a sudden end as I steered back and gave my attention to tarmac and automobiles and the real-time journey on which I found myself.

My arrival at Peekskill came, as planned, an hour before the appointed time. I familiarised myself with the streets and practised parking. The town was built on steep hills by the Hudson, and it soon became clear that the principal hazard facing drivers was that of sliding down towards the river – indeed, it was my impression that the fundamental challenge facing the whole community was to resist the immense gravitational force drawing all of its constituents, organic and inorganic, towards the watery abyss that constantly came into view. This struggle appeared to have taken a toll on the townspeople, who hung out in front of unaccountably run-down dwellings and wandered through barren shopping precincts with the lassitude of a population in shock. There seemed to be an abnormal concentration of impoverished black residents and a bizarre absence of the satisfied middle-class whites I associated with outposts of the City, as New York is called by people living in such places, and all in all I was put in mind of a town in East Anglia I'd once visited with my wife: arriving there at night, I was taken aback, in the light of morning, by a scene of exclusively white people, all colour and shape drained from their faces, shuffling here and there with an ill-omened, idiotic slowness, so that it seemed to me a species of zombie had established itself in that place. This inexcusable dread did not escape Rachel, who quietly said, after I had passed some comment, 'There's nothing wrong with these people.'

My driving examiner on this occasion was a polite old white guy who asked me in a bizarrely defeated voice if I had foreign driving experience, and I told him that, yes, I had. He beckoned the car forward, made me turn a corner, and asked me to park. I did so clumsily, anxious not to violate the ridiculous rule whereby the slightest contact between tyre and kerb results in automatic failure.

'Not great,' I suggested.

'Yeah, well,' the old guy said. 'I always used to tell my students, take a bogey on the parking. Never screw around with the out-of-bounds.' He directed me back to the starting point, and only after I'd come to a stop did I realise that he was intent on giving me my licence.

'Thank you,' I said, a little overcome.

'Drive safely,' he said, and got out of the car.

I was examining my temporary New York licence when there was a rap on the window. It was Chuck Ramkissoon.

I watched with astonishment as he opened the door and sat beside me. He removed his India cricket cap – sky blue streaked with the saffron, white and green tricolour – and paused for effect. 'What?' he said. 'You think I'd miss my student's moment of glory?'

Chuck, who'd agreed back in August to supply his car for the test, was not one to forget a date; and a call to my office had told him all he needed to know.

'I took the train,' he said. 'You're going to have to drive me back.'

What was I supposed to do? Throw him out?

'Yes,' Rachel says. 'That's exactly what you should have done.'

Nothing was said as Chuck and I got under way. Then, hard by the river at the outskirts of Peekskill, there appeared two immense semi-spherical roofs escorted by a thin, strikingly tall chimney: from our angle, two mosques and a minaret.

'Indian Point,' Chuck said.

It felt good to swing away into the countryside. Chuck turned off his phone. He said, 'You know, I never finished telling you the story of my brother.' He was looking into the hollow of his cap. 'My mother was destroyed by my brother's death,' Chuck said. 'She was inconsolable for months. Literally. Nothing my father could say would make things better. One day they had a terrible argument. My father, who had taken some rum, got so angry he ran out into the yard and came back with a chicken in one hand and a cutlass in another. Right there, in front of all of us, he chopped the head off the chicken. Then he threw the chicken head at my mother. "Go," he said. "Take that with you."'

Was I hearing this? Was he really telling me one of his stories?

Chuck reached for the handkerchief in his back pocket and mopped his mouth. 'The fight,' he said, 'was because my mother wanted to take part in a Baptist ceremony for my brother. You know who the Baptists are? You know about Shango?' Self-answering as usual, he said, 'The Baptist church is this Trinidad brew of Christian and African traditions – you'll see them in Brooklyn on a Sunday, wearing white and ringing bells and trumpeting the spirit. They believe spirits take possession of you. Sometimes one of them will catch the power on the street, shaking and trembling and falling to the ground and speaking in tongues. It's a spectacle,' Chuck said, holding out his arms and wobbling his hands. 'The other thing people associate with Baptists is sacrificing chickens. So you can see why my father did what he did. He was angry my mother was falling for this black people's voodoo.'

'You owe me an apology,' I said. 'An apology and an explanation. I don't want to listen to this.'

Chuck put up assenting hands and said, 'There's a place that the Shango Baptists like to go, called the Maracas Waterfall.' Running east–west across Trinidad, he explained, are the mountains of the Northern Range. In those mountains are remote and wild valleys, and one of these, the Maracas Valley, is the site of the famous Maracas Waterfall. Chuck said, 'It's quite something: the stream flows to the edge of the mountainside and drops three hundred feet. If you go there, you'll see the flags and chicken-heads left by Shango Baptists. It's pretty spooky if you don't understand what it all means.'

Leaning back in his seat, he told me that the waterfall may be reached only by walking for a few miles along a trail through one of the last virgin forests in Trinidad. It is in this highland forest that you may hear, and if you are lucky even see, he said, one of the most wonderful songbirds of Trinidad, the violaceous euphonia, known to everybody on the island as the semp. The male semp is a golden-yellow bird of four inches or so, and for as long as anybody can remember, according to Chuck, the children of Trinidad have trapped and caged it on account of its beautiful call, a practice that has resulted in the species now being close to extinction. Chuck said that it shamed him to admit that a large part of his own boyhood had been spent trying to capture songbirds, usually the seedeaters and finches that were then common in the grassy plains around Las Lomas. 'There are many ways to catch birds,' Chuck said. 'My own method, with the semp, was to use a caged semp as a lure. I fixed a stick to the cage and spread a gum, laglee, we call it, on the stick.' The semp, attracted by the song of its fellow creature, would land on the stick and become stuck in the gum for a few seconds. 'This was my window of opportunity: I'd jump out from my hiding place and grab the bird before it could fly away.'

Chuck, squinting in the sunlight, put his cap back on his head. It was a bright day. Autumnal colours were firing in the woods.

322

One day, he told me, he travelled to the Maracas Valley to catch a semp. He was thirteen or fourteen. He was slightly familiar with the area, having previously accompanied his father on a hunting trip there. It was a weekday. Young Chuck – or Raj, as he was called – walked in solitude up the path to the waterfall. On both sides of the path grew the immense trees of the forest. About a mile or so into the forest, he came upon a spot that suited his purpose. He deposited the caged semp on the edge of the path and crouched behind a tree at the side of the road. From down below, in the valley, came the sound of water running and falling on rocks.

After a short while, the semp began to sing. Chuck sat still, waiting.

It was about then that he noticed something unusual: a small dirt track, going into the forest, clumsily covered by branches. Chuck followed the track. It led to a tree. Stowed by the tree were farming implements and materials – rakes, hoes, fertiliser, a cutlass. Chuck noticed something else: seedlings in a cup. He knew straight away what this meant. A friend had only recently shown him: you put the marijuana seeds in a cup, and they germinated.

At exactly that moment, Chuck heard voices coming up the trail, the voices of men. It came to him immediately that these were the marijuana growers. The voices grew louder, and then he saw them through the trees, coming up the main path – two black men, one with long dreadlocks, the other an East Indian with sunglasses covering his eyes. 'The fear I felt at that moment,' Chuck said, 'is something I'll never forget. Never. It felt like a kick in the chest. Those sunglasses were terrifying. They were black, black – the kind Aristotle Onassis used to wear.' He shook his head. 'I knew I was in danger,' he said. 'These men are ruthless. They wouldn't hesitate to chop me. Some men can kill so easily. I knew the semp would alert them. A semp in a cage, left out in the open like that? Everybody knows what that means. So I began to run – down the mountain, toward the sound of water. It was the only way to go. I heard shouting behind me, this noise of branches and bushes. They were coming after me.'

The moment you stepped inside the forest, according to Chuck, you were under a thick, almost unbroken canopy. Where a tree had fallen down, the sunlight came through; everywhere else was dark. 'So you have these brilliant columns of sunlight in between the trees. That's where you'll find undergrowth. Otherwise the ground is almost bare. People think of virgin forests as jungles, but they're nothing like that, not these mountain forests. I could run freely; I had to grab on to saplings to slow me down, stop me from falling down the hill.'

Chuck stirred. 'God, I nearly forgot: the snakes. This forest is the domain of the mapepire snakes – pit vipers.

There are two kinds, the z'ananna and the balsain. There is an antidote for balsain venom, but the z'ananna, the bushmaster, fifteen feet long with diamond markings on its back – boy, if one of them bites you, it's certain death. They're night animals, but it's easy to disturb them. So while I was terrified about the men running after me – who I couldn't hear, by the way, I just sensed them – I was also terrified about snakes. My God, when I think back . . .' Again, Chuck shook his head. 'I remember the sound of the stream getting louder. I come down to a dry ravine, a gully. I jump across the ravine and climb up the bank, holding on to roots to pull myself up. Now I'm heading down again, straight for the stream. It's a clear stream, very rocky. I don't have to worry about snakes any more. I don't hesitate: I go downstream. I have no choice – upstream are these huge rocks, and straight ahead is a sheer escarpment, then more snakes. But the terrible thing was, I couldn't see where I was going. Fronds, thick heliconia fronds, hung over the stream, and I had to fight through them. I had a horrible feeling those men knew of some short cut – you know, I'd push aside the fronds and they'd be waiting for me. Anyway, I just kept going down the streambed, walking through these cataracts, trying not to slip on rocks. Then – and here's where it really gets like a movie – the stream dropped twenty feet into a pool. I tried to edge down the side of the waterfall, but it was no good. No way down. Then I heard voices, not far away, not far away at all. "Dread! Dread! He down there!"'

Chuck paused. 'Let me ask you this: have you ever run for your life? I don't mean what happened at that cricket match, although that was pretty dangerous. I mean, a real do-or-die situation?'

I didn't humour him with an answer. But we didn't have too many do-or-die situations in The Hague.

In a wondering voice, he said, 'What I think about now, when I look back, Hans, is how, when you're running for your life, you have this strong sense of luck. You don't feel lucky, that's not what I mean. What I mean is, you feel luck, good and bad, everywhere. The air is luck. Do you understand what I'm saying? I tell you, it's a horrible feeling.'

He paused, frowning. 'Anyhow, I decided to jump. We're talking twenty feet, into water that may or may not be deep. It was a real situation, because I couldn't swim – I still can't. And let me tell you, I can barely walk up a staircase without getting vertigo. But somehow, I forced myself to jump. Lord, the fear I felt as I dropped . . .' Chuck shivered heavily. 'I was lucky. The pool was deep enough to break my fall, but shallow enough for me to splash out. I banged my knee, but I could walk. I struggled onto the rocks and kept going. I was exhausted, finished. But I pushed myself on, trying to breathe, trying to forget about the pain in my knee. What I can't understand, now,' Chuck said, 'is my pursuers. I was running for my life – but these men? So much determination, just to catch a boy? Why, Hans? I wasn't any threat to them. I was just this small kid with a semp . . . All I can think is, it has something to do with hunting. The hunt triggers some deep instinct within us. These men were hunters, for sure.

'So on I went,' Chuck continued. 'Walking and stumbling. About twenty minutes later, I started to see cocoa trees. I thought about leaving the stream, but my fear of snakes returned, because a cocoa plantation is a favourite habitat of the bushmaster. I ran along the edge of the water, sometimes in the water, sometimes on land. Then I came to a place where huge tree trunks had fallen across the stream. I climbed over one and finally sat down to catch my breath. I was broken, I tell you. There was no sign of the men. But I couldn't be sure they were gone, because the fronds blocked the view. Then, I'll never forget this, a blue morpho, a blue emperor butterfly, came flying through the sunlight.' He turned to face me. 'Are you – what's the word – a lepidopterist?'

I almost smiled.

'I love that word. Lepidopterist. Well, anyhow, I head off again. I come to this faded old trail. Did the men know about this trail? Were they ahead of me, waiting? It didn't matter any more. I was too tired to care. I followed the trail up this steep embankment, steep like this' – he made an angle with his forearm – 'and found myself in an abandoned tonka-bean estate. You know tonka beans? The seed was used for perfume, snuff. Nowadays, they've got synthetic products, so the old plantations are returning to forest. Same thing with cocoa. That business stopped because of the snakes. People were no longer prepared to gamble with death. Anyhow, I come to the top of the tonka-bean hill. Down below are the houses of Naranjos, this mountain village. The people there are farmers and planters, a mixture of black and Spanish, almost red-skinned. Some have deeds going back to the Spanish time. They have Spanish names – Fernandez, Acevedo. And the village itself, Naranjos, is named after the orange trees they planted between the cocoa trees. I'm calling this place a village, but we're really talking about farmland with a house here and there, you follow me?' Chuck drew breath. 'It was still a full hour's walk to the actual centre of the village. So I limp along for an hour, and at last, at long last, I come to a rum shop. I tell you, I've never been so happy to see a rum shop in all my life. I stay right there, next to a bunch of guys shit-talking and drinking puncheon. Guys that make you feel safe. You know what,' Chuck said, leaning forward and slapping the dashboard, 'I still remember what they were talking about. Let me see, they were talking about a man who rode on his bike from Sangre Grande to San Juan with a pet snake wrapped round his neck – a boa constrictor. Dumb idea. The snake started to choke him and he fell off his bike, totally blue. Lucky for him somebody came by and pulled the snake off.' Chuck gave a soft merry gasp. 'Then I rode down to the shore in the back of a pickup truck carrying a load of coffee. And that was it. End of story.' He laughed. 'Or beginning of story.'

The car advanced us ever closer to New York.

Chuck said pleasantly, 'I've never spoken to anyone about that before.'

It wasn't my sense that he was misleading me. 'Why not?' I said.

He rubbed his jaw. 'Who knows,' Chuck said, suddenly looking tired.

Very little was said during the rest of that journey to New York City. Chuck never apologised or explained. It's probable that he felt his presence in the car amounted to an apology and his story to an explanation – or, at the very least, that he'd privileged me with an opportunity to reflect on the stuff of his soul. I didn't take him up on this. I wasn't interested in drawing a line from his childhood to the sense of authorisation that permitted him, as an American, to do what I had seen him do. He was expecting *me* to make the moral adjustment – and here was an adjustment I really couldn't make. I dropped him off at a subway stop in Manhattan. We had no further contact until the day I rang him and told him that I was leaving. It was only to make life easy for myself that I then agreed to meet him on Thanksgiving.

'I find it incredible,' Rachel comments, 'he travelled all that way to see you.'

'That was just like him,' I say.

'He must have valued you,' she says.

Between us we have drunk a bottle of claret, and what Rachel has just said makes me happy. Until she adds, 'I mean you were valuable to him. He wasn't interested in you.' She says, 'Not really. Not in *you*.'

By way of reply I stand up and clear the table. I am too tired to explain that I don't agree – to say that, however much of a disappointment Chuck may have been at the end, there were many earlier moments when this was not the case and that I see no good reason why his best self-manifestations should not be the basis of one's final judgement. We all disappoint, eventually.

In the following days and weeks I phone Detective Marinello repeatedly because I have, so I think, relevant information about Chuck Ramkissoon. Unbelievably, it takes him a whole month to get back to me. Marinello takes down my personal details – address, phone numbers, employment. At last, infuriatingly, he asks, 'So, you have some information pertaining to Mr Ramkissoon?'

He leads me through my statement. I tell him everything I know, even facts that are potentially troublesome for me, and over the course of an hour Marinello carefully records every word I say. This makes it all the more surprising that he immediately signs off, with no follow-up questioning, 'Thank you, sir, that's great.'

'That's it?'

Marinello sighs. Then, maybe because I'm in England and beyond the jurisdiction, or because he's made me wait a month, or because cops do this from time to time to make life easier for the good guys, he tells me something 'off the record': they know who did this. 'We just don't got the courtroom evidence,' Marinello says.

'Evidence?' I say blankly.

'Witnesses,' Marinello says. 'We got no witnesses.'

For the second time I say, 'That's it?'

'That's it,' Marinello says. He sounds satisfied. He feels he has taught somebody a lesson in realities.

Whether or not this is true, I feel I must persist. At the weekend, I ring Anne Ramkissoon again: this is when I find out the Ramkissoon home number is no longer operative. I dig out an old diary and with it Eliza's home number. A man with a Hispanic accent answers her phone. Eliza is out, he tells me. 'This is her husband. Can I help?'

So that he doesn't get any wrong ideas, I tell the guy exactly who I am. Either he's wary or not especially interested, because he barely reacts. 'I'll call another time,' I tell him.

I don't, however. I leave it there. Sure, I have my theories – Abelsky is an unlikely killer of Chuck, I tentatively conclude – but Marinello's indifference to me suggests that I have no personal connection at all to the relevant facts. Chuck Ramkissoon was involved in things categorically beyond my knowledge of him.

A month passes, and then another. Then, in July, there is an unforeseen development. I read somewhere that Faruk Patel, the millionaire guru whom Chuck claimed as a backer, is in town on a speaking tour. I decide to call Faruk's publicist and ask for a meeting. 'Tell him it's about Chuck Ramkissoon,' I tell the publicist.

Within an hour – this takes me aback – she calls with an appointment.

Faruk is quartered in a suite at the Ritz. An assistant escorts me into his presence. He is wearing, as the Faruk brand requires, a white tracksuit, white T-shirt and white sneakers. He democratically joins me on a large white sofa and tells me that I'm lucky to catch him since he comes to London infrequently and is very busy when he does.

'Tell me,' he continues, leaning back and waggling a foot, 'what exactly was your relationship to Ramkissoon?'

'He was a personal friend,' I say. I sketch my role as assistant groundsman. 'I had nothing to do with his business.'

Faruk seems amused. 'He told me you were a director

332

of his company. Then he told me you were a non-executive director. Then he told me you were involved, but only informally, and that you would show yourself once we got permission to build.'

I laugh. 'Well, it's possible I might have,' I said. 'Who knows?'

Faruk also laughs. 'He was an intriguing chap. That's why I became involved in the first place. My advisers told me not to touch it. But I wanted to know what this funny fellow would do next. One never knew. I captained my university team, you know,' he suddenly boasts. 'Sometimes I think I should have been a professional cricketer.'

Somebody pours us tea. I say, 'Do you think it would have worked?'

'The New York Cricket Club,' Faruk says, raising his eyebrows, 'was a splendid idea – a gymkhana in New York. We had a chance there. But would the big project have worked? No. There's a limit to what Americans understand. The limit is cricket.'

When, out of loyalty to Chuck, I say nothing, Faruk says emphatically, 'Look, he wanted to take the game to the Americans. He wanted to expand the operation, get them watching it, playing it. Start a whole cricketing revolution.'

'Yes, I know.'

Faruk says, 'My idea was different. My idea was, you

don't need America. Why would you? You have the TV, internet markets in India, in England. These days that's plenty. America? Not relevant. You put the stadium there and you're done. Finito la musica.' He drinks up his tea.

We rise to our feet. 'It's a tragedy,' Faruk Patel solemnly says, putting his hand on my shoulder: we are brothers in sorrow. 'Ramkissoon was a rare bird.'

That night, I cannot fall asleep. I get out of bed, go down to the kitchen, help myself to a glass of mineral water. The family laptop is on the kitchen table. I switch it on.

I go to Google Maps. It is preset to a satellite image of Europe. I rocket westward, over the dark blue ocean, to America. There is Long Island. In plummeting I overshoot and for the first time in years find myself in Manhattan. It is, necessarily, a bright, clear day. The trees are in leaf. There are cars immobilised all over the streets. Nothing seems to be going on.

I veer away into Brooklyn, over houses, parks, grave-yards, and halt at olive-green coastal water. I track the shore. Gravesend and Gerritsen slide by, and there is Floyd Bennett Field's geometric sprawl of runways. I fall again, as low as I can. There's Chuck's field. It is brown – the grass has burned – but it is still there. There's no trace of a batting square. The equipment shed is gone. I'm just seeing a field. I stare at it for a while. I am contending with a variety of reactions, and consequently with a single brush on the touchpad I flee upward into the atmosphere and at once have in my sights the physical planet, submarine wrinkles and all – have the option, if so moved, to go anywhere. From up here, though, a human's movement is a barely intelligible thing. Where would he move to, and for what? There is no sign of nations, no sense of the work of man. The USA as such is nowhere to be seen.

I shut down the computer. I drink a second glass of water and begin to study a sheaf of work papers I've printed out. I'm wide awake.

While Cardozo rushes by Underground to Sloane Square and his fiancée-to-be, I stroll across Waterloo Bridge with my jacket suspended from a hooked finger. I am happy to be walking. Although it's early evening, it's still very warm: this is, after all, the summer of the great heatwave. The English summer is actually a Russian doll of summers, the largest of which is the summer of unambiguous disaster in Iraq, which immediately contains the summer of the destruction of Lebanon, which itself holds a series of ever smaller summers that lead to the summer of Monty Panesar and, smallest of all perhaps, the summer of Wayne Rooney's foot. But on this evening at the end of July, it feels like summer simpliciter, and it's with no real thought of anything that I detach myself from the mass whose fate is Waterloo Station and go down the steps to the river-bank. It's a scene of good cheer on the esplanade, where the wanderers are in receipt of that peculiar happiness a summer river bestows, a donation of space, of light and, somehow, of time: there is something regretful in Big Ben's seven gongs. I go under Hungerford Bridge and its sunny new walkways and am overwhelmingly confronted by the London Eye, in profile. Here, by the tattered lawn of Jubilee Gardens, is where I've arranged to meet wife and son. Rather than crane up at the Eye, I pass ten minutes watching the waters of the Thames. It's hard to believe this was exactly the stretch where, in January, with television helicopters buzzing overhead and millions following its every sinking and surfacing, a whale swam. Chuck the birder taught me the term for such a creature: a vagrant, to be distinguished from a migrant.

My son's voice calls out. Daddy! Turning, I see my family and its super-long shadows. We are all beaming. Reunions in unfamiliar places have this effect, and maybe the great wheel itself is infectious: the stupendous circle, freighted with circumferential eggs, is a glorious spray of radiuses. In due course a security guard waves his wand over our possessions; an egg hatches Germans; and a gang of us boards. According to officialdom, we are flying counter-clockwise at less than two miles per hour. Jake, berserk with excitement, quickly befriends a six-year-old boy who speaks not a word of English. As we rise over the river and are gradually presented with the eastern vista, the adults also become known to one another: we meet a couple from Leeds; a family from Vilnius (Jake's pal is one of these); and three young Italian women, one of whom has dizziness and must stay seated.

As a Londoner, I find myself consulted about what we're all seeing. At first, this is easy – there's the NatWest tower, which now has a different name; there's Tower Bridge. But the higher we go, the less recognisable the city becomes. Trafalgar Square is not where you expect it to be. Charing Cross, right under our noses, must be carefully detected. I find myself turning to a guidebook for help. The difficulty arises from the mishmashing of spatial dimensions, yes, but also from a quantitative attack: the English capital is huge, huge; in every direction, to distant hills – Primrose and Denmark and Lavender, our map tells us – constructions are heaped without respite. Riverbank traffic aside, there is little sign of life. Districts are compacted, in south London especially: where on earth are Brixton and Kennington and Peckham? You wonder how anyone is able to navigate this labyrinth, which is what this crushed, squashed, everywhere-spreading city appears to be. 'Buckingham Palace?' one of the Lithuanian ladies asks me, and I cannot say. I notice, meanwhile, that Jake has started to race around and needs to be brought to order, and that Rachel is standing alone in a corner. I merely join my wife. I join her just as we reach the very top of our celestial circuit and for this reason I have no need to do anything more than put an arm round her shoulder. A self-evident and prefabricated symbolism attaches itself to this slow climb to the zenith, and we are not so foolishly ironical, or confident, as to miss the opportunity to glimpse significantly into the eyes of the other and share the thought that occurs to all at this summit, which is, of course, that they have made it thus far, to a point where they can see horizons previously unseen, and the old earth reveals itself newly. Everything is further heightened, as we must obscurely have planned, by signs of sundown: in the few clouds above Ealing, Phoebus is up to his oldest and best tricks. Rachel, a practical expression all of a sudden crossing her face, begins to say something, but I shush her. I know my wife: she feels an urge to go down now, into the streets and into the facts. But I leave her with no choice, as willy-nilly we are lowered westward, but to accept her place above it all. There is to be no drifting out of the moment.

What happens, however, is that I'm the one who drifts – to another sundown, New York, to my mother. We were sailing on the Staten Island Ferry on a September day's end. The forward deck was crowded. There was much smiling, pointing, physical interwining, kissing. Everybody looked at the Statue of Liberty and at Ellis Island and at the Brooklyn Bridge, but finally, inevitably, everybody looked to Manhattan. The structures clustered at its tip made a warm, familiar crowd, and as their surfaces brightened ever more fiercely with sunlight it was possible to imagine that vertical accumulations of humanity were gathering to greet our arrival. The day was darkening at the margins, but so what? A world was lighting up before us, its uprights putting me in mind, now that I'm adrift, of new pencils standing at attention in a Caran d'Ache box belonging in the deep of my childhood, in particular the purplish platoon of sticks that emerged by degrees from the reds and, turning bluer and bluer and bluer, faded out; a world concentrated most glamorously of all, it goes almost without saying, in the lilac acres of two amazingly high towers going up above all others, on one of which, as the boat drew us nearer, the sun began to make a brilliant yellow mess. To speculate about the meaning of such a moment would be a stained, suspect business, but there is, I think, no need to speculate. Factual assertions can be made. I can state that I wasn't the only person on that ferry who'd seen a pink watery sunset in his time, and I can state that I wasn't the only one of us to make out and accept an extraordinary promise in what we saw – the tall approaching cape, a people risen in light. You only had to look at our faces.

Which makes me remember my mother. I remember how I turned and caught her – how could I have forgotten this until now? – looking not at New York but at me, and smiling.

Which is how I come to face my family with the same smile.

'Look!' Jake is saying, pointing wildly. 'See, Daddy?'

I see, I tell him, looking from him to Rachel and again to him. Then I turn to look for what it is we're supposed to be seeing.

Significant portions of this book were written at Ledig House and at Yaddo. In the matter of artistic sanctuary I am also deeply thankful to the Bard family; to John Casey; and, most deeply of all, to Bob and Nan Stewart.

p.s.

Ideas,
interviews
& features ...

About the author

Read on

All Over America
Travis Elborough talks to Joseph O'Neill

I wondered if we could begin by talking a little about where and when the notion for a novel about New York cricket came to you. As I think has been well documented, it wasn't initially an easy sell and several publishers turned it down, but James Wood in his review of *Netherland* in the *New Yorker* suggested that you must have had a sudden eureka moment when the idea first occurred to you. Did you?

It's very hard to say where the ideas come from. I only get an idea for a novel once every ten years. I just thought here was an enormously interesting and, to me, *new* world – this marginal world of New York cricket and New York immigrants. I felt there had to be a story there somewhere. I'm not sure that 'Eureka!' was the exclamation that came to my lips. Even though the novel presents cricket in quite an impressionistic, aesthetic way, I always felt that it was a dangerous and potentially disastrous subject; the danger being, of course, that a story involving this tiny community of sportsmen (and told by a *Dutchman*) would be of no interest to anyone – which is what it felt like when the book started accumulating rejections.

One of the many things I love about the book is the way it operates in two time zones. Through Hans we, in effect, learn about both New York's largely forgotten Dutch immigrants and the challenges that their contemporary equivalents, whose stories are also a neglected facet of the city's make-up, face now. Part of the reason that duality works so well is that Hans is such a compelling voice. How far was the book composed with that first person narrative in mind?

Voice is immensely important. It was my ambition, if I had any kind of clear ambition, to write a novel that hinged on a voice. My favourite novels are like that. It almost doesn't matter what happens or what is said, the reader just wants to remain in the company of this voice. The question then, of course, is what constitutes a voice? And that is a terribly complicated, mysterious question. But I wrote a first draft of *Netherland* and essentially abandoned the second half of it because the book was fatally undermined by a preoccupation with plot. I found that whenever I tried to write towards plot points it completely deflated the central power of the narrative, such as it was. So I decided to stay with the voice and see what came out of it.

And, to turn to the question of time . . . From my own personal experience as I've grown older, I've always felt – and without wishing to sound like Heidegger – that the business of consciousness and the business of life itself, and our spiralling apprehension of it, are more and more mysterious. As a consequence I've become increasingly preoccupied by what it means to make a conscientious statement about the world. And I suppose that this carefulness, a philosophical carefulness, is an important part of Hans's voice. There are a ▶

❛ Hans is constantly looking. He is always trying to gain a perspective on what is happening to him, the world and the people around him. ❜

All Over America *(continued)*

◄ lot of things he resists saying. He seems much more comfortable in the world of description and he's much more certain of himself in those areas. He is, by profession, an analyst and a bystander. And furthermore the novel is fundamentally concerned with his quest to see. Hans is constantly looking – glancing through windows and peering under things. He is always trying to gain a perspective on what is happening to him, the world and the people around him. And, in a possibly rather over-obvious symbolic moment, the book, of course, ends with the scene at the London Eye.

One vantage point Hans has, of course, is memory. One of the things that concerns him throughout the book is the meaning of memory – what we're supposed to do with specific recollections, and what bearing they have on the life that we then should lead.

Another issue the book considers in some depth is what constitutes the American identity or what it means to be an American. Why do you think this topic, which recurs in many classic American novels, remains such fertile ground for contemporary fiction writers?
The American identity is more than a question of legal nationality. It involves, and historically right from the beginning has always involved, a sense of unique possibility: firstly spiritual and secondly economic. I think the emphasis is more on the latter these days, but America still has a special resonance. When we look at Hans and Chuck, Chuck self-consciously and squarely accepts being an American and the received ideas of what that

means – although he feels it authorizes him to act in ways that are illegitimate. Hans, on the other hand, has a much more complex, private and hesitant relationship with New York, not to mention that he feels completely alienated by the rest of America.

Could it be argued that New York is, in many respects, a rather atypical American city? In my, albeit limited, experience, it certainly seems to be the American city that Europeans feel most at home in.
New York is a world city. Over 40 per cent of current New Yorkers were born outside the United States. And historically it always has been a European obsession. The Dutch of course invented New York, though before that it was an Indian locality. But the city itself was a Dutch one, then an English one, then … what? It's interesting.

It's funny, I actually think Europeans identify much more readily with New York, and the narrative of New York, than most Americans do. For many of them, New York City is this hostile place with an incomprehensible and distasteful set of values.

You yourself were born in Ireland, educated in Holland and Britain, and today live in America. Do you think of your book as an American novel? *The Great Gatsby* is clearly a work you admire and is referenced in the text – do you see *Netherland* in something like that lineage?
Well, all of us who write about America are wandering in Fitzgerald's luminous ▶

❛ The American identity involves a sense of unique possibility: firstly spiritual and secondly economic. ❜

5

All Over America *(continued)*

◄footsteps whether we want to or not . . . I'm clearly indebted to Fitzgerald, and *Netherland* is clearly having some sort of conversation with *The Great Gatsby* – saying goodbye to it, perhaps, and to some of the notions associated with that wonderful book. This is by way of explanation of the fact that I actually see the book as a post-American novel. It is told from the perspective of a man who has left America. Hans is *over* America, even though he is still fascinated by it. Nick Carraway, by contrast, has moved back to the Mid-West.

I increasingly think that the integrity of the United States, the idea of the US as this special, sealed-off zone of opportunity and freedom, is anachronistic. Globalization has undermined the exclusiveness of the American experience. It remains an extraordinary and exceptional place but our attitudes to it have changed. The veneration certainly isn't what it used to be. I believe some of that has been precipitated by the behaviour of the United States internationally in recent times. But I also think that the way economies are developing, with the global flow of information and money, the importance of nationality and national boundaries is diminishing. I am not saying that nationalism is not a very powerful force, clearly it is. But it seems to me that history is running in the direction of a weakening of national identities – and America has been affected by that.

For many years as a novelist, I felt it was a huge disadvantage that I was of no fixed abode – certainly of no fixed abode imaginatively –

but now it seems that my personal circumstances, my physical and cultural mobility, are reflective of an interesting global development. I no longer think too hard about whether I am Irish, American, Dutch, Turkish or whatever. It seems of limited significance.

The milieu of the book is one you know intimately, and you, like Hans, live in the Chelsea Hotel and play for the Staten Island Cricket Club. You've previously written a family memoir, as well as novels. Could you, say, have written a non-fiction account of your experiences of playing cricket in New York? I think it was Philip Roth who once complained that everyone always assumed his novels were autobiographical and when he wrote a memoir people accused him of making it all up. Where does the boundary line between art and life lie for you?
There was never any question of it being a non-fiction book. None of the incidents in the book occurred in real life. One of the reasons it took seven years to write was because I had to make it all up. Circumstantial elements of the book are obviously personally familiar. If I'd been living in Pittsburgh, I may well have written a book set in Pittsburgh. As a novelist you use and take an interest in everything that is around you. But there isn't a single incident in the book that I have personally experienced. What I would say is that real events authorize you to imagine. For example, when I was a lawyer, I went to Trinidad and met a campaigner against the death penalty who was self-taught, very articulate and a ▶

‘ I actually think Europeans identify much more readily with New York, and the narrative of New York, than most Americans do. ’

Author photograph © Lisa Ackerman

LIFE
at a Glance

I was born in Ireland in 1964, in Cork. I grew up mainly in the Netherlands, where I attended French and British international schools, then studied law at Cambridge University. In 1990 I began full-time practice as a barrister, combining that with the writing of books. In 1998, I moved to New York, where I live with my family at the Chelsea Hotel.

All Over America *(continued)*

◄ really charismatic man. And it was this sort of encounter that authorized me to come up with Chuck Ramkissoon. I use the real world as a basis for imagining.

Reading the book for the second time, I couldn't help feeling that Chuck's scheme to build a cricket stadium in America actually seemed less far-fetched than it had first seemed to me. How plausible do you think it really is, though?
I think that there will certainly be someone who succeeds in installing a cricket stadium in the United States. But Chuck's ambition to get a significant number of Americans to play cricket is surely a non-starter. Unless, of course, this current immigrant generation, which is from South Asia, seeds the game in the United States. And then it could well become like lacrosse or rugby, a minority pastime, but nevertheless one that is played to a high level.

Though I completely accept your own definition of the book as a post-American novel, I am struck that there is a far greater tradition in American letters for utilizing sport, either as a metaphor for the state of the nation or even simply as a setting for drama, than in, say, British or Commonwealth literature. I can't, for instance, really think of an English footballing equivalent novel to Don DeLillo's *End Zone*. Why do you think this might be?
I am not much of an authority on sport and metaphor. But, yes, it is slightly amazing that there's never been a great soccer novel

written – and I mean anywhere. And it is the greatest sport in the world. I do remember a wonderful novel for young adults, I suppose, or maybe for adults, that I haven't read since I was a teenager, by Barry Hines, who wrote *A Kestrel for a Knave*, all about a football player. *The Blinder*, I think it was called. Barry Hines himself had actually been a professional sportsman, unless I'm mistaken. But you would have thought someone would have done something else. I do believe, though, that sport is a fantastically important part of the culture. It is a way of perpetuating the world of childhood and creating a sort of refuge, a refuge reality if you like. Needless to say it's overwhelmingly men who are the refugees. What's the matter with us? ∎

A CAPRICIOUS XI OF FAVOURITE BOOKS

U and I
Nicholson Baker

Herzog
Saul Bellow

Invisible Cities
Italo Calvino

Invisible Man
Ralph Ellison

Catch-22
Joseph Heller

Portrait of the Artist as a Young Man
James Joyce

The Silent Woman
Janet Malcolm

Collected Poems
Sylvia Plath

The Emigrants
W. G. Sebald

Collected Poems
Wallace Stevens

Of the Farm
John Updike

A Writer's Life

When and where do you write?
I have a little office in the West Village, New York City, where I go most mornings and hole up, in a daze more idle than industrious, for the rest of the day. My most productive times have come when I've escaped to a cabin in Ontario owned by friends, and write more in two weeks than I would in two New York months. I do this a couple of times a year, all being well. Solitude can be a wonderful thing.

Why do you write?
It's mysteriously compulsory.

Pen or computer?
Laptop.

Silence or music?
Both.

How do you start a book?
As inadvertently as possible. Then I continue as accidentally as possible.

And finish?
Exhausted.

Do you have any writing rituals or superstitions?
I like to have a putter handy, which I then swing as if it were a lob wedge. The green is somewhere beyond the kitchenette.

Which living writer do you most admire?
John Updike. It's not that I love (or even read) everything he writes, but rather that he's

fearless about following his imaginative impulses into artistically risky and socially disgraceful territory. Philip Roth has the same courage. Of course, Updike has the edge in the matter of sentences.

What inspires you?
The English language.

What's your guilty reading pleasure or favourite trashy read?
I don't ever feel guilty reading. ■

Have You Read?

Other Books by Joseph O'Neill

Blood-Dark Track: A Family History
In this spellbinding memoir, Joseph O'Neill examines the lives of his two grandfathers – one Irish, one Turkish – both of whom were imprisoned during the Second World War in mysterious circumstances. The result is a brilliant personal exploration of the ties and limits of kinship.

....

This is the Life
Narrated by James Jones, an introspective solicitor obsessed with his former tutor Michael Donovan, an illustrious and well-remunerated barrister who seemingly thwarted Jones' earliest professional ambitions, O'Neill's debut novel is an enjoyable study of envy, insecurity and the traps of hope.

....

The Breezes
O'Neill's second novel is a wonderfully dark and hilarious tragicomedy that charts the Breeze family's most hellish fortnight – a time in which insurance policies, security systems and lucky underpants are pitted against redundancy, burglary and relegation.

If You Loved This,
You Might Like …

A Fan's Notes
Frederick Exley

Seize the Day
Saul Bellow

American Pastoral
Philip Roth

The Sportswriter
Richard Ford

The Damned United
David Peace

Beyond a Boundary
C L R James

Desperate Characters
Paula Fox

Away
Amy Bloom

The Locusts Have No King
Dawn Powell

The Tenants of Moonbloom
Edward Lewis Wallant

The Fundamentals of Play
Caitlin Macy

Summerland
Malcolm Knox